Do you have to be a monster to fight one?

Erin Evanstar is a demon hunter, a protector of humanity from nightmarish predators that feed on people's fears and flesh. They are settling into their dual life of being a teen and hunting demons.

When a tentacled horror abducts Erin's partner, José, Erin and their family go on the hunt to get him back. But Erin gets an ultimatum: help the Fallen Angels bring on the apocalypse or watch José die. Erin will do anything to save José, but fighting monsters comes with a grim price—becoming one themselves.

I0583779

POWER

INVERSION

The Evanstar Chronicles, Book Two

Sara Codair

A NineStar Press Publication

www.ninestarpress.com

Power Inversion

Printed in the USA

Print ISBN: 978-1-64890-036-5

First Edition, June, 2020

Also available in eBook, ISBN: 978-1-64890-035-8

Warning: These warnings contain spoilers.

This book has depictions of violence, death, death of a minor character, temporary death of a main character, mention of past abuse, mention of miscarriage, pregnancy of side character, self-harm, suicidal ideation, guns, grief, kidnapping/abduction, alcohol use, brief depiction of humans enslaved by a supernatural creature.

Chapter One

"Prophecies are fickle and convoluted. People tried telling me that for centuries, but I still sought out the most renowned seers, Elven and Human alike. It wasn't until I miscarried the twins and started having visions on my own did I realize how unreliable an art prophecy is.

Thankfully, the visions faded after I delivered Liam and Lucy because they caused me more stress than anything else.

I could tell Liam this a thousand times, but if he is anything like me, he won't realize it until he experiences it. Let him follow his dreams until he discovers they are hardly probabilities, let alone definite futures. In the meantime, don't worry over much of what he tells you. Seeing himself die the same way more than once makes it less likely to happen."

—A letter from Niben to Seamus Evanstar, confined to the archives shortly after Liam died.

White graduation caps fell from the sky like flakes of vaporized Demon. High school was a beast, and I'd vanquished it like every monster I'd fought, with one exception—myself.

This moment deserved savoring.

Breathing deliberately, I slowed my perception of time until the caps seemed as if they were falling through cold honey on their way to the ground.

The late-spring sun beat down on me, but a breeze kept the temperature bearable. Some tassels lilted southeast—away from the towering clouds bruising the northwest sky. The weather wasn't going to hold much longer, but I was okay with that. Thunderstorms awoke something wild in me—a pulse-racing, dance-around-like-no-one-can-see-you kind of wild—a rush of adrenaline almost as good as what I'd get from battling a Troll or sparring with Mel.

With my sense of time slowed down, the distant thunder sounded like a lion purring. The clouds glowed purple as lightning forked through them like an X-ray, temporarily revealing a mass of tentacles undulating in the clouds.

Mel, did you see that? I thought as loudly as I could, hoping my telepathic cousin would hear me.

I'd seen a lot of different Demons in the three months I'd been hunting them, but based on the stories and the *Lexicon*, the massive tentacled ones only materialized in oceans, and they certainly could not fly. Yet, every time lightning flashed, there they were, waving as if violent updrafts were a gentle breeze.

My heart sped up. My hands closed into fists. Mel didn't reply.

I shut my eyes, opening my mind so I could feel all the energy around me. Most humans were blobs of buzzing heat, but Mel, a hybrid of human, Angel, and Elf, had a hotter, more intense aura with a spritz of simultaneously depressed and optimistically peppy texture. I found her near my Elven grandmother, who felt like a condensed thunderstorm.

Mel? Niben? Can you hear me? Did you see that?

Of course, there was a good chance they were both shielding. What telepath would have their mind open to other people's thoughts when there were so many other people around?

One who hasn't been able to properly shield in months. Mel's melodic yet squeaky voice was a welcome presence in my mind. *Shut down the hyper drive. You're giving me a headache.*

I exhaled over the course of ten seconds, willing my sense of time back to normal.

A garbled din of stretched-out voices morphed to something more akin to a clattering avalanche of pots and pans. A shoulder jostled mine. The corner of a graduation cap crashed into my head.

Erin? What had you wanted to tell me?

There were tentacles in the clouds, I thought at Mel, turning in the general direction I sensed her in.

I crashed into José, who, of course, stood right next to me.

"You okay?" he asked. Tears glistened in his midnight eyes and trickled down his sun-kissed cheeks. One snagged on the crooked tip of his nose. He clutched two graduation caps, his and mine, so tight that the scars on his knuckles were visibly stretched.

"Yeah. Are you?" I wondered if I should tell him what I'd seen. He'd been hunting Demons longer than me, but he also thrived on keeping school and the supernatural as two separate entities. And what if they hadn't been tentacles? What if the storm had just appeared that way with the lightning in slow motion? I didn't want to ruin his day if there wasn't an actual threat.

"I'll miss everyone." He stuffed the caps under his arms and hugged me. While I wanted to celebrate because I'd made it out alive, he mourned the loss of a place that had been a haven to him for four years.

I leaned my head on his shoulder, listening to his heartbeat, trying to let his steady warmth calm the worry growing in my mind. José's body was a rock in the sense that it was hard and athletic, but also because it anchored me when I felt as if my mind was running away.

Have you ever watched a storm with time slowed that much? asked Mel.

I shook my head before I remembered there were dozens of people between her and me. *No. Do storm clouds in slow motion look like tentacles?*

José kissed my hair and whispered, "Are you talking to Mel?"

I nodded.

"Is she okay?"

"She's having trouble shielding. We should go meet up with her and the others anyway." I stepped away from him and walked uphill.

Students, who wore white graduation robes, and their parents, who were dressed mostly in summer dresses, slacks, and collared shirts, were clumped all over Saint Patrick's sprawling lawn.

José draped his arm over my shoulder as I wove around groups of people. The pressure was calming, lulling panic monsters back to sleep with its warm weight. I glanced up at the clouds. They were closer and darker. The wind sped up, stealing programs from a dozen people's hands. The clouds lit up with lightning, but I didn't see any tentacles.

Mel's voice popped back into my head. *I don't sense anything in the clouds, and neither does Niben. I guess she's been restraining the storm for half the ceremony. Perhaps you were seeing her power mingled with it?*

Maybe. Some tension unraveled from my chest. I'd heard stories about my grandmother, Niben, controlling storms, but I'd never seen her do it. In fact, I'd never witnessed her do any magic unless she was modeling something she wanted me to try. She'd come on a few hunts, but she'd just watched with her unblinking feline eyes and later quizzed me on what I did right and wrong. For all I knew, her fabled storm magic could resemble tentacles.

Her magic manifests as roots or vines. Don't let her hear you compare it to tentacles.

Mel's bell-like laugh tickled my ears. I followed the sound around a large family and found Mel giggling under my favorite oak tree wearing a white-and-blue-floral maxi dress that covered her feet and touched the ground.

Once upon a time, looking directly at my cousin with my Sight open, my ability to see around illusions would've left me seeing spots, but today, only a dull thin haze of white light surrounded her. Rippled pink scars covered half her face, and her hair, once down to her waist, was just starting to regrow.

"You made it. Congrats." Mel pushed herself off the tree and hugged me, followed by Grandpa and Niben, who had been standing to the left of her.

"Where'd everyone else go?" I asked. Mike, my aunty Lucy (Mel's mom), and my aunt Rita (my mother's sister) had been here earlier.

"They decided to go in before the storm got too close," said Mel. Mentally, she added, *Mom and Niben kept debating how long it was safe to hold the storm off for.*

Is there anything those two don't argue about? I thought back to Mel.

I'm happy my mother and grandmother are talking at all. For years after your dad died, they didn't. Mel winked at me and shrugged.

"Congratulations." Grandpa hugged me. He was as dressed up as he ever got with khaki slacks and a short-sleeved blue button-up shirt. His ocean-colored eyes squinted, and his lips twisted into something halfway between a smile and a scowl: his "why can't you people talk out loud so I can hear you" face.

Niben, who wore the same dress as Mel only with reddish-orange flowers, glowered at the thunderclouds. Her pointy ears, which appeared as normal ears to humans who couldn't see around her glamour, twitched. The gusts pulled strands of red hair out of the two buns she'd braided it into. The strands flailed around like tentacles writhing in the wind.

Maybe I had just seen cords of her power in the clouds. Sometimes, when I saw magical things for the first time, I saw them how my brain could most easily process the latest shift to its reality. The tentacles could've been ropes of magic tethering the updrafts and downdrafts.

"That storm is moving in with a vengeance now. Shall we hurry up and take pictures before we are all drenched?" Niben turned her back on the thunderheads and pulled a bulky DSLR out of her bag. She loved photography. Apparently, it wasn't a thing in Faerie, so when she was on Earth, she had to get her picture-taking fix.

"Are you still controlling the storm?" I asked as I stood next to José, watching it over Niben's shoulder.

She adjusted the focus on her camera. "No. The longer I hold it off, the worse it will be when it hits, and

I've already restrained that one far longer than I should have."

The shutter clicked.

"Stand a little closer together, and, José, stop slouching." She took a few more pictures and asked Mel to go stand where José had been.

I counted as I exhaled, gradually slowing my perception of time, staring at the cloud behind Niben.

Mel smiled at the camera. *It's only a storm.*

I slowed my perception more, so when lightning flashed, the cloud remained lit up for a whole seven seconds. There was slow movement in it like drenched, dirty cotton balls shifting in a bag as someone dumped water in it.

Lightning forked again.

Something slithered near the bottom of the cloud and vanished.

*

The postgraduation reception, which was supposed to happen in the tent once the chairs were packed and the stage was broken down, had been moved to the gym. The tent would've been fine if it were merely a passing rainstorm, but the lightning was wild, and for a few minutes, hail pounded the roof.

I made it through the whole hour without snarling, jumping, panicking, hurting myself, or simply short-circuiting in the crowd of people and their voices echoing off the floor and walls. Without the foul-tasting Elf potions I used to manage anxiety, depression, and ADHD, I would've been clawing at my skin ten minutes after José pulled me away from the snack table to socialize.

An hour was enough.

The severe storm had faded to a steady rain and distant rumbles of thunder. I walked halfway to the tent and just stood in the middle of the field, letting warm rain drench my curls and clothes. People rushed out of the gym in groups. Some had umbrellas. Others fled to their cars.

"You want to go hang out in the tent?" José walked up to me with his graduation robe held over his head even though it didn't do much to shield him. His khakis pants and polo shirt were nearly as drenched as mine.

I smiled. "You don't have to leave your friends because I'm out here."

"I'll see them later." He dropped the robe and rested his hand on the small of my back. The tingling shivers it evoked kept me from cringing at the thought of having to play nice with Jenny Dunn.

For most of senior year, José's ex-girlfriend, Jenny Dunn, had bullied me every chance she got. But since I saved her life in March, she had been trying to not only earn my forgiveness but also become my friend. I forgave her, but I wasn't sure I'd ever be her friend.

When José and I got to the tent, he draped the drenched robe over a chair and hugged me. Standing with my body touching his leached tension from every muscle. It reminded me of sinking into a hot bath on a cold night after a grueling sparring session. A few months ago, this feeling had terrified me; it had made me feel weak and powerless. Since then, I'd learned to trust José to not take things further than I wanted them to go. I'd also developed a better understanding of why I didn't always want them to go further.

Between José and my therapist, I'd figured out I was somewhere on the ace spectrum, though I'd yet to figure out exactly where I fell. And although José was the epitome of hot, the core of my attraction to him came from the long friendship we'd had before it'd ever shifted to romantic. Don't get me wrong, I love kissing him; however, being so psychically attracted to him didn't necessarily equate to whether I was sexually attracted to him.

And my sexuality made up only one piece of the puzzle. The other part included the idea of sex immediately stopping me in my tracks. It wasn't something I never wanted to have. I just couldn't picture being so intimate with a partner if I didn't 100 percent trust and love both my partner and myself. José had earned my love and trust, but sometimes, I still despised myself.

José pressed his forehead to mine and whispered, "I love you."

"I know," I said, resisting the urge to tell him he shouldn't.

I listened to his heartbeat and felt his breath tickle my lips.

He cupped my cheeks in his hands. "Can I kiss you?"

My skin grew all warm and fuzzy as hormones chased my doubts away. I grinned. "Yes, but it's your fault if Sister Marie dumps a bucket of holy water on us."

"You'll freeze it before it's out of the bucket." He gently pressed his lips to mine.

My face, no, my entire body hummed as I breathed him in, my lips moving with his. I wrapped my arms around him and pulled him closer. Everything else faded away until the clanking of chairs falling like dominoes ruined the moment. I leaped away from José and shifted my weight like I would if I were being attacked.

"I'm sorry," said Jenny Dunn, backing away from me like I was a monster ready to lunge at her. "I didn't mean too...I just..."

"It's okay," I said, relaxing my posture and smoothing out the involuntary snarl the clanging had evoked. "You scared me. I'm not good with noises."

"That's an understatement." José squeezed my hand. He turned to Jenny. "What's up?"

She watched the two of us, opening and closing her mouth. Tingling cold crept through my veins, and my stomach twisted into knots. It was the feeling I always got when something I dreamed, or something related to a dream, was going to happen.

Please tell me you didn't dream something about tentacles. A Fallen Angel plotting an apocalypse is bad enough without storm-riding cosmic monsters. Mel's voice was a jarring intrusion.

Not all my dreams are about Demon attacks, I reminded her. *Where are you?*

I just passed the tent on my way to the archives.

I'm going to shield, but stay close in case this goes south.

I'll wait in the church. Let me know when it's okay to head downstairs.

I closed my eyes, imagining myself in a spaceship's cockpit, and raised my deflector shields to full strength as if I was expecting a mental attack. I knew something upsetting was going to happen, and Mel had enough to deal with. She didn't need to feel fallout from whatever emotional bomb Jenny was about to detonate.

"I—I wanted to talk to José alone," said Jenny.

I started to step away, but José moved with me instead of letting go of my hand. "If you want to say something to me, you can say it with Erin here."

Chills slithered through me like frozen eels.

Jenny folded her arms and stared at his feet. "José, I think it would be better if they weren't here for this."

"I don't want Erin to leave." José's voice crackled. He stared at the ground too, looking as small and defeated as Jenny.

It broke my heart every time I saw him that way. It woke the rage monsters that lived in my gut. I wanted to find the monster that was hurting him and fight it, but I was the only monster around.

"Please? Can we just talk you and me?" asked Jenny.

The déjà-vu ice eels slithered into my brain, slapping it with their tails. They turned to snakes, hissing at me for not connecting the dots before reverting to eels, but the electric kind. The weight Jenny had gained, the way her breasts were larger, her hips wider, and her tummy stuck out a little wasn't only because she was finally beating an eating disorder.

"I don't hide *anything* from Erin. Say what you need to say," said José.

The only things he'd ever hidden from me were the existence of Demons and the true extent of his dad's abuse. I would've been fine with less details of his sex life from before we started dating and about how the first time he slept with Jenny Dunn, he'd been wasted. Maybe he had been too drunk to remember a condom.

"I...I'm..." Jenny closed her mouth and her eyes. Tears dripped down her cheeks. "I'm..."

"A little over three months pregnant," I said, fearful she would drag it out forever.

Jenny stared at me.

José squeezed my hand like he was delivering a baby. "Pregnant? By who?"

I closed my eyes, dredging up a shard of dreamed future from my memory, one fleeting moment of peace between stretches of earth-shattering violence: Jenny smiling at a baby that had her glacial eyes with José's dark hair and dimpled chin.

"José, it's yours," I said when I tired of waiting for Jenny to say it.

Jenny gaped at me like I had sprouted a glittering horn from my head. "Erin, how do you know all that?"

"You dreamed this, didn't you?" José pulled me back to him, half laughing and half hyperventilating.

My hands curled into fists so tight my nails dug into my palms.

José kept talking. "I'm glad Erin said something because I thought this was going to be a completely different conversation. I'm an idiot, and the only thing I know about fathers is what they should never ever do. I don't know if I will make a good dad, but I will never be like my father. I'm assuming if you're this far along, you're keeping it?"

"Dreamed? You're a psychic?" Jenny stepped closer, visibly ignoring every single thing José said after he implied I had a premonition.

A hopeful smile clashed with her pained expression as she inched nearer. I flinched away, but there was nowhere to go because my back was literally pressed against José, who, despite his optimistic words, clutched me like a shield.

"I used to talk to a phone psychic, but Mom found out and made me stop. She said psychics were connected to Satan." Jenny grinned inches away from my face.

My skin felt like electrified maggots. I wanted to rip it off, and if José weren't holding my arms so tight, I might have. No meds and no half-truthful sessions with human therapists had equipped me to cope with this.

"They prefer to be called a prophet, not psychic," said José.

"I prefer you not to tell anyone," I growled through gritted teeth. I tried to step away from José, but his rigid arms were squeezing me tight.

Jenny was right in my face, staring at me like I was some kind of miracle freak. The creepy-crawly buzz trailed from my neck to my hands to my toes. I knew one way to make that stop. My heart raced. My feet frantically tapped the ground harder and harder until it was shaking both José and me.

José's rigid muscles softened, but he didn't let go of me. "Erin, I'm so sorry." He took a few slow, deep breaths. "Jenny, you were right. We should talk alone. Can you give Erin some space? I need a minute with them before you and I talk."

Half-dazed, Jenny nodded and went and sat down in a chair on the opposite end of the row.

"Erin, I'm sorry. That was the last thing I expected her to say. Are you okay?" José slid his hands off my biceps and wrapped his arms around me.

I was trapped, and my chest felt like it was going to explode. "Let go of me."

His lips brushed my ear. "If I do, are you going to hurt yourself?"

If I answered that question honestly, he wouldn't let me go, but I couldn't breathe. I needed him to let go of me. I needed to hurt, but if I ran hard enough, if I went to the training room under the convent and vented my rage on one of Sister Marie's punching bags, maybe I'd resist cutting.

"Erin, answer me."

"They're already hurting themself." Mel walked into the tent in a soaked, bedraggled dress. She pointed at my hands, which were balled into fists at my side and probably bleeding. "Go talk to Jenny. I'll make sure Erin doesn't hurt themself worse."

He let go.

I bolted.

"You know where to find us," Mel yelled to José as she ran after me.

*

Mel hit a light switch, illuminating a room with a floor entirely covered in mats. My skin still buzzed, but the burning in my legs from the short sprint over here kept the urge to cut at bay. A punching bag hung from the ceiling in each corner. The walls were lined with weights, practice swords of many styles, staffs, boxing gloves, ropes, Pilates balls, yoga mats, and a couple duffle bags filled with workout clothes.

Mel opened one of the bags and threw a tank top and gym shorts at me. "Change out of your binder before you start hitting things."

Still shaking, I turned my back to her while we changed into clothing more suitable for an intense workout. As much as I wanted to keep my binder on, I knew it wasn't safe to exercise in it.

"Thank you," I said to Mel, then aimed a right hook at a punching bag.

I swung at it again, not bothering to think of form.

Mel caught my wrist midswing. "You break bones when you go at punching bags like that. You've broken fingers, smashed up your knuckles, and one time you fractured your radius."

I spun around, yanking my wrist from her grip, a snarl growing on my lips. "I did not."

"You did, but you thought it was just sore." Mel threw a bamboo practice sword at me—the ones she'd altered for lightsaber sparring matches on the beach.

I barely caught it. My nails dug into the hilt. "You're saying I've broken my own bones, and instead of telling me and making me go to the hospital, you healed them even though it takes a shit ton of your Angel mojo?"

"Yes, and I don't have enough 'Angel mojo' to heal you now." Mel swung her modified Shinai at me so fast I had to jump backward because there was no way I would've blocked in time.

"You're sparring with me" was all the warning she gave before whipping the sword toward my skull.

I blocked it. Barely. "Mel, I'm too upset. I could hurt you."

She swung again. Her sword thundered against mine. "We always had the best matches when we were both out of our minds angry."

"But, you—" I started before having to block a blow that could've knocked my teeth out.

"What? I'm weak?" Her sword whipped at me.

I parried.

"Wounded?" She feigned a swing at my shoulder. She whacked my thigh.

I swallowed the mind-numbing rage that blow evoked.

Mel snarled and came at with a complicated series of attacks. "Everyone has been treating me like I'm glass that is going to shatter any moment. Grandpa has done a full switch and is babying me and sending *you* out to fight Demons with only José for backup."

I only blocked half of them. "For someone who doesn't want to have to heal me, you are being awfully aggressive."

"Then stop reacting and fight back. You'd be dead if this were a real battle," she said with her sword pressed against my throat.

She stalked over to the middle of the room. "I can feel what's in your head. Take all that rage and confusion out on me and let me vent mine at you. I need this as much as you do. This is how we always worked through our shit."

My breathing finally evened out, and my chest didn't feel like it was enduring a never-ending series of heart attacks.

I grinned. "I might actually win this time."

"Doubtful," said Mel as she ran at me.

This time, I was ready for her.

*

By the time José found us, Mel and I were lying head to head on the mats, panting and laughing hysterically, surrounded by shards of bamboo.

"What the hell happened in here?" he said, starring down at the two of us with puffy red eyes. He scanned the fragments of the practice swords.

"Sparring match. Obviously." I glanced at the shattered hilt of sword I'd practiced with for at least two years and started laughing.

José's frown deepened as he spoke to Mel. "Hadn't you brought those to Faerie and had Niben do something so this wouldn't happen?"

"That was last year. Erin is stronger now." Mel stretched her arms out, then rested her hands under her head.

José lowered himself to the ground beside me. "Does this mean you two will go more than a few days without having telepathic arguments?"

I grinned. "It means we're going to have a lot of bruises tomorrow."

"No, *you* are going to have a lot of bruises." Mel rolled to her stomach and started stretching.

"So, Mel won?" José arched his eyebrows.

"Yes, but only I wasn't shielding, and she wanted me to try reading her mind, which I cannot do." I sat up and reached for my feet, savoring the burn of the stretch.

"Yet." Mel grabbed her ankles and pulled them toward her head. "How'd the rest of the conversation with Jenny go?"

José ran his hands through his hair. "It was the most terrifying, awkward conversation I've ever had. I'm so scared I threw up my lunch as soon as I got away from her, but I'm also kind of happy, which makes me more scared, and, Erin, if I ever turn into my father..."

"You won't turn into your father. You are nothing like him." I took a few deep breaths, trying not to think about where he was going with that sentence.

José sat up, made eye contact, and held a hand out to me. "I don't want this to be the end of us."

I stared at his hand, at his scarred knuckles that for once in his life weren't scabbed or bloody from fighting Demons and his father. I could take his hand and muddle through this with him. Or I could walk away.

The thought of doing the latter made it hard to breathe.

"Please. I'm sorry. I never should've been with her in the first place. You were my friend. She was bullying you before I started dating her, and I know that made it worse. What I did hurt both of you. But these past three months have been the happiest, and I don't want it to end. I understand if this is too much, or if you need time but..."

"Can I kiss you?" I asked, cutting him off midsentence.

"Always." His face lifted to a smile.

I tangled my fingers in his hair and kissed him until Mel started giggling.

My heart was beating fast when I pulled away. "José, if I left you, who'd protect you from all the other monsters out there?"

He squeezed my hand. "I should tell you what Jenny and I talked about. There are a ton more details to work out, but if you're in this with me, I want to know what you think."

"Yes, but not until after we go home, and I eat all the cookies you baked this morning," I said.

He almost smiled, but then he glanced down at our hands.

Mel, sitting on the floor, studied José and me with a smirk on her lips and a glint of mischief in her eyes. "José is debating whether or not to tell you that Will and Jenny still want to go ahead with that postgraduation movie night you reluctantly agreed to."

"We don't have to go," he said.

I squeezed his hand. "But we will. If we're going to be part of this kid's life, then I'm going to have to learn to deal with her. Plus, you want to go."

"I just want a night out to be a normal eighteen-year-old. You've been training so hard, which is great, but also scary because you're training with..." José clamped his mouth shut, but he mustn't have stopped himself from thinking it because Mel leaped to her feet.

Mel snarled. "Fire. Erin, you lied to me."

I stood up and crossed my arms. "Yeah, and how many times have you lied to me? How much are you still lying to me?"

"Why?" Mel gasped as she paced around the room, breathing harder with each circuit.

"I'm doing it because it's a skill I need to learn. I lied because it gives you panic attacks about...the night you saved everyone." I got in front of Mel and put my hands on her shoulders, recalling a memory of her winning a sparring match on the beach and projecting toward her. "Look at me. Focus on what I'm thinking."

For a few minutes, she stared at me, tense and struggling to breathe. I closed my eyes, focusing on every detail of the memory, imagining images, smells, and feelings traveling down my arms, out through my hands, and up her neck to her brain like it was flowing through a telepathic HDMI cable. Finally, her breathing and heart rate slowed, and her shoulders relaxed.

She asked, "Do you need to siphon energy from fire?"

I put my hand on her scarred cheek. "I don't want you to get hurt like this again. Niben says I'm a sponge for raw energy. Fire is only another form of it."

José walked over and draped an arm over each of us, but he looked at Mel. "You don't need to play at being Erin's guardian Angel anymore. Let them watch your back for once."

Mel just stared at him, and then she stared at me.

I really wished I could read *her* mind.

"It's been a long day." José closed his eyes. His arm grew heavy on my shoulder.

I worried that if one more thing happened, he'd fall apart. I was glad I hadn't told him about the tentacles.

Chapter Two

"The Confluence is a place that exists outside of time. It is said to be a place for Angels, but some Angel-hybrids have allegedly traveled there through a combination of dreams and astral projection. Most describe it as standing on a transparent platform in outer space, surrounded by a cosmic river. Reports indicate that the river contains memories and potential futures. Most of the hybrids can view their past and see whatever potential futures the universe decides to show them. Approximately ten percent can control what they see, and of that ten percent, only one percent can access the pasts and potential futures of other beings."

—The History of Hybrids, 3rd edition, published in 1984 by Amena Nasser. A copy is available in most archive locations.

"Erin, you don't have to walk in there if you don't want to." José squeezed my hand.

I took a deep breath, hoping I didn't sound like I was huffing and puffing in frustration. "I wouldn't have come if I didn't want to."

"You're good at a lot of things but lying isn't one of them." José crossed his arms and stopped in the middle of the sidewalk.

People rushed by us. Someone's oversized purse brushed against my shoulder. I took a step toward the glass doors and gestured for José to follow me. "We don't always have to do what I want. In fact, I think we've been doing too much of what I want and not enough of what you want."

"I'll be equally as happy if we go home and watch a movie, just the two of us," he said.

I kept walking. "For someone who has had a lifetime of practice, you're a horrible liar."

I got to the movie theater door ahead of him and held it open.

"I never wanted to lie to you, but I didn't have a choice," he said as the door closed behind us.

"Mel didn't have a choice. You did."

José sighed like a balloon deflating. "I guess. Dad always found a reason to hit me anyway, so yeah, I guess I had a choice, one that might have alienated the only adult who ever made a small effort to *protect* me from him."

His words were knives twisting in my gut. "I'm sorry. I shouldn't have said that."

"It's okay," he said.

"It's not." I squeezed his hand, wishing that Elven ADHD and antidepressant potions also stopped me from saying stupid, hurtful things. But meds couldn't fix me being the monster everyone denied I was.

"José, we're over here," said Will.

Will, a lanky blond guy, sprawled in a faded-red armchair in the lounge outside the movie theater's small bar. His dark, crisp jeans so tight I wondered if he could move. He wore a T-shirt with Cthulhu written below an image of a giant, evil octopus with its tentacles wrapped around the planet. Why did he have to be wearing something with tentacles on it? I really, really hoped that Lovecraft had completely made that up and not gotten inspiration from something that actually existed. Usually, if a supernatural creature existed in pop culture and reality, the real version was worse.

Will cocked his head. "Erin, why are you staring at my shirt?"

"Is that a Tardis?" I asked, hoping if he geeked out about *Doctor Who*, I'd stop thinking about tentacles.

"Seriously?" Will laughed so hard he almost knocked Jenny off her perch on the chair's arm. She wore black leggings and a loose pink tunic that appeared to be made of the same soft, stretchy fabric as her leggings. She clutched a tub of popcorn but didn't eat any.

José folded his arms and smirked at me.

Will winked at José. "I could go for a beer, especially if Erin is going to be teasing me about *Doctor Who* all night and making it obvious they've never watched a single episode in their entire life."

"They'll card you," I said.

"This should be plenty of popcorn for all of us, but I'll let you carry it." Jenny handed me the big tub.

"Thanks." This was a peace offering of the best kind.

"You don't know that they'll card me," said Will. "José rarely gets carded. He could get us beer."

"They'll card both of you." I winked at Jenny.

"Listen to Erin," she said.

José gave me his puppy-dog eyes.

I shook my head. I hadn't dreamed anything about tonight, but he didn't need to know that.

"José is going to be a dad in six months. He needs a beer. I need one too because my girlfriend is having his baby," said Will. He and Jenny had started dating shortly after José had broken up with her. It had started as her revenge plot, but now she and Will were falling in love. Unfortunately for me, that meant José and Will rarely hung out without me and Jenny.

"Now you're being ass." I couldn't think of any better way to call him out. Were Sam here, she'd have some witty comment about the patriarchy or misogyny.

But Sam was in a psychiatric hospital. I'd committed perjury to keep her out of jail after she'd tried to shoot Jenny and got me instead. Jenny, who was grateful for me saving her life and feeling guilty about bullying me, agreed to tell the police the same story I did: Sam aimed the gun in the direction I had been fighting Jenny's assailant. She missed.

The police didn't realize Jenny had brought the unregistered gun to the scene. Everyone stayed out of jail. It was perfect until Sam attempted suicide.

"Erin, are you still with us?" asked José.

"I miss Sam," I whispered and leaned my head on José's shoulder while hugging my tub of popcorn.

José pressed his lips to the top of my head. I savored thirty seconds of peace.

"Erin, do you know how the movie is going to end?" asked Jenny.

I glared at José as I answered Jenny. "I don't know everything."

"I know the movie is going to start soon," said José, walking toward the person checking tickets.

I followed him. Jenny edged up beside me and whispered in my ear. "Do you know what gender my baby is going to be?"

"No. I do not know what gender is going to be assigned to your baby any more than I know if that assigned gender will be the right one." I sped up while she slunk back to Will.

Just a few feet away from the relative safety of the actual theater, a chill danced across my arms. Anxiety buzzed in my chest. I observed my surroundings, trying to connect this place to a dream, but I couldn't. Still, something didn't feel right.

José jogged to catch up. "Erin, what's wrong?"

"I just got super anxious."

Behind José, Jenny leaned her head on Will, tears leaking out of her eyes.

José frowned. He draped his arm across my back, eyes widening in surprise when his hand tripped on the hilt of my sword. "Why are you armed? Did you dream about something other than us getting carded?"

I glanced down at my worn Chucks. "I lied. I didn't dream anything about tonight, but I had a weird feeling when we were leaving the house."

Perhaps I should've mentioned the tentacles from the thunderstorm in case they weren't manifestations of Niben's power as Mel implied. Instead, I apologized for lying.

He hugged me while the others caught up. "Should we leave?"

"No." I was probably mixing up emotions, but if something was going to attack the theater, I needed to be there to stop it.

I took out my phone and typed a text to Mel: *I have a bad feeling about this.*

I hit send.

*

My skin pricked when we got into the theater. It was old and small and hadn't been renovated with the big spacious chairs like some of the cinemas outside the city. Still, I had the aisle seat. José sat next to me, Will next to him, and Jenny next to Will, but my skin buzzed how it would if I were sandwiched between strangers and off all my meds.

My phone vibrated with a message from Mel: *What is "this?"*

I wrote: *A future I didn't dream? Tentacles you think I didn't see.*

I deleted it and sent: *It could be because I'm at the movies with Jenny. I shouldn't have bothered you. It's nothing.*

Mel had probably just gotten home. I didn't want her to drive all the way back up here from Cambridge, Massachusetts, based on what was most likely anxiety.

It's never nothing. I'll alert Sister Marie and Karen.

"I agree with her," said José, glancing over my shoulder.

"You always do," I muttered.

"Whether you believe it or not, she loves you, and I love you."

"I know," I said in a normal volume before dropping my voice to a whisper. "But you shouldn't."

José sighed.

"Did they Han Solo you?" asked Will.

"They do that several times a day." José laughed. It was convincing, but the harsh edges told me it was fake even if no one else realized. His and Will's banter gradually got louder and more obnoxious until the movie started, and Jenny shushed them.

For a while, I let myself get swept away in snarky dialogue and unrealistic fight scenes that made me want to push my newfound abilities. Questions shot through my mind. How fast could I move? How high could I jump? Was that flip off the wall necessary? Could I do it if I wanted to? Could I call lightning from a storm and not only from wires? If I kept practicing, how much control could I gain over elements like fire and water?

Eventually, even the weird questions faded, and I was completely caught up in the action. Suspense wasn't what kept my attention; the heroes always prevailed in these movies. I only had to guess how and at what cost. Honestly, I was entranced because the scenes were colorful, loud, and graceful—more dance performance than an actual battle.

I literally jumped to my feet with my fists up in a defensive position when José poked me. I sat back down in a second but not before a few people grumbled at me.

"Will said Jenny wants to know if she can wear your sweatshirt," said José.

Jenny already had his sweatshirt on.

José's Elf Stone glowed green in the dark. He was using his Sight. What was he looking for?

"I want to use yours as a blanket," she stage-whispered across the boys.

I shook my head. I didn't want to use glamour to hide my sword, and I was freezing. When I exhaled, I saw my breath.

"I'm too cold," I said.

"Maybe we should go complain to the manager. Someone must have put the AC on the wrong setting," said Jenny.

A person behind us shushed her. I leaned toward José, whispering, "ACs don't make it this cold."

People complained to one another in hushed voices. José squeezed my hand. "Do you see anything?"

Opening my Sight, I stood up and considered the theater. Regular humans and their food filled every seat. Emergency Exit signs glowed red over closed doors. I opened my mind, mentally feeling past the bodies humming with a normal amount of heat to the empty hall leading to the exit to another hall where more humans buzzed with life. The walls thrummed with the electricity powering the lights, projectors, sound system, climate control, popcorn machines, and other appliances.

"Nothing seems unusual except for the fact that I'm freezing, my skin is crawling, and my gut is churning," said José.

"I don't see anything either," I said.

Jenny squeaked. "Erin, something bad is going to happen, isn't it?"

My phone buzzed even though it was set to silent.

"Mel?" asked José.

I held the phone up so we could both see the message: *I went to The Confluence. The time stream changed... IT'S STARTING!!!!*

So many swears fought to come out of my mouth at once that I coughed instead of cursing. A time stream was what most people would think of as a timeline, but to someone like Mel, who saw time as a fast-moving, swiftly changing river with infinite tributaries, a stream seemed more accurate than a line.

"What's starting?" asked José.

"The damned apocalypse," I said, not caring who heard now. I started typing a reply to Mel as crazed giggles burbled up from my gut. I eyed José. "Jenny having your kid is kind of irrelevant if we're all going to die."

"Erin, what's going on?" Jenny leaned over Will, staring at me expectantly.

I answered with panicked laughter.

The emergency door by the screen opened, and air rushed outside into a void even colder than the air inside. The power went out, plunging the theater into darkness, killing any chance I had of drawing electricity from the wall. A storm of complaints and questions erupted around me. The only light in the whole theater came from my phone.

Jenny stood up. "You're serious. This is the apocalypse."

"Shut up and sit down," I hissed.

Jenny obeyed.

José took his phone out. Thanks to Mike, Mel's genius fiancé, the shielding he put on the phones to prevent me from accidentally draining their batteries or frying them when I was throwing electricity around shielded them from whatever took out the power.

I pocketed my phone. "Call for help."

Fire flashed near the door. A gunshot rang out. Jenny and everyone else screamed. A buzzing life turned still and cold. More bangs followed in rapid succession. More people died. I leaped to my feet.

José grabbed me and pulled me down as more bullets ripped through the theater. "What the hell are you doing?"

"Trying to save us," I hissed as my breath came too quickly, and my heart beat too fast. I needed to breathe. I needed to stop the shooters and stop the dying.

I counted as I inhaled, forcing my breaths to go slower each time.

"Erin, they're firing automatic weapons."

"It doesn't matter what they are. I need to stop them." I closed my eyes, drowning out the screams, the whimpers, the prayers, and the rapid fire until I only heard the beat of my heart.

I leaped up, opening my eyes. Bullets soared toward me faster than I expected with my perception of time slowed so much. Three people fired from the front of the theater with a Puppet Master, a Demon resembling an oversized, bleached Gumby, looming over them, controlling them with inky strings. More dark energy trailed from the heat-sucking void outside. Two black streaks climbed toward my face at a steep angle. I slid down inches before one had the chance to rip through my skull. Someone screamed behind me, and their life force winked out of existence.

"No," I gasped, shaking, breathing harder than normal.

Someone died because I dodged a bullet.

The person next to them wailed, full of raging grief that shattered my soul. Another gradually faded, clawing for every breath until they were gone. I balled up on the floor. I needed to do something, but I couldn't breathe. I couldn't move.

"Erin!" José climbed on top of me, pinning my shoulders to the floor. "Focus. What did you see?"

"Puppet Master controlling the shooters," I gasped.

"Shit."

"Let me up," I growled, still shaking.

"So you can get yourself killed?" José's voice was steady, but drops of sweat beaded on his forehead.

I grit my teeth. "People are dying."

"Let Erin go." Jenny crawled over to us.

"Jenny, shhh," hissed Will as if being quiet could save

her.

Jenny ignored him. "You were standing right near Sam when she pulled the trigger. You got to me before the bullet. I know it sounds impossible, but you did. You can do it again, right?"

I nodded.

José lightened the pressure on my shoulders but didn't get off me. "You need to slow your perception of time until you're supersonic if you want to reach the shooters. You can safely sustain that for thirty-three seconds real time."

"That is plenty of time. When the bullets stop, get Jenny and Will to the Jeep. Arm yourself. Wait for me in the car," I said, hoping the Jeep's wards would keep them safe until I returned.

"What if you don't come back?"

I focused on my breathing, on gradually slowing my perception of time.

"I'll wait ten minutes once I get them in the car, and then I'm coming for you," he said, and then he started counting to help me focus.

The syllables of each number stretched out. I counted the seconds between each. I listened to blood swoosh in my veins and how each of my heartbeats came slower. When the space between sixty and sixty-one grew so long that I got frustrated and gave up counting, I slithered out from under him in half the time it took him to blink, unsheathed my sword, and slid it to him because I knew there were more Demons lurking around.

His lips twitched, but before he finished a word, I dove down the stairs, speeding under and around a barrage of bullets moving like bumble bees perusing a garden. I wanted to stop and redirect them all, so they hit no one, but there were too many bullets and not enough time. I stepped on a man, pushing him off the man he shielded with his body, so the bullet passed over them both.

I jumped onto the seat in front of me, calling soda and ice from three extra-large cups, and rearranged the molecules until I had a long blade with a spark of my own energy trapped inside. I used the contents of another cup to make a frozen knife and threw that at the Puppet Master as I leaped, landing between two of the shooters. The knife landed half buried in the Demon's chest. It hardly had time to react before I took its head off and shouted a banishing.

The shooters collapsed to their knees, wide-eyed, staring at the guns in their hands before dropping them like they were burned. Silence hung over the theater for the space of one of my breaths before garbled noise broke out as people realized the shooting was over and fled.

I wanted to run to check on José, but I stayed where I was, letting my perception of time quicken.

Defeating the Puppet Master had been too easy.

Three inky tentacles lashed out from the open door, snapping the shooter's necks. I sucked in a sharp breath and clenched my fists as fear and rage tore through me. The cold lurking outside, the Demon controlling the Puppet Master, was what I truly had to worry about.

"You are correct, little one," rumbled a deep violent voice. The creature's laughter shook the ground. Icy tentacles twined around my legs.

If I survived tonight, Mel, Niben, and Grandpa were going to have a long talk with me regarding what existed and what didn't.

If I survived being the key phrase.

I leaped and kicked, trying to shake the tentacles off, but they tightened. I stabbed at them with my frozen-soda sword, but it shattered on contact. As the little pieces fell, I sped up their molecules, directing the liquid to my skin and freezing it in a thin barrier of ice between the tentacle and me in case this monster was the same kind of deep-sea Demon that destroyed Aunty Lucy's legs.

The Kraken? They merely imitate me. Fear not, little one. I was ordered to deliver you whole.

I closed my eyes for half a second, just long enough to erect mental deflector shields so my thoughts stayed private. The Demon, if it even was a Demon and not something else entirely, laughed while dragging me outside.

Even though it was June, the air was as cold as a January night while a polar vortex sucked the life out of Maine, leaching every drop of humidity from the air, leaving it the kind of dry that made my skin itch. Struggling against the tentacles was useless. The more I flailed, the tighter they got, but I refused to panic again. I let my body go limp. Maybe this beast would think I'd given up and let its guard down.

Momentarily opening a crack in my shields, I stretched my awareness as far into the theater as I could, collecting and freezing whatever liquid I found. I wasn't precise. I couldn't be while being dragged by a mass of tentacles that resembled the monster on Will's T-shirt more than anything from a Demon hunter story.

I bombarded the shadowy Cthulhu-like Demon with needles of frozen soda as it dragged me over the roof's edge to a small lot sandwiched between the theater and a bank. I cracked my phone's case, drained what little energy was in the battery, and zapped the monster. The tentacles loosened for three seconds. Two gulls screeched and flew out of a nearby dumpster. I didn't hesitate to summon electricity from the battery of the lone car and shoot lightning bolts at the tentacles.

The tentacles loosened more this time. I got a hand free and then a leg. Tears, shouts, and panicked gasps for air echoed from the streets around the corner. Hopefully, José was in that crowd, making his way to the Jeep. I needed to end this beast before José came searching for me. What chance did a couple of handguns and a sword have against such a monster?

I couldn't tell what the tentacles were attached to.

I got my other leg free. My other arm next. My feet hit the ground. Air rushed into my lungs. Moonlight silhouetted telephone poles and their wires, but they were as impotent as the wires in the theater walls.

I didn't see a single light on anywhere.

No sirens wailed.

Great. First an Incubus stalked prey online. Now, this Shadowhulhu beast had triggered an electromagnetic pulse or something similar to one.

I stepped over one limp tentacle and ducked under another, navigating a maze of stunned appendages. Three steps away from clear space, the tentacles snapped back together, but instead of squishing me, they formed a cage.

"My servants told me you preferred fight to flight," rumbled the Shadowhulhu, "yet you choose to run away from me and leave hundreds of innocent humans at my mercy."

"I wasn't running," I lied. There was no electricity to vaporize my enemy with. No aid was coming. Mel was too far away and too drained to help.

The monster laughed, and the Earth quaked. The screams echoing from the streets raised all the hair on my body. The cage stunk worse than the inside of a Troll's mouth.

"Try to escape. Fight me." The cage shrunk until I could barely stand without hitting my head on the top.

"What are you?" I asked, even though knowing might not make a difference.

"What are you?" If power flowed through the high-tension lines, this would be over, but this monster knew that. It feared me enough to disable a weapon I wielded effectively, so maybe I could win.

"What—"

A tentacle twined around my throat before I could finish the question, squeezing hard enough to cut off my oxygen supply without breaking my neck.

Dropping my shields again, I plunged my awareness downward past concrete and dirt. My consciousness dug through four feet of asphalt and soil, mingling with strangled roots and water molecules a couple of feet away—where the tree-lined street met the alley and the gas main connected to the buildings. I tangled my energy around tree roots and water, pushing up against a gas pipe until it breached the surface of the already cracked pavement and broke in half.

Even if I could've breathed, I wouldn't have been able to smell the gas over the monster's stench, but I felt it rushing around us. I needed a spark or a tiny flame. My brain was unraveling. Ideas didn't click together. My body went limp. Molecules were blurs I could no longer focus enough to touch. All I had was inside me. I pushed energy out of myself—a piece of my life, a spark from my soul—and ignited the natural gas.

The tentacle loosened. The ground flew up from under me, knocking the cage away and exposing me to my flames. I pulled excess energy into my body. Heat seared under my skin. The pain nearly overwhelmed me, but dammit, I was alive. The fire turned to light and sank into my skin until I felt like I was going to melt. I pushed the energy outward, engulfing the monster in golden flames.

The tentacles retreated to a dense knot of shadows. I grit my teeth against the heat assaulting my skin; I kept pushing the flames forward. I hadn't learned a banishing spell for anything like this creature. I wasn't sure one existed. So, I willed it to be gone as I had done to the Incubus in March.

This monster didn't explode into a thousand shards I could scatter across the multiverse. It spun until it became a black hole, sucked up the flames, and disappeared.

Chapter Three

I sleep so much better next to Erin than I ever did in my father's house. I come home from school knowing no one is going to hurt me. When I respond to Demon sightings, Erin is always with me. They destroy the Demon. All I have to do is say the banishing. They've become my shield, my safety, and my home. But everything has a cost. Erin would train until they collapse if I didn't make them stop. They'd live off bacon and cookies if I didn't cook for them. I hold them at night when they wake screaming from a future too horrible to put into words.

—From the journal of José Estrella, written in May 2018, confined to the archives the morning of his high school graduation.

I rolled to my stomach and pushed myself up onto my hands and knees with shaking arms. Dirt, roots, and twisted conduit surrounded me. I didn't have the energy to stand, let alone climb out of the crater I'd made. Everything hurt, especially my churning stomach and throbbing head. The gas didn't help.

Now was a good time for José to find me. The monster was gone. It was safe for José to help me out of this crater and support me while I hobbled to the Jeep.

I waited, but he didn't come.

Maybe the monster had brought Demons along to keep José from helping me. He could handle a few with a sword and a handgun, especially if Sister Marie or Officer Karen had gotten Mel's message and come to help.

He'd be here any minute. Right?

I dug my phone out of my pocket. The screen and case were wavy from melting and hardening. Apparently, the new case could keep electricity from frying the phone, but it wasn't fireproof. I shoved it back in my pocket.

There was still no sign of José.

He'd never leave me to fend for myself unless he was injured or still fighting his way to me. What if he was hurt and drained too, wondering why I wasn't coming for him? I grabbed a root, grit my teeth, and pulled myself to my feet. My arms and legs shook; my tired muscles screamed for rest.

I breathed too deeply and gagged on sulfur and rotten eggs. I reached for another root and stuck my foot in a crevice. I wedged the next foot onto a thicker root, slowly but surely using roots, footholds, and pieces of conduit to pull myself up. I was only six or seven feet down, but with my body so drained, it felt like climbing three times the distance.

My head breached the surface. A nervous simmer of sobs, angry questions, and a few sputtering engines echoed from the parking lot.

My hips broke the surface next. I rested on crumbled pavement before pulling the rest of me up. A flashlight shone around the corner. The dark-blue uniform told me the person was a cop. Their badge reflected moonlight nearly as bright as the flashlight. I needed help, but crawling outside the door the shooters used right next to a crater created by an explosion wasn't an ideal situation to be found in by the police. I pushed myself up and collapsed flat on my back.

"Amelia? You got here quick! Are José and Erin with you?"

Relief lightened me as I realized the voice belonged to Officer Karen, the police officer who volunteered to help supervise dances at Saint Patrick's on her nights off, who was both half-Demon and a Demon hunter. I mustered enough energy to sit up and peer around, but I didn't see my cousin and her telltale glow. My Sight was definitely open because Officer Karen's skin was ghostly white, and her eyes dilated wide enough to hide brown irises and half the sclera.

"José isn't here. Where is Mel?" On a dark night, it was hard to miss someone who glowed even if her glow was faint.

Officer Karen paused, shining her light in my face. "Erin? I thought you were your cousin."

"Have you heard from her?" How did she mistake me for Mel? Was I somehow glowing from my stunt with the fire?

"I guess she and Mike are still on their way. Are you okay?"

"No." I took the hand she offered and let her pull me to my feet even though my muscles burned in protest. I had to lean on her to stay upright. "José was supposed to leave the theater with Will and Jenny. He told me he'd wait ten minutes before looking for me."

"I just left those two. He wasn't there."

"Did they say when they last saw him?" I hobbled away from the crater first, relying on her for support and eventually walking on my own. Barely.

"They lost track of him in the crowd and went to their car since they didn't know where you parked. I found this on the ground beside your Jeep." Officer Karen stopped walking and took a broken sword out from under her jacket, the one I had given José right before I went after the shooters.

*

Bolstered by a surge of panicked adrenaline, I stumbled through a crowd that resembled a cross between a funeral and a riot with Officer Karen trailing behind me. Hundreds of people from the theater and neighboring restaurants filled the streets, aiding those who were injured, starting cars with mixed luck, or staring at their powerless phones as if their best friend had betrayed them.

"Stay here and help them," I shouted with little conviction. The people needed help. I wanted her help finding José. I was so tired I feared if I stopped moving for a second, I'd pass out.

"Erin, wait!" Officer Karen caught up as the crowd thinned. Her energy was a few degrees cooler than that of the humans.

The Jeep was a beacon of green hope parked in front of an office building. A new dent graced the driver's side door. I yanked the handle, but the door didn't open. I patted down my jeans, but my keys weren't there.

"Where do you think you are going to go?" she asked.

"To find him." I hoped I didn't fall asleep behind the wheel.

My head swam as I knelt down and searched the undercarriage for the magnetic box I kept my spare key in. My legs burned as I climbed up into the driver's seat, but they sang with relief as I sat. I yawned. My vision darkened even though I didn't close my eyes. I pulled a brownie out of my center console with one hand while I started the car with the other.

The engine growled to life. No lights illuminated the dash. The headlights wouldn't turn on. I shifted to reverse, nearly crashing into the car behind me as I backed out mid-yawn. I shifted to park, shoved half the brownie in my mouth, and pushed the shifter to forward only to realize an abandoned Tesla car blocked the road, horizontally like it had skidded when the EMP fried its circuitry. Stepping on the brake, I turned my wheel hard, but Officer Karen stood in the middle of the street with her arms crossed. I put the car in park and finished my brownie, barely swallowing as my throat burned with frustration and tears leaked out of my eyes. My whole body shook.

Exhausted.

Trapped.

I needed to find José.

The driver's side door creaked as Officer Karen opened it.

"Why are you here? Should you be trying to contain the chaos?"

She shrugged. "There were doctors and nurses in the theater, and they can do more for the wounded than I could. Plus, Sister Marie would have my head if I let you blindly drive off after José alone."

"What are we going to do?" I croaked over unwelcome tears.

"Eat." Officer Karen pulled a protein bar out of her pocket and handed it to me.

Peanut wasn't my favorite, but it was food, which steadied my hands and distracted me for a whole two seconds.

A motorcycle purred in the distance.

Officer Karen handed me a package of saltine crackers.

The purr grew to a rumble as I chewed.

A trio of Pixies, one red and two blue, illuminated Sister Marie, who was clad in a vintage bomber jacket, weaving a 1940s motorcycle around stopped cars and panicked pedestrians. She squeezed around the Tesla and stopped the bike with the engine idling. "Hop on."

Officer Karen grabbed me as I stumbled out of the Jeep. She held me by the arm and walked me halfway to where Sister Marie waited on the motorcycle, then turned me so I was facing up the street. "Stand still."

She backed a couple yards away from me before removing the Taser from her utility belt. "Try to actually absorb the energy instead of temporarily holding it."

I'd done that with fire a few times. I closed my eyes, breathing slow, with my hands and mind open.

Sister Marie kicked her kickstand down and got up. "Karen, are you sure—"

Officer Karen fired. I snatched the prongs out of the air with my right hand. My arm twitched, but my body was so used to taking in huge amounts of electricity that calming and channeling it was muscle memory.

The harder part came next.

The electricity raced across synapses, buzzing under my skin. Normally, I could let it mingle with some of my own energy and then shoot raw power at whatever Demon I wanted to destroy. But right now, I needed the energy. It wasn't the same as a big meal and a good night's sleep, but it would keep me going a little longer.

I counted the space between heartbeats, willing the energy to slow down with my perception of time, to sink into my tired muscles and stimulate sleepy parts of my brain. The buzzy feeling faded. My legs steadied, and my head cleared. I opened my eyes and used my left hand to yank the prongs out of my right hand, feeling guilty at the rush I got from the little bit of skin that came away with the metal until someone pressed an alcohol wipe onto my cut palm.

"Don't want you wasting energy fighting off on infection. Now, arm yourself and go find José." Officer Karen patted me on the back.

I returned to the Jeep. My hands were steady as I opened my tailgate and the spare-tire compartment concealing my weapons. José must not have had a chance to unlock the car because all the guns and blades were still there. I strapped a katana on my back and belted three sheathed knives to my waist.

"There are two handguns if you want them," I said to Officer Karen

"I'll take them." She unzipped her jacket and stowed them in two empty shoulder holsters.

Did that mean she'd fought her way here?

An engine revved behind me.

"We don't have much time." Sister Marie bared her teeth, handing me a sleek helmet that matched the one she wore.

I put it on and then sat on the back of the bike. A smartphone tracking José's phone partially obscured an antique speedometer.

"Hold on tight. This baby doesn't get to see open road much these days, so she's raring to go." Sister Marie kicked the kickstand.

I hugged her waist, which was covered by her brown-leather bomber jacket, probably as old as the bike. Her handguns were modern, but her shotgun belonged in my history textbook.

It reminded me how old the nun was. Last year, Sister Marie had a seventieth-birthday celebration at school, but in reality, she was over two hundred years old. As an Elf-Human hybrid, she wouldn't live millennia like a full Elf, but her life could still quadruple that of the average human. Officer Karen was nearly as old, but she posed as someone in her late forties.

A few blocks out from the theater, Sister Marie took a sharp turn. Stopped cars clogged the road while others tried to navigate around them without the use of headlights or blinkers.

People roamed the streets.

Dogs barked.

Children cried.

We'd only gone a couple miles from the theater, but I could see the end of the EMP radius. Closer to the water, the lights were all on. The road we were on was still dark with some stopped cars, but there weren't looters or crowds of panicked people. Police and ambulances worked their way through while tow trucks moved the cars that wouldn't start.

No one noticed as we swerved between cones and a police perimeter. Back beneath streetlights, we wove in and out of traffic and ran red lights. At first, the GPS led us to the waterfront along a street crowded with restaurants and shops. We took a sharp right, zigzagging up to another section of town in the blackout zone. The tracker dot paused. We zoomed toward that spot and stopped in front of an alley: the same one I had fought the

Incubus a few months ago. I leaped off the bike, ready to charge in.

Sister Marie grabbed my arm. "You don't know what is in there."

The red and blue Pixies who had been following us dimmed their light. Air from a fluttering wing brushed my cheek. The Pixie returned a few long seconds later, claiming it didn't see anything in the alley.

Sister Marie's head tilted, and her eyebrows furrowed as she translated. I ran ahead, not seeing so much as feeling for any sign of life. A lone source of electricity radiated from a pile of litter. I kicked food wrappers and flyers with my foot until I saw a phone.

"His phone is here, but he's not." After carefully picking up José's phone, I dusted the screen off on my pant leg.

Sister Marie's three Pixies illuminated the alley as they escorted her into it. She stalked forward, aiming a shotgun at the shadows as I unlocked José's phone. I sucked in a breath of cold air, clenching every muscle in my body. Had he been tracking a Demon assuming I'd catch up? Had he been taken, and for some reason, this point was where they realized he had the phone and ditched it? Had he ever been here at all? What if he'd disappeared into a blackhole with the tentacles and some other Demon had brought the phone here to throw me off?

I looked at the screen.

It was white.

Black letters appeared:

THE CLOCK IS TICKING.

SURRENDER OR HE DIES.

To who? Or what?

A time appeared on the screen counting down.

6 DAYS, 23 HOURS, 59 MINUTES, 55 SECONDS

The Demons that wanted me had José. He was the bait to lure me into a trap. Could I spring it, save him, and get us both out alive? Did faking a surrender to save him mean ushering in one of the visions where I ruled a scorched Earth with him beside me in chains? Or were all the potential futures I had seen now erased and replaced with possibilities I had yet to glimpse?

Don't surrender, don't...like I... A familiar frog-like voice whispered in my head, but the words were static and garbled. I spun around, sword out, ready to fend off the Incubus. I saw evanescent cloud. *You're stronger...both realize.*

Sister Marie's footsteps thundered down the alley.

Crawlers...coming...after...run! The cloud dissipated.

Chapter Four

Grandpa's always been weird about Erin and me dating people. He's protective in an old-fashioned way, but modern in the sense he doesn't discriminate based on gender. Boys, girls, and enbies all get the same intimidation tactics. But Mike was different. The first time they met, Grandpa was getting his ass kicked by a rather large Spike. Mike shot it without a second's hesitation, saving Grandpa's life.

—An entry from Amelia Evanstar's personal journal, written in 2014.

"Erin, don't even think of letting them take you." Sister Marie grabbed my arm, yanking me toward the alley's opening.

"I wasn't going to, yet." I shrugged my arm free and followed her, peering around for remnants of the white cloud. Had the Incubus warned me against its own master? Why?

"When we locate him, we'll plan a proper extraction," she said, not easing up her grip on me.

"I know." I had a week to find another way to get him.

"Do you have a way to do that, other than tracking his phone?"

I didn't have any clues regarding his physical location, but as I had been reminded multiple times today, I was a prophet. I dreamt the future. Hopefully, one of my apocalyptic nightmares would contain some hint of his location, or even better, a way to find him.

Sister Marie frowned. "If we can find...shit."

A six-headed, winged Demon landed on the ground in front of us. All six of its mouths moved at once, speaking in screechy singing voices. "If you come with us now, the old nun lives, and you find your lover. Fight us now, and we eat her and try to take you."

Sister Marie blew one of its heads off with her shotgun. I unsheathed a sword and rushed it.

"Dinner time!" it sang with the other head and lunged at us as a horde of Crawlers leaped off the roof and scurried down the walls.

I bisected a Demon with the body of a spider, two mosquito-like heads, and eight human-ish arms. Crawlers came in an amalgam of shapes and sizes. They could do a lot of damage on their own if they got close enough, but their lack of intelligence made them easy to kill.

A six-legged beast leaped off the wall, teeth and claws scratching for me, and practically landed on my sword. I yanked the blade out just in time to block the claws of another. Sister Marie kept firing up until the Demons were practically on top of her. She whacked one with the shotgun as two blades popped out of the side forming a fork.

When I first joined the Demon hunters, I thought fighting alongside my high school principal would be awkward.

There wasn't much time to think about awkward during battles.

Cold pain in my calf tore my attention away from the gun. I growled and slashed my sword at the beast that had wounded me.

Blood soaked my pants. It *hurt*, sparking a slumbering psychological beast. I swung twice as fast and stabbed harder at every monster that came at me. Pulling what little electricity was stored in Sister Marie's flashlight, I sent two concentrated bolts of energy flying toward two Crawlers.

They turned to snow.

I laughed.

While I decapitated a nine-eyed bug, a puddle became a storm of icicles taking out three more Demons.

"Easy," shouted Sister Marie. "Save the party tricks for the big guys."

"Big guys? Don't tell me there's a Troll." I had yet to take down a Troll without electrical assistance.

A jaw full of teeth flew at me. There wasn't another puddle or flashlight, so instead of trying something that required more of my already depleted energy, I kept slashing and hacking until the pain in my leg faded to a dull throb, and Sister Marie and I stood back to back, fending off a seemingly endless onslaught.

How many of these damned things were there?

An engine whined, barely audible over the hordes snarling and hissing. Tires screeched. Electricity hummed in lights and in a car engine that radiated far more power than one with a normal battery.

Erin, don't even think about messing with that. Mel's voice was a welcome intrusion into my mind.

The tentacles were real. They took José, I thought as my sword pierced a bowling-ball-shaped skull.

Brace yourself for a power surge and keep the worst of it off Sister Marie.

Energy flared. Electricity forked through the alley, vaporizing Demon after Demon. I reached out and grabbed the bolts that came near Sister Marie and me. The raw energy singed my skin and rattled my bones as I channeled it through myself, shoving supercharged lightning toward whatever Demons remained.

Thirty seconds later, I was laughing knee-deep in snow-like disintegrated Demon. My lungs burned and everything hurt. Mike stood at the mouth of the alley, holding a smoking canon—not the kind that shot metal balls. This looked like it should be shooting lasers off a spaceship. Hair the color of honey stood up straight, classic mad scientist.

"Can I have one of those?" I coughed as I collapsed to my knees.

You don't need one.

I could hear the eye roll in Mel's voice. I couldn't see her anywhere.

"Wouldn't 'thank you' be the appropriate response?" Mike lowered the smoking weapon to the ground and leaned it against a brick wall.

"Yes. Thank you," said Sister Marie.

Mike grinned. He always bragged about his Demon-killing weapons, but I'd never seen him use one. Mel never let him out her sight when Demons were around.

I can see him.

Where are you?

Locked in the damned DeLorean.

Mike snorted. Apparently, Mel was broadcasting loud enough for us all to hear.

The last of my battle high faded and reality sucker punched me.

Tears washed bits of Demon flakes off my face as the adrenaline receded, leaving me cold and drained, again. José was just as gone, and I had even less clues as to where he was than I had a few minutes ago. At least I knew he was alive and would stay that way for a few more days. Assuming the message on the phone wasn't lying.

He's not dead. I don't have as strong a connection to him as you and Mike, but I've healed him enough that I'd feel it if he died. Get in the car before more Demons, or tentacles, show up.

I followed Mike to the car. He opened the rear hatch, one of many things not original to the car, and put his cannon in the small cargo area behind the back seats.

"I'll meet you kids at the convent," said Sister Marie. Her bike growled and she sped off with her three Pixies in tow.

I squeezed past Mel's seat, but as soon as I was in the back, she was there too.

"Let me see your leg." She knelt on the seat next to me in gray sweatpants and a *Star Trek* T-shirt she wouldn't have worn if she'd planned to see me.

"It's fine." I scooted away from her.

"I can still check it."

I crossed my arms.

Mike hit a button to start the car. The engine, another thing definitely not originally in his wannabe time machine, started with a quiet hum.

Huffing and puffing, Mel dug into an archaic magazine holder attached to the back of the passenger seat and pulled out a first aid kit. She opened that and removed alcohol wipes, gauze bandages, tape, antibiotic ointment, and a green tube labeled Skin Glue.

"I can treat your wound without healing it."

"Fine." I should've thanked her, but I was exhausted and lost. As much as I loved my cousin, or perhaps because I loved her, it was too easy to be mean.

"I'll take that as an apology." Mel rolled my shredded pant leg up and cringed. I didn't look to see how bad it was.

I gritted my teeth, but I still yelped when she sanitized the wound. I focused on the front of the car, specifically on the screen that replaced what in my parents' generation would've been an eight-track player. It displayed the dotted map Mike used to track supernatural activity in the area.

It was completely devoid of Demon activity, but it showed a few hunters and an Angel hovering nearby.

Mel squeezed something cold onto the wound on my calf, which thankfully numbed that part of my leg a little, so I barely felt Mel pressing my skin together.

"This is surgical glue I made for people like us. It will help you heal quicker." Mel covered the now glued skin with a gauze pad and taped it to my leg. When she was done, she said, "Show me what happened."

I leaned my head against the window's cool glass, watching lights blur by outside as I replayed the memory from the shooters' deaths.

"I'm sorry I didn't believe you," she said.

I shrugged. "Do you have any idea where José is?"

Mel shook her head. "I don't know where to start searching other than in your dreams and the Confluence."

"Assuming we can get there, we can follow the time stream from when he and I split to the present." Twice, when I'd been sleeping, Mel had pulled me out of my dreams and brought me to the Confluence, a place that resembled a rainbow river in outer space.

Mel claimed it was a metaphysical plane where all the time streams converged. There, we could potentially see the past, what is happening in the present, and millions of possible futures. If Mel could get me there, and if the time streams cooperated, then locating José would be possible. Most of her attempts to get me there failed, and alone Mel could only see potential threads of her future. I was the one with the ability to control what we saw.

"Is there any way we can track him? A spell or something?"

"We can't. A Witch *might* be able to." Mel rummaged around in the part of the car she had pulled the first aid kit from and handed me a bag of chocolate-covered bacon.

"We need to try the Confluence again."

There were very few human Witches alive. The skilled ones had grudges against Niben and refused to deal with her grandchildren. According to the Incubus and my nana, Sam was technically a Witch, but she didn't know much about the supernatural and probably hated me as much as the other Witches hated Niben.

I finished the chocolate-covered bacon, curled up with my back to Mel and my forehead on the window, and closed my eyes, hoping I'd fall asleep and dream of how to rescue José, but exhausted as I was, my brain refused to shut off.

*

I was relieved to see the lights were on at Southern Maine Rehabilitation and Nursing Center. The blue-and-white sign was a beacon, and the warm light poured out from the windows, almost making it cozy with shadows hiding the brick walls.

"Thank you," I said to Mel as the DeLorean doors lifted. Mike got out and moved the seat forward, so it was easier to get out of the back. Mel stood next to the door with a hand extended. I considered her strangely until I put weight on my injured leg, and my nerves assaulted my brain with stabbing pain signals. She snickered and let me lean on her as we walked toward the building.

Mike stayed behind. I looked at him, then at Mel.

"He is itching to hook José's phone up to one of his computers to see if he can get anything useful off it. He has enough tech in the car to get started." Mel looked over her shoulder at him, took a deep breath, and strode toward the building.

Technically, visiting hours were over, but the person at the front desk was too busy watching a newscaster report on the movie theater shooting and the power outages to notice us.

Mel and I took the stairs up to the second floor. My leg throbbed, but the pain was better than taking the elevator. Since I'd learned how to manipulate electricity, I'd been terrified I would accidentally short out an elevator while I was in one and get trapped.

I winced with each step I took. Of course, setting foot in a medical facility at all was a risk. Although 99 percent of the time I was in control of my abilities, there had been one time when I became overwhelmed with rage, light bulbs exploded and electricity arced out of the socket like I had summoned it to fight a Demon. And if that happened here, the consequences could be dire for patients relying on electrically powered machines to survive.

You were cornered in a locker room by a group of bullies. Mel's voice was a welcome intrusion to my anxious thoughts. *That isn't going to happen here. We're fine.*

I nodded, hoping she was right as I continued to hobble up the stairs, letting the sharp stabs of pain silence the doubt anxiety whispered in my head.

As we emerged into a wide foyer, our footsteps echoed off the tile until we reached the hall lined with doors to the rooms. Then, the buzzing and whirring of IVs, monitors, and oxygen machines masked our footfalls. The people at the nurse's station never glanced away from their screens.

I limped past several open doors, trying not to look in, but the blurs in my peripheral vision were too difficult to avoid. The first showed an elderly woman watching a game show with her mouth hanging open. Another showed someone so casted and braced, I really had to try not to stare in a pointless attempt to see who they were. They had the news on their TV. A reporter stood in front of a dark street. Her mouth moved, but the volume was too faint for me to hear what she said. The coverage switched to another reporter standing in front of the movie theater, which was finally empty of victims and crawling with law enforcement and military vehicles.

When I got to Mom's room, I sped past her roommate, wishing I could manage walking while glamouring myself invisible at the same time. I also wished I didn't have to hear the reporter on her TV rattling off death tolls between interviews with sobbing teenagers.

When I visited Mom, I rarely kept my Sight open. Without it, she still looked like my mother: the brown roots pushed their way out from under dyed-blonde hair, and brown eyes with wrinkles extended from the edges resembling the curvy lines from waves breaking onto sand.

But with my Sight open? Hurricane cataracts swirled over her eyes, and the flaking points of Elven ears seemed to shrivel up more and more every day. Mom might appear to be sleeping because she wasn't hooked up to any machines and could breathe on her own. However, she could only chew and swallow when someone fed her. She blinked and squeezed hands, but she didn't talk. Her facial expression never changed. She couldn't stand or sit up on her own.

I wanted my mother back.

But with Mel's healing abilities out of commission and Demons triggering EMPs, shooting up movie theaters, and prepping for an invasion I no longer knew how to stop, I wasn't sure I'd ever get my mother back.

This might be goodbye.

Mel hovered in the background while I sat beside Mom and held her hand. Although unsure if she could understand me, I'd gotten in the habit of telling her everything. A tale of what happened tonight poured out of me with tears I could no longer restrain.

Mel leaned over me and put her head next to mine and whispered, "Maybe we should try to put wards around the room."

"Is something coming?"

Wards weren't as effective around individual rooms as they were around houses, but they'd still deter some Demons from trying to get in here to hurt Mom. None had tried to harm her in the months she'd been here, but Demons had done a lot of unusual things today.

"Not yet. But it's getting late, and we need to meet up with the other hunters. You need to tell them what happened tonight."

"All right. Just give me another minute to rest first." I yawned, leaned back in the chair, and closed my eyes.

I wasn't in Mom's room anymore. I was in my nana's. I'd been to visit her several times in person over the past couple months, but the only time I could ever make some sense of what she wanted from me was when she visited me in dreams.

"Erin!" Nana sat up, stiff and electric. Her black eyes were filled with swirling galaxies. "You've tarried too long, depending on others to do your work for you, overconfident in your ability to read the time streams."

She grabbed my wrist, gripping it with bony fingers. The lights in the room flickered. Static made my hair stand up. "Get your Witch, break my curse, and free me. Do not make your father's mistakes."

She vanished, and I was sitting beside my mother's bed while Mel stared at me, squinting like she was dissecting my brain. If she'd been reading my mind, then she should've seen the vision too.

"Mel, is she talking about Sam?" I stood too quickly. Pain shot up from my leg. Both the room and I wobbled as I toppled forward. My shoulder slammed into Mel's chest. Her sneakers squeaked as she stumbled backward, wrapping her arms around me to keep me from falling onto my mom's bed.

"I think so, but we can't exactly walk in a psychiatric hospital and walk out with Sam."

I sucked in a sharp breath. We could do just that if we had a strong enough glamour. Mel might be too weak to pull it off, but my grandmother, Niben, would have no trouble keeping us hidden from human eyes.

"Is everything okay in here?" A man in scrubs poked his head in the room. He was short with warm skin and hair that was a dozen shades of blond, identical to Mel's hair. His badge labeled him a CNA, but I didn't recognize him.

"Are you new?" I asked at the same time Mel whispered, "Dad?"

Confused, I opened my Sight. White light seared my eyes. Even at its brightest, Mel's light had never been this luminous. Perhaps that was the difference between a young half Angel and an ancient Angel. I shut my eyes and my Sight. Black and purple spots danced under my lids and obscured my vision when I opened them again.

Mel stepped forward with her arms raised like she was about to hug the being that now resembled a normal human but stopped when a nurse stepped into the room behind him, saying, "Michael, can you help me get her out of bed?"

Okay, he wasn't only wearing the uniform. He actually worked here.

If you two don't leave soon, you'll draw Demons here. Michael's voice was a low, melodious whisper in my mind.

Mel squeezed my hand. *Let's go.*

I looked at my mom one more time, whispered goodbye, and backed out of the room, holding Mel's hand. Once we stepped into the hall, anxiety crushed my chest with the pressure of an ocean. "Mel, what does it mean that your dad is here?"

She stared straight ahead as we walked past the nurse's station. "Demons won't come anywhere near this place."

"But why is he all of a sudden here now?"

Mel's lips pressed together. "He started working here around the time your mom transferred in but told me not to tell you."

"Why?" I opened and closed my free hand as I walked, struggling not to leave it clenched in a fist.

"I don't know," said Mel. "I asked. He gave me one of his cryptic looks and changed the subject."

I hadn't actually seen Mel's dad before today, but based on what she'd told me about him, he wasn't very good about answering questions. Mel paused in front of the elevator, reaching for the button. I let go of her hand and hobbled toward the stairs. Going down would hurt. I was okay with that. It made it easier to stop thinking.

Chapter Five

At one point during the war, we were all lovers—me, Seamus, Marie, Karen, and Aelfric. But it didn't last. Aelfric and my winter cousin, Phineas, disappeared after defeating the Fallen. The Cold War consumed Karen's attention. Marie resumed running her school and summer missions. I could have and probably should have gone home. But Faerie didn't feel like home anymore. Seamus did.

> —From the personal journal of Niben of the Summer Elves, written shortly after the birth of her children, Lucy and Liam.

I stumbled, propelled by Mel, into the chilly parking lot. The DeLorean hadn't moved. The air shimmered in front of us, and for a moment, the veil between this world and Faerie parted. A big, shaggy dog charged forward, pulling Niben out of a lush forest onto the cracked pavement. She let go of the leash. The gateway closed behind her. Bessie charged forward, stood on her hind legs, and slobbered my face.

Keeping my eyes on grandmother, I knelt so Bessie wouldn't knock me over while Mel tackled Niben with a hug. Niben's brown pants were torn at the knee, and the edges of her long-sleeved green shirt were smeared with dirt and blood. A storm cloud of a bruise covered the skin around her left eye.

"Where is Grandpa? Did you get attacked too?" I asked.

Immediately after graduation, Niben and Grandpa had left on yet another quest to track down some old friends who might know how to deal with the Fallen Angel that was behind the apocalypse. Both Niben and Grandpa had been alive the last time one tried to invade, but they'd been on the sidelines and in the background of that fight. They were searching for those who had been on the front lines, Elves and hybrids neither had seen in decades.

"He's safer than us right now. He is trying to persuade an old friend, Aelfric, to help us. He wanted to rush back after the Pixies reported what happened, but I convinced him to stay, telling him I'd go right to wherever you were. When I stopped at your house, I ran into a group of Demons."

"I'm glad you made it here okay." My words were distorted by Bessie licking my face.

"Me too." Mel chewed her lip. "Grandpa never mentioned anyone named Aelfric."

"There is a lot Seamus has either lied to you about or outright refused to think of since Liam died," said Niben.

I tilted my head, watching Niben. It was old news that Grandpa hid stuff from me, but I thought Mel knew *everything* about our family.

"I'm aware of that, but *you* never mentioned this Aelfric either." Mel stood between Niben and the car with her arms crossed, eyes narrowed, and lips pressed tight together.

Niben mirrored Mel's posture. "Aelfric didn't want you to know he existed."

The car doors lifted. Mel huffed, but she stepped aside while Niben gracefully glided into the car. I limped, then stumbled in beside her and ended up with all one hundred pounds of Bessie on my lap. Mike sighed, still focused on his screen.

Mel climbed in the front and peered around to the back. "So, who and what is Aelfric, and why do we need his help?"

Niben leaned her head on Bessie's back and closed her eyes. "There may be a way to find José, but it requires a certain amount of Angelic power, which you are not in any shape to provide, but Aelfric, a distant cousin of yours, one of the rare Angel-hybrids whose life span has surpassed that of a human, has plenty to spare."

Mel stared at Niben with her head cocked and her mouth open. "Niben, I would've liked to have met this cousin a long time ago."

Angel-hybrids were not common. Except for the few born without healing powers, most of them died young because they overused their abilities. Mel didn't know any who were older than her. I hadn't been aware of it until recently, but she'd come very close to death several times in the past few years. An old Angel-hybrid was a big deal.

Niben smirked, but her eyes looked sad. "You would've been disappointed."

"Do you think he'll help?" I asked. That was all that mattered now. The more people we had on our side, the better out chances were.

"I hope he will," said Niben.

I scratched Bessie behind her ears with both hands. "How much do you know about what happened tonight?"

Niben stared at the car's floor with her brow furrowed and her pointy ears pressed to her head. "The Pixies saw the Many-Tentacled Destroyer arrive at the theater and got as far away from it as they could. They informed me that José was missing and how you and Sister Marie found José's phone and were ambushed."

I took a deep breath. The Many-Tentacled Destroyer must be the creature I had deemed Shadowhulhu. "I think I saw it earlier today in the storm you were holding off."

Niben nodded. "You very well may have. It's an ancient entity, one I didn't believe was still capable of manifesting on Earth, and it is beyond my ability to detect it if it wants to remain hidden."

If a three-hundred-and-something-year-old Elf, who could control thunderstorms, couldn't sense Shadowhulhu, then how was I going to find it and the person it took from me?

*

Saint Patrick's grounds were dark and silent. It was hard to believe that earlier today I'd walked across a stage here and gotten a diploma. I'd kissed José under the tent, and just when all in the world felt right, Jenny came and told us she was pregnant. That had upset me so much, but now, it seemed so insignificant. José was missing, and the world was about to end. Nothing mattered if we were all going to die.

"We can still save him and the world," said Mel, responding to my thoughts from the front passenger seat of the car.

I nodded, but my throat was too tight for me to speak. There had to be something we could do, but I had no clue where to start. Even if we did manage to stop the apocalypse, there were so many things that could go wrong in the process.

"What if when whoever abducted José realizes I'm not coming right away, they start sending me body parts? Things a person can live without like fingers or ears."

"He won't be good collateral if they break him," said Niben as we drove into the convent parking lot.

"Niben is right. These are Demons, not humans," said Mike. He pulled into a parking spot in front of a plain brick building. "The cruelest monsters I've seen were human. There are people I fear more than any Demon I've seen since I started hunting with the Evanstars."

The car turned off, but Mike still gripped the wheel so tight veins bulged against tendons in his wrist. He didn't move. In the rearview mirror, he stared unblinking and pasty until Mel put a hand on his shoulder, and he collapsed inward like a dying star. Bessie pawed the back of his seat. Her hind paws dug into my legs when she tried but failed to climb into the front. My growling stomach was the loudest thing in car. If Mel and Mike were discussing whatever thought had triggered his panic attack or flashback, they were doing it in their minds. Awkwardness and curiosity crawled over my skin and strangled my stomach.

Up until March, most, if not all, my conversations with Mike had been about video games, comic books, or movies. Other than that, I knew very little about him aside from him being four years older than Mel. I also knew he was a genius working toward a PhD at MIT. Based on that information, I guess I'd always assumed naivety was the source of his light attitude toward Demon hunting. But perhaps I was mistaken, and Mike's history was as violent as the hunters.

I picked at my lip, then sat on my hands. If I didn't get out of this car, if someone didn't say or do something,

I was going to start clawing my skin off. Bessie made a noise that was something between a moo and a howl. She licked my face. Something hummed as the door finally lifted, and a cool breeze carried the scent of bacon from the convent to my nose.

I flew out of the car and would've literally ran to the door had Niben not grabbed my arm. "Mike is embarrassed enough. Don't make it worse by being childish and running."

Bessie barked her agreement as she trotted up alongside me.

Nodding, I slowed down even though I wanted to get inside as quickly as possible. Maybe once I ate and calmed down, I'd think of something I could do. Maybe Sister Marie would know something the rest of us didn't. I leaped up the three steps to a small porch. Wood boards creaked under my feet. I reached for the door, but it opened before my hand touched the knob.

While I frequented the gym under the convent, I'd only been in the main building a few times, and on those occasions, only Sister Marie and Officer Karen had been home, so I was surprised to see a boy a few years younger than me open the door.

"It's Jeremy, right?" said Niben in a voice more grandmotherly than I thought she was capable of.

"Yes." The boy nodded. His 'fro was a halo of black accentuated by golden light. His skin was warm brown and glowing. Not quite bright enough to make me squint, but enough to tell me he was an Angel-hybrid. Jeremy took a step backward with his hands clasped behind him. "Ca...can you both shield?"

I closed my eyes for a moment, envisioning myself in a spaceship cockpit, flicking a lever to put deflector shields up. I didn't always need to go through the whole mental image, but it made it easier when I was tired.

"Thank you," he said. "It's hard to focus on talking when I can hear other people thinking. Sister Marie is expecting Erin. And the Pixies keep dive-bombing the cake."

He turned around and jogged up the hall like he couldn't get away from us fast enough.

"Mel never mentioned there being another Angel-hybrid so close," I said to Niben.

"I know of him from Marie and Karen, not from Mel," said Niben.

Jeremy turned around a corner. Niben and I followed him into a warm kitchen lit by Pixie light and vintage lamps. I wanted to sink into a chair at the kitchen table, but there was no food on the table.

I jumped as Sister Marie slammed her coffee cup down, leaped up from the table, and hugged Niben. "I'm sorry I was so stubborn about the storm."

"It's insignificant in light of current events." Niben held Sister Marie tight until the old nun pulled away.

Sister Marie wore a loose-fitting T-shirt and sweatpants. Her short, gray hair was a tangled mess. She ran her hands through it as she turned and looked at me. "Erin. How are you?"

"Tired. Lost. I don't know what to do." I unclipped Bessie's lead and looked up. A spider web stretched from the particle board ceiling to a dusty light. A fly was caught in it, twitching as the spider climbed toward it.

"Your head will be clearer after you eat. There is chocolate cake, and the boys are making bacon." Sister Marie pointed to where Jeremy stood with one hand on another boy's back.

The second boy was half Demon with the same pale skin and dark hair as Officer Karen. He jumped when Bessie licked his hand. He patted her but didn't take his eyes off the bacon he was cooking.

"Allen is Karen's little brother, but he calls her his aunt. Jeremy is Allen's boyfriend." Sister Marie guided me toward the food.

I glared as a Pixie dive-bombed a chocolate cake and left with a face and fist full of frosting. Jeremy flinched when I grabbed a knife. A big slice of cake would settle my stomach. I'd think better if it didn't feel like it was trying to digest itself.

Sister Marie put her hands on her hips, frowning at Jeremy. "They're not going to stab you or the Pixies. Why are you acting like I just let a Troll into my kitchen?"

"I don't need telepathy to see how angry they are," stammered Jeremy.

Shaking her head, Sister Marie walked over the far corner of the room and started a hushed conversation with Niben.

Jeremy snatched two pieces of bacon right out of the pan, absorbing the heat without getting burned, then chewed them both much more slowly than I would ever chew bacon while he continued to stare at me. "I'm sorry if this sounds rude, but what kind of hybrid are you?"

I chewed a mouthful of cake. "Lately the question I've been asking is 'what am I not?' Niben's my grandmother, and Grandpa is mostly human, but he had an Elven grandfather. My maternal grandmother was Elf and Angel."

Jeremy glanced back and forth between Allen and me. "And your maternal grandfather?"

"Never met him. My mom hardly remembers him. Nana hardly remembers him, though half the time I see her, she doesn't know who I am. I want to think he was only human." I chewed the last few bites of my cake so hard I bit my tongue. I'd thought a lot about this since I started training, and I had a theory I'd been too afraid to mention to anyone. The possibility that I could be part Demon was the last thing I wanted to think about right now.

I reached toward the bacon, trying to absorb energy from the pan. I purposely didn't take enough to stop it from burning my fingers a little as I snatched up three pieces, letting the pain distract me from my inability to go out and do anything.

"Jeremy, are you okay?" Allen turned off the stove and pulled Jeremy closer to him. Jeremy's eyes were closed. His hands curled into shaking fists.

"I am but not Mel and Mike. Mel wants Erin to stop shielding so she can talk to them, but I don't want to hear Erin's thoughts."

"I don't want to hear my thoughts either," I muttered, staring at the little red marks where my fingers had touched the hot grease in the bacon pan.

Jeremy leaned into Allen, who buried his face in Jeremy's hair and kissed the top of his head. Had both forgotten I was standing a few feet away from them?

My eyes stung with the threat of tears. I swayed, wishing I could lean against José's solid chest, feel the weight of his arms around me, and let him carry some of my weight while I ate and recouped my strength. He was likely terrified, wherever he was.

"Mel says not to eat all the bacon. And that I need to practice shielding more because she is coming up with

Mike, who had a big panic attack, and the closer he gets, the harder it is going to be for me to be around his thoughts because he's too upset to shield, and that Allen and I should play video games with him, but no first-person shooters and no games with spies." Jeremy spoke fast, repeating things as Mel thought them at him.

"Do you have *Super Smash Brothers*?" That game often helped me stop thinking. There was a part of me that wished I could play too. That I could just forget about everything. But I knew that wouldn't help me figure anything out.

"Mel says you need to tell the old people about your fight with the tentacles." Jeremy glanced across the room at Niben and Marie, who were still having some hushed conversation they didn't seem to want anyone else to hear. Neither reacted to the "old people" comment. I needed to give them a detailed account, but all I really wanted to do was eat and sleep so I could dream where José was.

But I was shaky, and my thoughts were going too fast to sleep. Fifteen or twenty minutes of mindless gaming would make it easier to sleep. Defeating virtual enemies would be therapeutic. Defeating virtual enemies with the lightning might make me feel better even if it were only for a few minutes. But the clock was ticking, and I couldn't lose any time.

I wanted to scream. I wanted to find the Demons that had José, electrocute the shit out of them, and scatter their remains across the multiverse. Had Shadowhulhu not knocked out all the power, I would've vaporized it. I would've stopped the Puppet Master in a couple seconds. José would be here. More people would be alive. Next time I saw that monster, or one who it worked for, I was going to destroy it.

A light bulb shattered.

A bolt of electricity flew out of the ceiling, hit me in the chest, and sent me flying across the room.

Everyone stared at me as I sat on the floor, digging my fingers into the linoleum as tears slid down my face and five Pixies swarmed what was left of my cake.

My chest burned. Monsters raged against the remains of the potions that had kept them mostly in check for weeks. I couldn't breathe. I couldn't *not* breathe. I wanted to tear the earth apart searching for José. I wanted to avenge the people who'd died because I was in the same movie theater as them.

I needed to do something. Ideally, destroy the monsters that had taken José. That had ripped him away from the sliver of happiness he had just tasted. I needed to obliterate them for stealing the lives of people who didn't even know those kinds of monsters existed. But I couldn't breathe right. My head hurt. My body was drained. My own dog was afraid of me. Bessie stared at me from under the table, ears back, whiskers singed off her nose.

"I'm sorry," I croaked, burying my face between my knees.

The floor creaked. Bessie skulked across the kitchen until her wet nose bumped my cheek. Mel slid into the room and squished Bessie and me into one hug. I let Mel hold me despite feeling shitty about that too. I could feel her in my head after she slipped past the ruins of my shields, trying to figure out what was going on so I wouldn't need to tell her even though it had to hurt her to feel all the raw rage in my mind.

In these moments when she didn't hesitate to get down on the floor and hold me with her body and mind, cradling my soul with her already depleted energy, I realized it wasn't badass powers, a migraine-inducing glow, or her father's DNA that made her an Angel. It was selflessness. A kind of grace I never understood.

"You're not the monster you think you are," Mel whispered.

I closed my eyes, praying that when my tears ran out, I'd fall asleep. Dreams might hold the answers that no one around me seemed to have.

Chapter Six

Half-Angel Child: An emotion cyclone of an eating machine, who is obsessed with fixing broken things. When raising one, budget for groceries as if you were feeding a family of ten. Be prepared for tears and pain, for the soul-stabbing job of teaching your child that she can't save everything, and of having to save her from herself over and over and over.

> —Lucy Evanstar's handwritten addition to the copy of the Demon Hunter Lexicon kept in the Archives under Saint Patrick's Church, South Portland, Maine.

A steaming mug of chamomile warmed my hands and loosened the tear-conjured snots clogging my nose. Mountains of unhealthy food crushed my monsters that were screaming at me to go out and tear the world apart until I found José. Giving in to the urge would get me killed or captured, so I stayed sitting at the table with Mel, Niben, Sister Marie, and a frazzled Officer Karen. The last had stumbled into the house shortly after I broke down, loudly cursing humanity's dependence on electronics.

Half-numb from exhaustion, I gave everyone as detailed an account of the movie theater tragedy as I could muster. When I narrated my fight with Shadowhulhu,

Niben bombarded me with questions and didn't offer any explanation of what my answers meant. Mel took over narrating when we got to the part where she met up with me. I filled in the details about my short dream. And when our story was done, Niben gave a history lecture.

I struggled to parse the relevant details from their reminiscing on events from decades before my parents were born. The hunters were trying to figure out if the Fallen Angel that the Shadowhulhu worked for could be defeated the same way that a different Fallen Angel had been defeated back in the 1940s. Niben, Officer Karen, and Sister Marie had not only been alive then, but they had actually been on the sidelines of the battle, creating a diversion while an Elf, named Phineas, and Aelfric, the half Angel, fought the Fallen. Unfortunately, they didn't know what Phineas and Aelfric had actually done to defeat it.

I zoned out for a few minutes, and by the time I wrangled my focus back to the conversation, the topic had shifted to Niben talking about how if Grandpa could convince Aelfric to help, then we could use some magic pool-map thing to track José. The rest was lost to me because I was too tired to process new information. My yawns grew more frequent and my eyes heavy.

Finally, I was ready to sleep. Mel quietly led Bessie and me away from the table and down a long hall to a closet-sized room with a cot in it. I plopped down on a thin mattress, not caring that I could feel the squeaky springs through it. My eyes closed. I rolled over, instinct prompting me to snuggle up to José's chest and listen to his heart. My arm flailed through the air. I flopped onto my back.

Mel dropped a heavy quilt on me. "Hopefully, I'll see you in a few minutes."

"That would be helpful." It was also unlikely.

I wrapped myself in a blanket, summoning memories of José. Him laughing at my attempts to glamour a sword so the blade resembled a lightsaber. His hands on my hips, and his lips brushing against mine. His smile while he stood at Mom's stove, stirring pasta and vegetables into a cheesy sauce. After months of living together, I couldn't picture life without him. I needed to find him and bring him home alive and whole.

Finally, I slept.

My consciousness flew through a thunderstorm. Clouds toppled, exchanging electrons until they rumbled like an earthquake farting out a mountain. Bolts of blinding electricity shot down, filling my body with raw power.

A burning building collapsed into a black hole.

Jenny Dunn lay in the middle of a seven-sided star while people chanted over her. Mel held my right hand.

Grandpa, appearing only a few years older than me, screamed in no-man's land, daring a horde of monsters to chase him. They did. And so did the corpses in the field. He hopped onto a motorcycle and sped through dirt and blood around foxholes and trenches and barbed wire while an army of Crawlers and zombies chased him.

José's Elf Stone was the only source of light. The green glow illuminated his face and thinned the shadows clinging to his folded hands and crossed legs. His eyes were closed. His hands squeezed his knees. "This isn't real," he whispered over and over and over.

Sam sprinted down a burning hall as the drop ceiling caved in behind her. Crawlers charged toward her from every hall and around every bend, snapping and clawing even as the flames obliterated them. Sam tripped over a nurse's corpse. She grabbed a needle off a toppled med cart and threw it at a Crawler that had been chasing her. It paused when the needle stuck in one of its seven eyes. Sam smiled. A toad-ish Demon unhinged its jaw as it fell from the ceiling. It bit her head off and swallowed it whole.

A blade in each hand, I hacked my way through a blockade of Spikes. A gray dome loomed half a mile away. I chopped on and broke through the wall, only to stumble into a shadowy mass of tentacles that snapped around my wrists and arms and legs and neck.

You were supposed to surrender, boomed Shadowhulhu's deep voice.

"Erin never surrenders," croaked another being in a black trench coat open over a snowy chest. Instead of legs, a cyclone of white dust held him up. He only had one arm.

"Vincent," I hissed, forcing air up my constricted throat. "Do your job."

Tentacles crushed my throat and whipped my body toward the gray dome.

*

Something sharp and hot stabbed my arm, forcing electricity into my body. Bessie's bark was a battering ram attacking my ears. My heart pounded as my arms flailed, colliding with Jeremy's glowing face. A few feet behind him, Mel, who was only a fraction as bright, laughed. She cried. She pushed the baffled boy out of the way and threw her arms around me. Bessie plopped on top of us both.

"If you die on me again, I swear, I will—I'll find—I'll—"

"Die?" I put my hands on Mel's shoulders and pushed her off me. "I died in a dream. I'm fine. I'll make sure it doesn't happen in real life."

Mel shook her head. "Your heart stopped for 86.21 seconds, the amount of time it took for me and Jeremy to run from the rooms on either side of this, crash into each other, rip a wire out of an outlet, and shock you with it."

Jeremy stood at the foot of the bed, still clutching a live wire.

"Isn't that way more—it's just raw electricity, not controlled like a defibrillator."

"You'd be dead if you were human," said Jeremy while Mel hysterically laughed and cried at the same time. "It worked because you're a teenage-mutant Demon-hunting video-game character."

"So, if I dream my death, I go into cardiac arrest?" I asked, unwilling to use the word "die." I hadn't been dead. If I was, I wouldn't have felt Jeremy stab me with that live wire before its current jumpstarted my heart.

"You did this time," said Mel.

My father had supposedly dreamed his death dozens of times before it happened, but the vision hadn't killed him. Maybe it was something specific to this dream, to this death? "Mel, did you see what happened in the dream?"

Mel shook her head. "I couldn't pull you with me to the Confluence, so I went alone, but I only saw myself getting hurt, dying, and failing to save people over and over."

"Do you want to see my dreams?"

"Yes, eventually, but not the one where you died." Mel wiped tears away from her eyes and walked over to the window. The sun was high, illuminating grass and vibrant green leaves.

"Umm, what should I do with this wire?" asked Jeremy.

"Hold it for a minute." Mike peered into the room. "I'll get some tools from the basement and fix it."

"Is there anything he can't do?" I asked as Mike disappeared down the hall.

"Plenty," said Mel.

"Right." I chewed on my lip, thinking of another death I had dreamed. "I think we need to go get Sam."

Mel closed her eyes and took a deep breath. "Sam was involuntarily committed. We can't just walk in and take her back out with us."

"Then we better not get caught," I said.

Mel crossed her arms. "She's attempted suicide three times that I know of. What makes you think she would or should come with us? What makes you think she isn't where she needs to be?"

"She'll get decapitated by a Crawler's teeth if she stays. And based on what everyone is telling me, I need her alive if I am going to save José. I've been waiting months for her to get discharged so I can try to convince her to help with Nana's curse. I can't wait anymore, and I don't care if she wants to come."

Mel walked toward me, so our noses were touching. "So, this is a kidnapping."

"Depending on what she says when we talk to her." I backed away from Mel and tried to duck between her and Jeremy, who clutched wire as he watched the conversation with his eyes wide and lips pursed together, petrified by awkwardness.

Mel grabbed my arm. "You'd actually make her come if she doesn't want to?"

I met her gaze and nodded

Her eyes filled up with shimmering tears. "You'd kidnap her from a place where she is getting help so you can coerce her into doing something she might not want to do."

"I'm also saving her from getting eaten. I'm saving José's life. In the process of saving him, I might also save millions of other lives by preventing an apocalypse."

Mel stared at the floor while biting her lip. "Did the dream have any hints about when this Crawler might eat her?"

I shook my head.

Mel glanced up. "There might be another way you could save her."

"No. I'm human enough to be a monster if that's what it takes to save José."

I expected Mel to say something, to tell me she couldn't help me or to argue I wasn't a monster.

She let go of me.

Mike came into the room with a toolbox and a handful of wire.

A tear dripped down Mel's cheek as I slid past Mike into the hallway. She didn't follow me to the kitchen, and she didn't show up when I started cooking bacon. At least Bessie stuck with me even if she was drooling all over my feet. I stared at the sizzling deliciousness, trying not to cry. I'd cried enough yesterday. Still, my eyes were wet, and my throat was so tight I was nauseated. I wanted to smash things.

Little bubbles formed in the melted fat, popping and splattering everywhere. I didn't flinch when drops of hot grease hit my face. The physical pain distracted me from what I felt in my heart. Part of me wanted to touch the pan until the burning overpowered the guilt and rage ripping me apart from the inside out. The scissors I opened the bacon with whispered temptations with their sharp edges.

Bessie growled at me. I scratched her behind the ears.

I thought I was getting better, that the potions were helping, but maybe they weren't. Perhaps I had adapted to my new life quickly, and I wasn't any better at coping with change and trauma than I had been a month ago.

"No one is good at coping with this kind of change." Mel trudged into the kitchen, sat down at the table, and held her forehead with her hand. "The Elf potions don't stay in your system the way human antidepressants do, and you've missed a dose. Chemical imbalance plus partner getting kidnapped equals psychological cluster fuck for anyone."

I turned the burner off, scooped bacon out with a fork, and put the plate on the table. When I sat, the bacon was between Mel and me.

Mel picked up a piece and sniffed. "We were so close. You learned to harness electricity and destroyed a horde with lightning. You banished the Incubus. We were getting a team together to neutralize the Fallen. I really thought everything was going to work out."

"It still could work out fine." Sister Marie joined us at the table.

"She's right. Even if we can't reach the Confluence, we still have my dreams, and those are a lot more focused now than they used to be," I said.

Mel glowered at Sister Marie with bloodshot eyes. "Erin dreamed their death."

"Which means I know how not to die," I said.

Mel hugged me with one arm. "Unless it happens again. What happens if you are alone next time?"

"A robot does what you did only more efficiently." Mike plopped a toolbox on the table, took a phone out of his pocket, and slid it across the table to me. He stood behind Mel and started rubbing her shoulders. "I'll pick up a heart rate monitor from a sports store and program it to talk to something Erin can wear, and if it senses their heart stop, it can shock them. They attract and conduct electricity unconsciously. Precision isn't necessary."

"At least someone is optimistic." Sister Marie snatched a piece of bacon off my plate.

I picked up the phone identical to the one I had melted. "Is there a point to this? Next time I get into a big fight, it's probably going to get destroyed."

"The case can handle electricity just fine. I'll have to think about the fire problem." Mike chewed a piece of bacon.

I unlocked the screen, happy to see the Bessie background from my old phone with all the app icons in their usual places. There were dozens of text messages and Facebook notifications. Ten missed calls from Jenny Dunn. A few from Will and José's other friends from school, including the ones he had hardly talked to from the past month.

Mel, Mike, and Sister Marie's voices dissolved into background noise while social media, a void familiar and alien, sucked my attention away.

> *Are you safe?*
>
> *Are you okay?*
>
> *Are you alive?*
>
> *Have you heard from José?*
>
> *Is he okay?*
>
> *Is he alive?*
>
> *Where is he?*

Where are you?

Please respond. No one has heard from you or José.

We tried to report you missing to the police. They said you weren't missing, and that you had given a statement after the shooting. Why aren't you replying?

We stopped by your house and no one was there. Bessie didn't even bark.

Those were just the text messages. Social media buzzed with stories and tears and hash tags about being strong. Images and videos showed candles lit and memorials for people who had died.

I didn't like any posts or add any comments.

I posted one status update: *I'm alive. I'm sorry.*

Mindlessly, I scrolled through more of the feed.

"Erin, take your medicine, put your phone down, and focus. We have people to find and extractions to plan," said Sister Marie.

When I didn't put my phone down, Bessie stood up on her hind legs, knocked it out of my hand, and stole my bacon. A Pixie dropped a potion in front of me. I uncorked the bottle and swallowed the foul-tasting liquid as fast as I could. It burned my throat like hard liquor, but in a few minutes, a blanket of warm water soothed my brain. My thoughts slowed down enough for me to compartmentalize them and not be overwhelmed. Sounds separated instead of blurring together.

I stared at the old nun. "Does that mean you agree with me about breaking Sam out of the hospital?'

"What?" Sister Marie nearly choked on her bacon.

I explained my dream and the argument Mel and I had had.

She rubbed her temples with her eyes closed. "Ethical questions aside, you're talking about committing a felony. If you get caught, you go to jail."

"I won't get caught."

Sister Marie snorted. "Your glamours are atrocious. Even if you don't physically get caught, police might discover what you did."

I made eye contact with Mike. "Then I'll disappear."

Mel snarled. "Erin, you don't know what you're asking him."

Mike put a hand on Mel's back. "The likelihood of getting caught is lower if we help."

Mel stood up and backed away from him like his hand was fire. "You're on their side?"

"Think of it as recon. You make a glamour. Erin powers it. The Pixies can patch me into the security system, and I'll loop the camera footage. You can talk to Sam and ward her room."

Mel took a deep breath. "I'll help you go in to *talk* to Sam. If she's willing to help, then she can request voluntary status and then request to be discharged."

I didn't think we had that much time, but I couldn't push Mel any further right now. I'd figure out the rest when we got there.

Chapter Seven

Curse: A focused stream of energy with a malevolent purpose. Curses are often bound to living beings but are sometimes attached to objects. They are more commonly used by Demon hybrids and Elves, though almost any being with the ability to manipulate energy is capable of creating one.

> —A Demon Hunter's Guide to Magik and Alchemy, published in 1856 and stored in most archives.

"Erin? What the hell? How are you here? What *are you*?" Sam stood in the middle of a small room, halfway between a tiny bed and a minimalistic armchair.

I glanced back and forth between her and Mel. Everyone we had encountered so far had been fooled by the glamour—the one that had made us invisible to everyone without the Sight.

Sam's hands clutched the edge of the chair. The fuzz around her undercut had grown out, leaving her hair choppy, uneven, and messy. Dark circles hung under her eyes. "Vincent said you weren't human, but these people keep telling me the supernatural stuff isn't real. Some bullshit about my brain making metaphors for things I didn't want to admit happened. I was almost starting to believe them because I'm still alive and here, and he said we both could die or be captured and tortured if we failed to deliver you, and you killed him and I got arrested and nothing came for me, and the charges were dropped and nothing came for me, so I wondered, but what the fuck are you? And why is your cousin glowing?"

I watched Mel. I couldn't form coherent words because my brain was too busy trying to figure out why Sam all of a sudden had the Sight. If she'd had it before, she hadn't used it the day the Incubus had followed her around Portsmouth unless she'd lied.

"I glow because my father was an Angel. Erin is a hybrid too, though their DNA is a little more mixed up. We're here because Vincent wasn't lying about you being in danger. You aren't safe here," said Mel.

"We need to get you out of here." I ran my hands through my hair.

"What? I can't just leave." Sam fidgeted with her pentacle necklace, twisting and untwisting the black cord the pendant hung from.

"Why is the staff letting you wear something you could choke yourself with?" I asked, wondering if I should snatch it off her neck.

Sam picked the pentacle up. "It was on the floor after Mom left this morning. I lost it the night I got arrested. I assumed Mom found it, was being sentimental by carrying it around, and didn't realize she dropped it."

"That explains how you got the necklace, not why you were allowed to keep it," I said.

"I've been tired all day, so I've been staying away from group stuff, and I've been doing better, so the staff are letting me stay in my room alone. I hid it when they checked on me, and even the time I forgot, the staff didn't notice," said Sam.

Mel stepped forward and studied the necklace. Faint light flared around the pentacle, illuminating an intricate pattern of soft whirling curves and sharp angled lines.

"Is that some kind of tracking device?" I asked.

Mel shook her head. "It isn't broadcasting any energy signature, but it is mingling with hers."

"So, if I'm in danger, why now? Why not months ago?" Sam stepped away from Mel to pace around the tiny room.

Mel frowned. "We banished a lot of Demons back in March. The Fallen Angel leading them might have been too busy regrouping to bother with you. But something bad is happening now."

And we're not the only ones who can see possible futures. Our presence here could be what triggers the future you dreamed. Mel's words were like icicles stabbing my thoughts.

Perhaps, but I've seen it, and I'm here. I can make sure she doesn't die. Ignoring it was a risk I was not willing to take.

"Do you think something planted this on my mom? If it's not a tracker, could it be some kind of magic murder device?" Sam took the necklace off and handed it to Mel. Sam spun around. "Where did you go?"

Mel returned the necklace to Sam. "Put this back on."

"Wow, that was weird," Sam said with her head tilted and a smile tugging on her lips. "This is letting me see through glamours."

"It appears so," said Mel.

"Do you know what a Crawler is?" I asked, unsure how much "Vincent" had told her about the supernatural world.

Sam's smile vanished. "Vincent said those were a cross between zombie bears and Hell hounds. They eat people."

I nodded. "In my dream, a Crawler literally bit your head off."

"I think Vincent is trying to protect you," said Mel. "That pendant feels like him."

I glared at Mel. Something about her words made me uneasy.

"Erin killed Vincent." Sam crossed her arms and glared. Her lip curled back as if she were a dog baring her teeth at me.

I stared at her brown eyes. "Demon's aren't alive enough to die. I banished him."

Sam glanced at the floor. "He said he wasn't a Demon. He was alive and you killed him."

I took a step closer. "Then he lied to you. He was a monster; a serial rapist that fed off fear and lust. You were only livestock to him."

Sam's hands curled into fists, and when she spoke, there was a growl in her voice. "No. The Incubus was those things. Vincent was trapped inside it."

"What did he say he really was?" Mel's fingers twined around her short tufts of blonde hair. Her finger kept twirling even though she ran out of hair to wrap around them. Her eyes were wide, swirling faster than normal.

"Does it matter?" asked Sam.

"Yes," said Mel.

Sam chewed her lip. "He tried to tell me, but some magic prevented him from explaining out loud."

Mel inched closer to Sam. "Did he give you any hints?"

"No."

Mel chewed her lip as she watched me. "Sam isn't lying. I think Vincent was telling the truth.

A fire alarm blared. A deep rumbling rolled through the building. The whole structure shook and rattled.

"We need to get out here now!" Mel grabbed Sam by the arm and yanked her toward the door.

Chapter Eight

Burnout: When an Angel-human hybrid expends all their energy and dies. (I hate that word. It makes us sound like light bulbs. I am not a damned light bulb.)

—The Demon Hunters Lexicon, a copy owned by Seamus Evanstar and annotated by Amelia Evanstar.

The tremors intensified. Metal studs groaned. The building rumbled like a fleet of freight trains charged through the basement.

"An earthquake?" asked Sam.

"*Run!*" screamed Mel as the ceiling collapsed behind us. Hot breath made the hair on my skin stand on end as something clawed its way out of the floor.

"Don't look, just keep running," shouted Mel as I glanced over my shoulder and saw a dozen Crawlers behind us.

"There's a lot of other people in here." I sprinted into a hallway. Patients and staff poured out of doors, rushing toward exits. A few tried to get the rest to exit calmly, but panic and fight-or-flight instincts had a tight grip on most.

"Sam is the target. They'll follow us outside. We can fight them there, away from so many bystanders." Mel ran with a hand on Sam and me. I could barely hear her over the blaring alarms and the din of panic.

At the movie theater, José was the target, and plenty of other people died, I thought at Mel.

That was a diversion—they knew you were there and would do anything to keep him from them. This is different.

I didn't believe her. She didn't care.

You get Sam out of here. I'll do what I can to make sure the others get out safe.

You're still healing. You're not ready for that.

I have to be.

Mel.

Help is on the way.

The building shook again.

Someone screamed.

If Mel was right about the Demons following Sam, then she would be safer from them if we split up, but I was more concerned with her healing people the Demons hurt.

Go! Mel's voice boomed in my head as she turned down a hall where someone was trapped under a large piece of debris.

I grabbed Sam's arm, and we sprinted. The Crawlers followed us and ignored Mel while she cleared pieces of shattered ceiling tile off a person and their overturned wheelchair.

I made it past two doors, three, and four. Another scream reverberated through the hall, accompanied by a gurgling growl and crunching bones. I skidded to a stop. Sam kept moving a few more feet before turning around and glaring at me. "Why did you stop? They're after me."

"Why did a Crawler eat that person instead of running past them to us?"

Sam paled. Her jaw hung open. She inhaled. "Shit. Was Mel lying to make us leave?"

"Possibly. But even if she wasn't, a Crawler lacks the impulse control to skip an easy snack." I pushed my mind open, feeling raw energy in all the electrical wires. I pulled. Bolts forked out of an outlet, meeting at my hands before being directed to the Crawler, vaporizing it in seconds. A dozen more charged us. Raw power surged through my nervous system, contained and controlled, so I didn't short myself. In less than a minute, the Crawlers were dust.

Water rained out of the ceiling's fire sprinklers.

"Umm, Erin, did you mean to do that?" Sam pointed at the wall.

Smoke poured from a hole where an outlet used to be. Flames licked its edges.

I said get out of here. Mel's voice was loud and clear even though she wasn't anywhere in sight. *Electrical fires will hurt as many people as Crawlers.*

I reached for the flame, siphoning energy until it was out, but as soon as I stopped, I saw melted wires still sparking.

Listen to Amelia. Get Sam away from here. Niben's voice was distant, but the words were clear. She was close. She'd help.

I grabbed Sam and ran to the stairs, arriving just as the door flew off its hinges. We came face-to-face with a snarling Troll reeking of a dead skunk rotting in an outhouse. I pulled electricity from an exit sign glowing above its head, directing the bolts down toward the Troll.

Its head steamed, but the bulky monster still raised a meaty fist and swung at me. Ducking, I lost my concentration and the surge of power stopped, leaving a smoking hole in the roof. This creature was three times as wide as the last Troll I'd fought, taking up most of the hall with its girth.

"What the hell is that?" Sam didn't shout: she paused between each shaky word.

"A Troll."

It opened its mouth, roaring and sending a fresh wave of stench at me. I backed up to Sam, fashioned an ice machete out of water from the sprinklers, and choked on a few smoke-filled breaths as I struggled to slow my perception of time.

The result wasn't ideal, but everything around me slowed enough for me to leap at the Troll before it had time to react. I shoved the ice machete into its oily eye, which squished, popped, and sprayed ichor all over me. I dropped to the ground as the Troll's hands moved toward its face. I reached out with my mind, trying to focus on the energy above me in the lights, not the shorted-out exit sign's circuit.

Glass shattered over the Troll before bolts rained down. I called more electricity, which tingled and burned while mingled with my own energy. I shoved lightning bolts at the Troll, growling and willing the damned thing to break apart. The Troll turned to dust that vanished as I pictured it scattered across the universe.

Panting, I turned around. Sam wasn't right behind me anymore; she was at the other end of the hall. I ran toward her. Perception of time still slowed, I caught up in seconds. We reached an intersection. Straight ahead was blocked by fire. Had that spread from my electrical fire? Or was it related to what had triggered the alarm in the first place?

Sam turned right. I followed her and let my perception of time return to normal.

"There's another staircase this way," she said. "Another way out."

"I'll follow you," I said.

The air was clearer. I didn't see or sense any people—hopefully that meant they had been evacuated in time and not eaten.

An emergency exit sign glowed ten doors away–a beacon of hope. I could've sprinted there in seconds, but Sam couldn't go that fast. I grabbed her arm, pulling her as I picked up my pace a little.

Something snarled behind us. I dragged Sam along to the door. The metal was cool. So was the handle.

The sign's light went out.

I opened the door anyways.

The stairwell was pitch black, but the air was fresher than that of the hallway. We charged in. The door slammed shut. We descended as quickly as we could in the dark. I reached out with my mind, sensing no life forces or demons in the stairwell. I hoped the lack of electricity was firefighters disconnecting power from the building, not something smarter than Crawlers taking away my favorite weapon.

We made it down two of the three flights when the building quaked again. I felt the disturbance, cold and violent, a second before a group of Crawlers swarmed up the stairs snarling and snapping their teeth.

I grabbed Sam and darted out the door into a foyer where three halls met. We gagged on smoke. We ran, stopping when the heat was too much. Flames ate a wall even though water poured out of the sprinklers. I used that water to make an ice sword just in time to bisect a Crawler that leaped toward me.

Sam sprinted down a burning hall as the drop ceiling caved in behind her. I ran, leaping over debris and trying to syphon energy from any flames that came close enough, using them to singe any Crawler I could reach.

Crawlers charged toward Sam from every hall and around every corner, snapping and clawing as the flames obliterated them. I coughed more than I breathed, counting the heave of my lungs until the ceiling fell in slow motion.

Sam tripped over a nurse's corpse, then grabbed a needle off a toppled med cart and threw it at a Crawler.

This was the moment I had dreamt about.

Sam was still a good fifteen feet away from me.

Slowing my perception of time again, I leaped over a mound of rubble just as the needle landed in one of the Crawler's seven eyes. I passed a door and juked to the side as something fell.

Ten feet.

Flames sprang up from the floor. I pulled energy from them as I passed through, but they singed my pant legs.

Sam smiled.

A toad-like Demon unhinged its jaw while falling from the ceiling. I dove forward, shaping raw energy into a spear and throwing it at the Crawler. The warty beast disintegrated on contact. I lost control of the dive and wound up flinging myself over Sam before slamming down hard onto the floor. Hard enough to crack tiles.

Pain shot through my ribs as I tried to sit up. Crawlers closed in on us. Sam scrambled to her feet.

"You stay down." I blindly shoved energy around the two of us at the Crawlers as I had when fighting Shadowhulhu at the movie theater, letting the fire mix with my own energy, spewing flames flecked with gold at any Demon that got within range.

They kept coming.

My aim was poor, igniting wall and Demon alike. Smoke stung my eyes and lungs. Sweat evaporated off my skin as quickly as it appeared. Sam was flat on the ground, and I didn't know if she was still conscious.

Chapter Nine

The inhabitants of the Faerie Realms have seeped into human mythology, but more often than not, the legends, the heroes, the gods, and the saints–those are hybrids. A prime example is Thor, God of Thunder. It is unlikely an Elf would be so dramatic as to carry a lightning-channeling hammer. If such a being existed, it was undoubtedly a Human-Elf-Angel hybrid. (If my grandfather is to be believed, Thor had more in common with the character in the comic books my children love reading than the being in human-recorded literature).

–Myth and Religion Through a Demon Hunter's Lens written by Dr. Phyllis Schwartz in 1956. A copy, annotated by Niben of the Summer Elves, is shelved in the archives under Saint Patrick's Church in Portland, Maine.

Soot and sweat dripped into my eyes, so I wasn't sure if I saw right when the flames in front of me parted, rose up in an arc, and formed a tunnel. A femme figure moved through it. She was a silhouette at first, then took on a more human, no, a more Elven shape.

Come! Niben commanded in my head.

I let go of the energy I was holding on to and dropped to my knees, partially from exhaustion and half to grab Sam's shoulders. "Get up!"

Sam half responded by attempting to crawl and scramble forward while I tried to haul her up but failed time after time. The tunnel moved closer, and we scuttled toward it, me half dragging Sam until we were inside. The air wasn't much cooler, but it was free of smoke. I could finally breathe.

My limbs still quivered, and my head swam when I stood. Sam rose to her knees, staring wide-eyed at the fire around us, gasping in greedy gulps of breathable air.

"We need to move," said Niben. "I can't maintain this long."

"Is Mel okay?" I asked.

Niben's simple brown leggings were stained with soot. A tear around her knee showed raw, scraped skin. Her arms, bare from the elbow down, were scratched and sooty. A shallow gash streaked from her right eyebrow to the top of her head. Her pointy ears were red and blistered.

"Are *you* okay?"

"I've been worse. Mel was outside last I saw. I believe you two are the only people left alive in here," said Niben.

I crouched down, stuck my unsteady hands under Sam's armpits, and hoisted her up. "Get up."

Sam wobbled to her feet and put her weight on my shoulders, straining my exhausted body. We made slow progress, me holding Sam up while Niben shielded us from the fire. Niben stopped, held her arms up, and threw them forward. Fire blew a chunk of wall off the second floor.

I held my breath. For a second, it seemed flaming debris was going to fall on the fire trucks, police, and the evacuated people who were behind them. I saw Officer Karen in the crowd in uniform, watching the building from the inside of the police tape. Her face paled as she stared up.

Could she do anything? Could I do anything? I started breathing slower, trying to buy myself more time to think.

Niben flung her arms out.

The flaming debris soared past the crowd, spread out, and dissolved.

"What now?" Sam leaned on me harder.

Excess energy floated back to Niben as she collapsed. Only ash fell on those below. We were so close to making it out alive. I only had to get a barely standing Sam and an unconscious Elf down from the second-story window.

"Erin?" squeaked Sam.

The firefighters might not have seen what happened to the debris, but they saw something because a fire hose turned right toward us. I further slowed my perception of time, so when the stream of water spewed from the hose, it moved like cold, half-crystalized honey dripping from a jar to a teacup. Feeling more than seeing, I focused on the water until I sensed it on a molecular level. I pulled energy out so the water molecules slowed down as they approached.

I commanded the water, willing it to bend downward while I pulled more and more energy, locking more of the molecules together in a crystalline structure. It froze in the shape of something relatively close to a narrow half pipe going from the window to the ground.

In other words, I made a slide.

Sam stared and shook her head. She sat and pushed herself forward before it was complete, barking out exhausted laughter as the slide formed in front of her before abruptly ending a few feet above the ground. I got my hands under Niben, pulled her onto my lap, and slid. We crashed into muddy grass.

I lay there, breathing hard as the mud cooled my overheated, overtaxed body. I half expected paramedics or cops to run over to us but no feet squished in the mud, and when I finally mustered the energy to turn my head, no one seemed to see us at all, except for Officer Karen, who was watching but not abandoning her post.

Niben opened her eyes. Her body heaved as she started laughing hysterically. I thought I heard her mutter something about having the best grandoffspring ever and how she was feeling alive for the first time in over a decade.

Under other circumstances, creating a slide from the fire hose water might have made me laugh too, but as I lay on the ground, guilt crushed my chest, a hurt that cut deeper than the burns and bruises.

Sam scrambled to her feet and limped toward the woods. She seemed to move in slow motion. My perception of time hadn't quite returned to normal.

"Please go find Mel," I said to Niben, assuming her cackling meant she was okay.

Everything swayed as I struggled to stand. I took a step toward Sam. Something wet tickled the skin above my lip. I touched it and realized it was blood dripping from my nose. I lurched forward. Even at my hobbling pace, I was catching up to Sam, but my brain hurt, and the blood coming out of my nose was flowing into my mouth.

"You should stop moving so fast," said a voice with a slight Scottish brogue. An aura of light more blinding than Mel's had ever been materialized at the edge of the woods.

Sam crashed right into it.

I assumed the light was an Angel-hybrid and the source of the warning. Maybe he was the one Grandpa had been trying to convince to come help us.

"What happened?" Grandpa stepped out from behind the hybrid's too-bright aura and caught me with a hug just as I tripped over a root.

I let my perception of time return to normal now that Sam had stopped running to shield her squinting eyes with her arm.

"I saved Sam from getting eaten. I might have lit a building on fire trying to electrocute a Troll. Niben saved us. Sam ditched us, and I chased her."

"I thought you were right behind me, and I worried those Crawlers might be too," said Sam.

"You didn't look." I turned away from Grandpa to glare at Sam but didn't fully let go of him, afraid I'd fall over if I did.

"We're all alive. That's what matters." Niben hobbled into the woods with a flickering Mel. They both had their arms around each other. I couldn't tell who was supporting who.

I let go of Grandpa and leaned against a sturdy maple, so no one noticed me swaying on my feet. Grandpa ran over to hug them both at the same time. "Is that an actual Angel?" Sam gaped at the light.

As my eyes adjusted to the glare, I saw a man with reddish hair and a gray beard, wearing a Hawaiian shirt over a kilt. He broke into laughter that shook his pot belly.

"Oh, no. I'm an Angel-hybrid like Erin's cousin. My name is Aelfric."

Aelfric held his hand out to Sam, who tentatively shook it.

Then he turned to me. "And you're the mystery grandkid Seamus tried to hide from everyone. I thought Niben would murder him for cutting her out of your life. She never seemed the forgiving type."

"Is this the guy you've been searching for all month?" I arched my eyebrows at Grandpa, who was a few feet away with Niben and Mel.

"We've been searching for Phineas. I knew right where this oaf was. Getting him to get off his drunk ass was another story." Niben broke away from Grandpa to hug Aelfric.

"I'm here now." His light enveloped Niben when he hugged her.

When she stepped back a minute later, all her wounds were healed, and his light hadn't dimmed.

"Erin, you want to go next?" asked Aelfric.

"Is that okay?" I asked Grandpa.

Aelfric's aura made me see spots, so I figured he had plenty of energy to spare, but I didn't know anything about him.

Grandpa nodded.

I tensed as Aelfric wrapped his hairy arms around me, and a surge of warm energy flooded my body. It didn't burn like the time Mel had healed me. This energy was a warm bath that bolstered tired muscles, soothed my headache, and healed wounds I'd been ignoring.

He patted me on the back before tromping over to Mel, studying her with his brow furrowed. "There isn't a lot I can do for you."

Mel's eyes watered as she stared at him. "I don't need your help."

Aelfric crossed his arms. They stared at each other for at least five minutes. I couldn't tell if they were talking telepathically or having a plain old staring contest. Eventually, Mel sighed and held out her hand to him.

His light flared around her. Too curious for my own good, I forced myself to watch even though it burned my retinas. The half-healed burns faded to smooth skin, and when Aelfric pulled his energy back, a thin blanket of light stayed with Mel. His light had dulled enough that it didn't hurt to look at him quite as much.

"It might be enough for you to start replenishing your own reserves if you don't squander it the next time someone gets a scratch," he said like he knew and cared for her even though Mel had just met him.

"If you're done with all this family drama, we should leave before more Demons arrive and try to eat us," said Sam.

"I missed you." I gave her an awkward half hug, then trudged further into the woods, toward high-tension wires and the access road the Jeep was parked on.

Mud squished under everyone's feet as we walked. Twigs snapped in the woods. Out of the corner of my eye, I saw a flash of white, but by the time I turned my head, it was gone.

We have a common enemy, whispered a voice I'd once associated with the Incubus. No one else reacted to it.

And we have a common ally. The voice was as faint as the tiny breeze stirring the leaves high up in the trees. The hem of a trench coat swished to my left and vanished a second later.

The thin trees and brush ended, revealing my Jeep, parked under wires thrumming with electricity. Mel and the others were too engrossed in conversation to notice the way Sam stopped and stared into the woods with her fingers absentmindedly tracing the edges of her pentacle. I let my gaze follow hers as the two of us watched the transparent outline of the trench-coat-clad man. Dust coalesced into a face, but it wasn't the Incubus's shark-toothed, black-hole-eyed face but the almost-human I'd seen before I knew how to consistently see through his glamour.

Except right now, my Sight was open.

And the dust?

It shimmered in the shade.

Demon fragments didn't glow.

Chapter Ten

Are you sure it is wise to bind the Map Room to your home? We have only scratched the surface of what it can do. You may not be able to power the tracking pool without Aelfric, but the room is tethered to realms unknown. It is disconnected from time as we perceive it, and it is supercharged with energy I do not understand. If you can send messages from it, I assume it can also receive them. I would sleep better at night if we could find a better place to hide it.

—An excerpt of a letter from Niben to Seamus Evanstar, written in 1949, confined to the archives shortly after.

6 DAYS, 9 HOURS, 52 MINUTES, 31 SECONDS.

I gripped the table hard enough that my fingers nails left little crescent indentations in the wood. While I watched the seconds of José's life tick away, Niben and Mel filled Sister Marie, Aunty Lucy, and Mike in on what happened at the hospital.

Mel leaned against Mike while she talked. His arms were draped over her like a protective vest, and she appeared so warm and content and happy that jealousy ripped up my guts. Not because I wanted to touch Mike, but because she had her partner, and I didn't have mine.

Even though healing energy had restored my body, my brain was exhausted. In these types of moments, I needed someone to share my load, to hold me and talk to me and keep my mind from spiraling out of control. I needed more than an antique table to support me.

"What is that thing?" Sam pointed at the countdown on the phone.

I sunk down into a chair and told her the whole story.

"That fucking sucks," she said when I finished.

"Thanks for listening." I leaned back and ran my hands through my hair.

"Thank you for saving me. I'd ask how you were holding up, but the fact that you are not shoving food down your throat tells me you're way beyond that," said Sam.

I started crying when she stood up and rummaged through Grandpa's cupboards like she would've at Mom's house. I'd thought even after I saved her from the Demons, she was going to hate me. That I'd have to beg, bribe, or threaten her into staying, but Sam didn't try to run away. She put a package of Oreos in front of me, pulled her chair up close to mine, and asked me if she could do anything to help save José.

I opened my mouth to tell her but decided to eat a cookie instead. I didn't want her to think I *only* saved her because I needed her help. It was part of it, but it wasn't the sole reason. I ate another cookie. José would know a smooth, tactful way to explain it without making her hate me. I ate another cookie. For all I knew, Demons were torturing José. I missed him so damned much.

My throat got too tight to keep eating. Air wasn't getting into my lungs quick enough. I forced myself to breathe.

"Erin, tell me how I can help you." Sam put a hand on my shoulder.

I flinched, but I didn't pull away. I took as deep a breath as my half-panicked throat allowed and managed to say words when I exhaled. "Did Vincent tell you that you're a Witch? That you have the potential to do actual magic?"

Sam let go of me. "Define magic."

"Umm, manipulating energy? Not the stuff you say you do with crystals and tarot cards. More like what you saw me do."

"So, you're a Witch too?" Sam snatched a cookie and leaned back in her chair.

"Witches are *humans*. I'm only a little human. Like Bessie is mostly golden retriever and Rottweiler, but she has a little Saint Bernard. However, Elves and humans aren't as closely related as golden retrievers and Saint Bernards." I shoved two cookies in my mouth and chewed as hard as I could. If I were stuffing my face, I wouldn't start hyperventilating.

Sam smirked. "Even with pointy ears, you're still you."

"And you never answered my question."

Sam glanced away from me and watched the window. "He said I was something rare, but it was while we were talking online, and I thought he was some college boy trying to get laid. When we finally met in person, he taught me how to summon him, but I thought anyone could learn if they believed it was possible."

I shook my head. "Summoning is a Witch thing like breaking curses and making them."

Sam bit her lip. "How did *you* know I was Witch?"

Tears leaked out of my eyes as I answered her. "The same way I knew a Crawler was going to try to eat you. And how I knew you were going to get into Brown and Bowdoin but not Boston University. And how I passed that last pre-calc quiz I didn't study for. The same way I know that someday, you and I might be friends again."

"Might?" asked Sam.

I sniffled, trying to stop myself from dissolving into the kind noisy ugly crying that made me want to puke. "Time is rivers and oceans and atmospheres. It's all currents and streams that change and shift as people make choices and do things. My brain is a radar, which picks up on probable tracks that relevant time streams could take. Sometimes I'm right. Other times, I predict rain, and we get a foot of snow."

The older folks who didn't look anywhere close to their ages were huddled in the living room, laughing at jokes I didn't get. Mel and Mike sat on the stairs, talking to Aunty Lucy, whose wheelchair was pulled up right beside the bannister.

The cookies were all gone.

Sam stared at the countdown.

I still hadn't told her why I needed her help.

*

Something about Grandpa's basement had always been simultaneously creepy and fascinating. As a kid, it had been like that room in a fairy tale that the main character was forbidden from entering and entered nonetheless. Except there were never any consequences for me aside from Grandpa jumping out from behind a box and scaring me, or if he was in a bad mood, he'd revoke a promise to buy me a giant chocolate-chip cookie from a local bakery.

Of course, there were *some* rooms I'd never been in, and as I got older, more and more doors were locked to me, for good reason. No one in their right mind would've wanted me in a room full of lethal weapons when I was suicidal and fifteen. The walls were lined with swords of every style, knives and daggers, pistols, machine guns, rifles, grenades, and more; some very old, others very new.

Beyond that, a battered, dusty wood door made of planks that didn't go together led to a room with mats, practice weapons, and a couple of punching bags. On cold rainy days, it was a much better place for a sparring match than the beach.

April had been a very rainy month, so I'd spent hours down here with José. The first time he asked me to spar with him, I'd been terrified I might hurt him. I could still picture him, standing in the middle of the room with loose black sweatpants and a fitted gray T-shirt, holding two practice swords loose by his side. "Every Demon I fight is stronger and faster than me. The more I train with allies who are stronger and faster, the more prepared I am."

"But I don't really know how strong I am. What if I go too hard by accident?" I had asked.

He had smiled. "You don't know your limits, but you'll figure mine out pretty quick."

He had been right. I'd learned his limits after a few rounds, and I'd also discovered that my favorite time to kiss him was after those matches.

*

I walked to the end of the room where one of his hoodies lay crumpled in a corner. I picked it up. It still smelled like him. When I closed my eyes, I saw him. Alone in a dim room, José meditated inside a star trap. His Elf Stone glowed green on his forehead.

"Erin?" called Grandpa. "You coming?"

The vision faded to the inside of my eyelids. I opened my eyes. The floor mats had been pushed to the side, and Grandpa held a trap door open. I hadn't seen it before, but I wasn't surprised. Grandpa's house was the type of place where the secret rooms had secret rooms.

I walked toward him, wondering if I'd had some kind of vision, or if I had imagined what José might be doing in captivity.

An attic staircase unfolded, heading down to a dark chamber with a faint-green glow in the middle, which warmed to something more yellow and intensified as Mel, Grandpa, Niben, and I went down into what resembled the map room out of an epic fantasy novel's castle. The furniture and wood paneling was dark, shiny, and ornately decorated. Old books with cracked leather spines lined the wall. Scenes of Elf battles were carved into the panels between shelves alongside portraits of people I didn't know. A table-sized stone pool filled the center of the room. Layers of fluid maps rippled on the water's surface.

Aelfric smiled at Niben, running his hands across a varnished rim. "I never thought I'd see this again."

"Where are we? What...?" Mel glanced around the room, eyes wide with confusion and arms crossed over her chest. "You mentioned a device, but..."

The more I studied the room, the more certain I was that I had been here before. The memory was fuzzy like most early childhood memories, but I recalled the sound of my dad talking to Grandpa even if I couldn't visualize any version of Dad's face that wasn't from a picture or dreamed memory.

The smell—a mix of musty, damp church incense over the decay of a vernal pool at the end of summer—evoked the feel of being tiny, held by someone bigger. The sounds of their voices were relaxed and confident since I was too young to remember what they said. Maybe they'd had no reason to lie to me back then.

Niben tilted her head and smirked at Mel. "Where do you think you are?"

"Not Grandpa's basement." Mel scrunched up her forehead in concentration. "Why have you never shown me this place before?"

"It's dangerous," said Niben. "You could lose yourself if you were here too long."

I closed my eyes, but instead of reaching outward, I searched inward, inhaling the smell as if slowing my perception of time. My head throbbed. I yawned. Fatigue smothered me. I didn't fall asleep exactly, but the memory sharpened as Niben prompting Mel with questions seemed to fade into the sound of Dad and Grandpa talking.

"Do you know anyone else who can power this?" asked Dad.

"In another fifteen or twenty years, Amelia might be able to," said Grandpa.

"We don't have fifteen or twenty years," said Dad.

Sound became clearer and darkness brightened, returning me to the same room we'd been in, but this version of Grandpa had less gray hair and slightly brighter eyes.

Red curls fell in my eyes as my dad shifted me from one hip to the other. Staring at him was like staring into a mirror showing a more human and more masculine version of myself. He had the same fiery-red hair as Niben and me, but unlike mine, it didn't spark as if it was literally about to ignite. We had the leaf-green feline eyes, but his irises didn't have any glowing bits. I reached up with a tiny hand and tugged his pointy ear.

"Aelfric was the last Angel-hybrid I knew who lived to adulthood *and* had the will to retain enough energy to power this. Most of the others born in the past fifty years burned out before they could legally drink."

My dad's arms stiffened around me. "Sometimes I wonder what the hell my sister was thinking."

Grandpa rolled his eyes. "Amelia will tell you if you give her enough sweets. She's very into chocolate-covered sour worms and finding out things she isn't supposed to know."

"That's not what I meant." My dad leaned forward and kissed my head, inhaling unhurriedly through his nose.

"I could ask you the same thing," said Grandpa, dropping his voice to a more serious tone.

My dad sighed. "What about my mother-in-law? Could she power this?"

"Did you forget about the curses? It drains most of her power."

"What if we paid Mom's debts to the Puget Coven and contracted them to break it?"

"They hate us. I doubt they'd ask a price we'd be willing to pay, and even if we strike a deal, Helen is sick and not responding to medication, human or Elven."

"Mom said there might have been a breakthrough."

"How many other times has she said that?"

My dad didn't answer.

Eventually, Grandpa said, "Mel might be grown up and able to run this by the time they figure out a potion to help Helen manage the symptoms."

"If Mel grows up," whispered my dad, clutching me to his chest a little too tight.

*

"Now that is what I call interesting," said Aelfric, patting me on the back so hard I stumbled backward.

Grandpa sat across from me on a worn leather armchair, face pale, eyes wet with tears.

Mel, did you broadcast what I was seeing?

Yes. Mel nodded. "Did Erin astral-project into their two-year-old self?"

Niben shook her head. "Even in a place this thin, Erin couldn't project themself back in time by accident. This was more akin to their dreams."

"Erin's never had that much control," muttered Mel.

Aelfric glanced back and forth between Mel and me. "I suspect this is the first time they tried to watch a piece of the past in this type of place. Erin, why do you think it worked?"

I took a deep breath, struggling to organize my thoughts. "The conversation I witnessed happened in this place. Time feels strange here. I'm exhausted, so when I meditated and slowed my mind down, I partially fell asleep. I saw the moment I had been trying to recall through the eyes of my past self."

"Could you do it again if you wanted to?" asked Mel.

"Maybe if I could think of another time I came here."

"That was the only time Liam brought you here, that I know of." Grandpa stood and shuffled over to the pool. He placed his palm on the surface of the water. Seven maps came into focus. Aelfric stuck his hands in the water and poured golden light into it.

The top layer morphed to a sprawling map of Earth. Aelfric raised his hands, and the water lifted out of the basin in the shape of a globe. Grandpa retrieved a strand of José's hair from an envelope. They'd collected it from his hairbrush. Grandpa tossed the hair into the basin with his free hand. It expanded into a splash of brown liquid as it rose, circled the globe, and sunk down.

That means he isn't on Earth.

Niben rolled up her sleeves. She stuck her hands in and raised water up like a lily encompassing the globe, closing and spitting out more spheres as it opened again. She arranged the four spheres around the room. The brown circled through them all over and over, going slower each time but never stopping until it returned to the basin, spiraling across the dark, shimmery dregs, which for all I knew may have concealed an infinite map of the multiverse.

"In most cases with this device, a sample of DNA, a piece of hair or skin, is enough to track a being through Faerie, human, Demon, and Angelic realms," said Niben. "Were José dead, the indicator would not have risen out of the basin; it would have floated on the surface like a dead fish in a pond."

"So, what does that mean?" I pointed at the spiraling indicator.

"I have no clue. It's never done that before," said Aelfric.

"There is an extremely small possibility that somewhere, a similar device is being utilized to prevent us from finding José," said Niben.

"What if he is being kept in a realm you haven't mapped? Or somewhere between worlds? The multiverse has far more than four dimensions. What if he is outside the four that touch?" Mel stepped closer to the basin to observe the still-spiraling dot and stared at it like a cat tempted to pounce on a bee even though she knew getting stung would hurt.

Chapter Eleven

I've destroyed more monsters than I count and never felt an ounce of guilt. Killing a man should've been different, especially since I didn't mean for him to die. Yet, I felt nothing. I paid him to unravel my mother-in-law's curse. It consumed him. She told me that would happen. I ignored her. I didn't pass on her warning for fear she was wrong, and he wouldn't try. He died. I feel nothing save pressure: the fate of humanity is crushing me.

—An undated entry from the hunting log of Liam Evanstar, confined to the archives after his death. Decoded by Lucy Evanstar in June of 2018.

"Everyone who knows anything more than me is dead." Aelfric sat at the kitchen table with Mel, Grandpa, Niben, and me. "A bomb fell on them. They burned out. The Fallen killed them. A Demon ate them. Their sibling murdered them."

His words about the tracking pool were not very encouraging. Not much in the room was. Mike had hooked José's phone up to a computer and was frantically typing as code streamed across the monitor. His frequent swearing told me he wasn't accomplishing anything. The only good things were the chicken pie and chocolate-chip cookies. As long as I kept eating, I wasn't panicking or rushing off to do anything stupid.

"I don't think Phineas is dead. I never believed you were dead," said Niben to Aelfric.

I swallowed a mouthful of steaming, savory goodness. "I've dreamed about him, but it's always been the past."

"We could try tracking him," Grandpa suggested.

Niben crossed her arms. "With what? We'd need a DNA sample."

"Can it be from a relative?" I asked.

"Direct offspring work if they've been born in the past century or two, but he never had any kids," said Aelfric.

I smiled. "He had a daughter with an Angel."

"Are you sure you interpreted the dream correctly?" said Aelfric. "Angels in female form rarely carry hybrid children to term. The fetus burns up inside them."

"Phineas carried the child. The Angel was male." After I spoke, I thought more about what Aelfric had said while everyone stared at me for a minute with their heads cocked and brows furrowed. His words implied that Angels, by nature, were genderfluid. I grinned, directing a thought at Mel. *Can hybrids change their gender?*

Not that I'm aware of.

I'd had such bad reactions to any human medications, ranging from antidepressants to antibiotics, that I hadn't dared to try hormone replacement therapy to ease the dysphoria I experienced about certain aspects of my body. With all the apocalyptic chaos going on, I hadn't had a chance to ask about more magical, Faerie methods of making my body more masculine.

"Phineas is transgender," said Mel.

"I wouldn't have guessed," said Grandpa.

Kind of the point, I thought but didn't say it out loud because I was too tired to explain or argue.

"Elves have more efficient methods for transitioning than humans without the prejudice humans harbor against transfolk. Did the dream reveal who his daughter was?" said Niben.

Her eyes were wide with curiosity. She chewed on her lip the same way Mel did when she was trying to figure something out. Either Niben had a fantastic poker face, or she didn't know. I hadn't told anyone but Mel what I'd pieced together.

I glanced at Grandpa. He shrugged. Part of me didn't want to tell them what my dreams had revealed. If this weren't about finding José, I might have kept it secret to get revenge for keeping me in the dark for so long, but now wasn't the time to be petty or childish.

"I saw his sister running from something in a dream and leaving a baby on the doorstep of the house where my nana grew up. His sister died. I had thought the baby was hers until later when I had a dream where I saw Phineas give her his baby and ask her to hide it for him. But what I don't get is how a family could raise a kid that wasn't human at all and not know?"

Grandpa's mouth opened and closed, but no words came out.

Niben, on the other hand, had plenty to say. "To someone without the Sight, Angels appear very human when they walk on Earth, but if whoever hid the child wanted it to be safe, they could bind an illusion to the child. One to make sure someone never noticed how her eyes swirled, or that her skin produced light. *If* that is true, we might be able to use Helen to track him, but we'd need to get to her first and bring her here. If we threw a piece of her hair in the basin, then it would just track her. She'd need to be present," said Niben.

"And to do that, we would need to break the curse. Was that what she meant when she told me I wouldn't find José until I freed her? Maybe she can lead us to Phineas and he can track the Fallen?"

No one answered me.

Sister Marie walked into the room with Sam and Aunty Lucy trailing behind her. While we'd been using the basin, they'd been trying to assess what Sam could and couldn't do with magic. Aunty Lucy wasn't in her wheelchair but walking on a pair of robotic legs that looked as if they came straight out of a *Star Wars* movie. They were new. With Niben in regular contact with the hunters again, Mike had access to Faerie metals and semiconductors that were better suited for making prosthetics than anything found on Earth. They interacted with magic, allowing her to control them with her mind, but they were only prototypes and didn't work consistently.

"Has anyone heard from Karen?" asked Sister Marie.

No one had.

Mike pulled up his system for locating hunters and Demon activity. Officer Karen's energy signature was nowhere on the map, but her phone pinged in the same alley we had tracked José's phone to.

My chest tightened. What if she had been taken?

"I'll bet you ten kegs that if we went and powered the pool back up and threw a piece of Karen's hair in it, it'd do the same thing it did with José's," said Aelfric.

Sister Marie already had her coat on and keys out. She strode toward the basement door.

"I'll come with you. It's probably a trap." Aelfric followed her.

"Wait." Mike got up, jogged down the cellar with them, and returned a minute later with a handful of metal balls. "Lightning grenades. In case there's another ambush."

"I like the sound of those," said Aelfric.

Sister Marie grabbed the shimmering metallic grenades and pulled Aelfric out the door before he could say anything else.

"Should I go too?" I asked a minute after I heard Sister Marie's bike tear down the driveway.

Aunty Lucy shook her head. "Those two can handle themselves. Right now, the most useful thing you and Mel can do is sleep and get yourselves to the Confluence."

Maybe tonight we'd finally get there, but if Mel failed again? I had a theory of another way we could try to reach it.

*

It took me three tries to open the top drawer of the one-hundred-year-old dresser where I kept a few pairs of clothing and pajamas. The fleece *Iron Man* pajama pants were a little tight because I'd built so much muscle with all the training I'd been doing, but the plain gray T-shirt, which had always been several sizes too big, was loose enough on my filled-out shoulders. The floor creaked when I walked over toward my bed. The sheets were cold. Still, sleeping at Grandpa's was much more comfortable than sleeping at the convent.

I had my own bedroom here with a round red door and a little window that went directly into Mel's. When we were kids, during the weekends we spent at Grandpa's, we'd leave it open unless we were mad at each other. Games and made-up adventures flowed freely between the two rooms. If I had a bad dream at night, I'd run to her, not Grandpa.

Things were different now. Our relationship was strained in a way it hadn't been back then. We were better than a year ago, but Mel was an adult, and I was on the cusp of child and not. Mike shared Mel's room, and if José were here, he'd be here with me.

I was awake enough tonight to feel José's absence. After months of him being next to me, his absence made me lonely, unsettled, and caught between the shivers and the buzzy frustration that made me want to rip skin off.

Last night, I'd been so tired that I passed out as soon as I lay down in the cot-like bed. That wasn't the case tonight. As exhausted as I was, my mind raced over the day's events and raged at my inability to go out and find him. Even Bessie had abandoned me. Last I saw, she'd been stalking a group of Pixies working together to remove a bag of cheese curls from Grandpa's pantry.

Hinges squeaked.

"Erin?" Mel called.

"Yeah." I sat up as she took a few steps into the room.

Mel sat on the edge of the bed. "Remember how when we were little if Grandpa told us a story that was too scary, you'd make me come sleep in bed with you?"

I nodded, having an idea of where this was going, not opposed to her being near me how I would've been a couple months ago.

"I know we're not kids anymore, but I'm worried, especially after your heart stopped this morning." Mel inched closer. "And if we're right next to each other, it could be easier for me to get you to the Confluence."

"It's okay." I scooted over to make room for her. Distance had never consistently affected whether or not she could carry me there, but her presence might make falling asleep easier.

For a minute, awkward space and four years of disagreements and broken trust filled the space between us, but then Mel rolled onto her side, facing me like she had when we were kids, and smiled. "Remember the time Grandpa told you that story about the Troll that climbed the observatory on the Penobscot Narrows Bridge?"

"A fairy tale cliché mixed with King Kong."

Mel nodded. "You swore it wasn't scary at all. It was silly."

"Until I was walking to the bathroom, and you screeched at me from on top of the big bookcase at the end of the hall, and I threw a slipper at you," I said, a laugh forming in my chest but never breaking out.

"Did a Troll really climb that?" Back then, I had thought the stories were all made up. I knew better now.

"A small one. I wasn't there, but I saw Grandpa's memories every time he told that story. The night was windy enough for the bridge to be closed, but it happened in summer, not winter, and your dad didn't climb the tower. Grandpa always left out the part where he started climbing it, but Niben showed up and made him get down. There were storm cells nearby, so she adjusted the wind currents and pressure until they moved directly over the bridge, and the Troll got struck by lightning."

"I guess that version isn't as suspenseful," I said, though from my current point of view, the new details made the story far more interesting. Controlling storms and lightning strikes could be very useful, but I also imagined that type of magic could have unintended consequences.

Microbursts. Squalls. Droughts. Tornados. If you don't know what you're doing, you'll mess up weather in surrounding areas. Niben has had centuries to practice.

I don't plan to try that anytime soon, I thought as lightning flashed, momentarily illuminating rain pouring outside my window. Thunder rumbled a few seconds later. The last time I remembered being curled up in this same bed with Mel during a storm, we'd whispered late into the night about things we didn't want to say in front of Grandpa. I had told Mel how I simultaneously had a crush on a ninth grader, Kimberly Hanscom, and her younger brother, Ezekiel, who was in eighth grade with me. And then I asked her if it was still a crush if I didn't want to hug either of them.

That was the beginning of the end, thought Mel with a hint of sadness.

She was right. I had a bout of depression in the spring. That summer was the last one I spent down the cape with her; the one when I kissed José. Freshman year was a disaster; one riddled with lies, spilled secrets, and broken trust.

Mel moved to Boston for college and met Mike soon after.

I was only forty minutes away.

She hardly visited her first semester. After that, she came home on the weekends to meddle and tell my mom every secret I shared.

I was trying to help. To stop you from self-destructing.

Which I did anyway.

I know.

But I'm still alive because you were a snitching pain in the ass, and I'm grateful for it. Thank you.

Can I hug you?

Of course.

Mel scooted close enough for her tears to soak my shirt. I was never much of a touchy-feely person, but after a few seconds of tense muscles and crawly skin, I relaxed. I might have cried a little too before she rolled over onto the other side of the bed and cocooned herself in the blankets. She giggled when I tugged them back, and after a few minutes of the blanket tug of war we'd played as kids, we had equal shares of sheets and quilt.

Sleep stole the brief reprieve Mel had given me.

"What were you thinking?" yelled my father at a seven-year-old Mel.

"It was dark, and we wanted to keep playing, and we didn't want to wake Aunty up," squeaked Mel as tears dripped down her face.

Liam knelt and put hands on Mel's shoulders. "Erin is different than you. It's dangerous for them to play with light how you do, especially since they are so small. They just turned three."

"So, we're not in trouble for staying up late? I'm in trouble for teaching Erin important things?" Mel squirmed away from him.

The dream faded to black.

I lingered in the dark until slivers of green light filtered through slats of a vent, ten feet up where the wall touched the ceiling.

José sat on a dirt floor with his back to a concrete wall.

A metal bucket loomed in a corner across from him. A plate of bread and cheese sat untouched in front of him. He reached for a cup and sniffed its contents, staring as if he couldn't decide whether drinking was more dangerous than risking dehydration. He took a tiny sip and waited. Nothing happened. He took another. He put the cup down. Dark circles sank under his eyes, and dirt smeared his cheeks, but he didn't have a single bruise.

The angle of the green light shifted as time passed. He opened his eyes and gulped down the rest of the liquid and then devoured the bread and cheese. The door groaned. José leaped to his feet and guarded his face with scabbed knuckles.

The image of José faded. I willed it to stay, clung to the vision as much as one can cling to something as intangible as a glimpse through time and space.

A ball of fire landed on the street across from Grandpa's driveway, creating a crater. Three figures crouched in it. Allen held two phones bearing the same countdown as José's.

5 DAYS, 19 HOURS, 22 MINUTES, 13 SECONDS.

Aelfric sprawled at Allen's feet, flickering and unconscious while Jeremy frantically shook him. Demons materialized all around the crater, accompanied by a cloaked figure I'd been dreaming about for months.

Crawlers leaped on Allen.

Tendrils of dark energy wrapped around the two half Angels.

The scene faded to a beach.

No. I needed to wake up.

My father and Lucy walked on damp low-tide sand. The full moon bathed the beach in silver light.

Wake up!! I mentally screamed while my father and aunt bantered. *Wake up!! Wake up!! Wake up!!*

*

Small but strong fingers dug into my shoulder, and I nearly flew over the foot of the bed and onto the floor as Mel yanked me upright.

"Erin, what's going on?"

"They're gonna die." I leaped off the edge of the bed. My heart raced. Sweat soaked my pajamas. My throat and lungs burned. Had I been screaming for hours?.

"More like five minutes." Mel followed me as I ran out into the hall and leaped down the stairs in a few bounds.

"Erin, who is going to die?"

"Watch." I walked to the kitchen table, projecting a replay of the dream to Mel.

5 DAYS, 19 HOURS, 26 MINUTES, 33 SECONDS.

I sprinted toward the basement,

Mel didn't ask any more questions. I grabbed the first two swords I saw and ran back up the stairs.

The Pixies were frenzied. The ceiling creaked and groaned as people got out of bed above me.

"I woke Niben and relayed the message." Mel and I ran out the door.

I stopped and put my hands on her shoulder, pushing her back inside. "Stay here, please."

I inhaled, starting the process of slowing my perception of time.

"Stay in the house," I repeated between breaths.

"Listen to them." Niben grabbed Mel's arm and pulled her further into the house. Grandpa took Mel's hand, and Niben joined me outside. She had two swords belted to her hips and a shotgun slung over her back.

I turned to run, but Niben grabbed my shoulder and spun me around so we were face-to-face, noses touching. "Last night, Allen asked you what you were. You left out a detail you were uncertain about. If your speculations were true, then for you, energy is energy. You can take it and shape it whether it is inside a person, a wire, or a monster. In a fight with Hanzel, that may be the difference between life and death."

She let go of me and sprinted down the driveway.

"Who is Hanzel?" I charged after her, slowing down time more and more until I caught up to her at the end.

"A hybrid—Angel, Demon, Elf, and human—who has allied himself with the Fallen in the past. He is a cockroach."

A car sped by. No animals rustled the brush. No tree frogs sang in the wetlands across the road. A cloaked figure stepped out of the trees.

Niben's hands blurred as she grabbed her pump-action shotgun and fired five rounds into its chest. The figure staggered back, laughing. "Oh, Niben. For an Elf of the most ancient lineage, you are so human."

"Hanzel, how many times must I kill you before you stay dead?" She reloaded.

I didn't know who or what Hanzel was, but nothing about him felt right. Cold and slimy energy radiated off him. He wasn't a Demon, but my instincts and Niben's lack of hesitation to shoot at him told me he meant us harm.

I focused on the energy humming in the overhead electrical wires, ready to summon it when fire bloomed between Hanzel and me. Pavement flew off the road as the raw energy dispersed, leaving three people behind. Allen, Jeremy, and Aelfric were all in the circle of crumbled pavement exactly how they had been in my dream, but now I could see how startled Allen was, staring at a handgun with wide, all-black eyes.

"Wake up, wake up, wake up." Jeremy shook Aelfric, who flickered.

Crawlers materialized in the shadows, growling at us.

"Stay down!" I screamed as I called lightning out of the wires.

I half cackled, half screamed as volts surged into me and danced out of my fingertips, obliterating the Crawlers.

Shots fired.

Why did Niben keep shooting and not attack Hanzel with magic? Or a sword?

I shot lightning at Hanzel, who caught it and yanked it like a rope and sent me flying like a discus. Pavement shredded T-shirt and skin alike.

That's why. Shield before he realizes you aren't shielding, Niben scolded right before her telepathic presence vanished.

The stinging and burning consumed me for approximately ten seconds, and then the monster in me woke up. I shielded and growled before charging toward the cloaked creep with a sword in each hand.

Excess electricity still hummed under my skin. Shadowy vines shot out from under his cloak toward Niben, who had a still-unconscious Aelfric slung over her shoulder. A human her size wouldn't have had the strength to carry him.

I ran faster.

Allen and Jeremy were ahead of her, walking backward in slow motion down the driveway while she screamed for them to run.

A few feet away from Hanzel, I raised my sword. The vine whipped away from Niben and wrapped around my wrist. I kicked. I tried to wriggle and flail free while more vines writhed, binding my limbs and torso. Thorns dug into my skin and seared my already-shredded back.

I wanted to rip this creep's face off.

"Looks like Grandma has no problem feeding Little Red to the wolves," said Hanzel. He leaned forward, revealing a skeletal face covered in red blister-shaped scars. His eyes were space-deep black filled with glittery stars and swirling galaxies.

"I am not Little Red," I snarled. I forced my lips into a grin, hoping I appeared as berserk as I felt. Referring to me as a victimized fairy-tale character was a mistake, but he was right about Niben leaving me behind. She and the others disappeared up Grandpa's driveway. Doubt and betrayal gnawed at my guts, but I refused to let this asshole see that. I had to keep talking to silence the doubt in my head. "If anything, I'm the wolf and you're Little Red. You've got red and a hood, so that definitely makes me the big bad wolf. I'm going to tear you to shreds. I'm—"

My words died as the vines twined tighter around me.

Hanzel shrieked as Niben stabbed his shoulders with a shimmering dagger in each hand. The vines loosened as her daggers tore through his back. Smoke poured out of the wounds.

I grinned. She must have returned while I was focused on Hanzel. She hadn't abandoned me after all. Wriggling out of the vines, I grabbed my fallen sword.

"Run! You'll be safe in the house!" she yelled.

I slashed at Hanzel, but his damned vines parried, ripping my sword in two.

A blur of dim light flew toward us from the driveway. My hands clenched into fists. Why had Mel left the house? She wasn't supposed to leave, but here she was, cutting through the vines with a glowing broadsword. Hanzel's abdomen smoked where she slashed it. She raised her sword, attempting to decapitate him when he got a vine around her wrist.

I stabbed at him with a broken blade, but I didn't get very close before he had a vine around each of my wrists and ankles. They multiplied. I closed my eyes, retreating into my mind's cockpit, and half dropped my forward shields.

The vines were cords of oily energy wrapping Mel, Niben, and me up in tight, slimy cocoons, making my skin crawl. Little Red was a freaking spider. I threw my shields back up. Grandpa came down the drive yelling for Mel. A tentacle-riddled shadow moved across the sky, cloaked the street in darkness.

Hanzel was bad enough. Now Shadowhulhu had arrived.

"Erin. Catch." Grandpa threw something at us.

A tentacle batted it out of the way

"No!" I screamed as the same tentacle snatched Grandpa up and vanished into a black hole. My chest tightened. A roar bellowed out of my mouth.

"Perhaps if you will not surrender for your lover, you will for your grandfather!" boomed Shadowhulhu. "If you swear to serve me and you come with me now, then no harm will come to either."

I writhed against Hanzel's tightening vines, straining toward the sky. "And if I don't come? Are you just going to kill him now?"

Shadowhulhu's tentacles whipped Grandpa's phone at me. "The prisoners will live until the timer runs out, but my master and I grow weary of restraining our servants. Beings such as Hanzel have very specific ideas of fun."

"I'd rather die than serve you and your kidnapping shithead of a boss," I snarled.

"So be it. The consequences of Hanzel's amusement are on you." Shadowhulhu vanished with Grandpa.

Mel screamed. Her light dimmed quickly as Hanzel siphoned energy from her.

I bared my teeth. "I'm going to end you, Little Red."

He stopped draining Mel's energy. His vines sucked power out of me as if they were tree roots taking water from the ground. Like I pulled electricity from a wire.

"Who's Little Red now?" laughed Hanzel.

"You!" I screeched. I closed my eyes, grit my teeth, dropped my shields, and yanked my own energy back. It didn't come as easy as electricity, but my ability to tug back surprised Hanzel enough that he gasped and staggered back. Mel and Niben thudded to the ground.

Hanzel narrowed his cosmic eyes. Telepathic energy shot toward my mind. Even though it was intangible, it made me think of slime. I retreated to my mental cockpit and fired lasers at him until the vines loosened. I slithered out of them and grabbed as many as I could. They were greasy, cold conduits that allowed power to flow from one being to another. Inside the conduit, pieces of Mel's energy felt like white-hot light, and Niben's were similar to a summer storm.

I pulled it all.

"Tell me where José is and how I can find him, and this will be over quickly," I said in the most monstrous voice I could muster. The energy was mostly through the conduit; another inch and it would be mine.

Hanzel drew power back toward him. "Arrogant child!"

I tugged harder. "Where is José?"

Icy pins and needles tickled the tips of my fingers.

"I don't know what you're talking about," he growled through gritted teeth as he struggled and failed to pull his power back.

"Where is José?" I shouted, channeling all my pain and rage and longing as I summoned energy out of his conduit. Fizzy cold surged through my veins, followed by searing heat. The more I took, the easier pulling became. I seized every ounce of stolen Angel fire and summer storm even though Hanzel's slime came too. With so much of his energy under my control, the vines responded to my will and twined all around him, squeezing his throat to the verge of snapping.

"Where is José?"

"The Bracken Bubble," he croaked.

"Where is the Bracken Bubble?" I asked.

He didn't answer.

I tightened the vines. "Where is the Bracken Bubble?

He stilled, hanging limp in his vines.

My vines.

Chapter Twelve

Erin thinks Mel is nothing like them. On the surface, that may be true. But at her core? Mel is just as depressed, angry, and self-destructive. The difference is in how they cope. Erin cuts. Mel heals. Lately, I'm more worried about Mel than Erin.

—From the hunting log of José Estrella, written in February of 2018, confined to the archives after his high school graduation.

Grandpa was gone. Shadowhulhu had another person I loved. I had a name for where he was, but that name meant nothing. The person who might have been able to tell me was a corpse crumpled on the pavement.

He was a corpse because I made him one.

I killed Hanzel. He was a monster that tried to kill Mel, Niben, and me, but he wasn't a Demon. He was a hybrid. Just like me.

My fingernails dug into skin that felt like millions of slimy maggots. I was a murderer. I pressed my nails in further until my skin stung, hurt, and bled, reminding me I was still Erin and still alive. I was a killer, but I hadn't turned into a collective of slippery slugs.

My shields were down, but Mel hadn't scolded me for hurting myself. She hadn't popped into my head to tell me I wasn't a monster.

Someone sobbed.

I turned. To say the shredded skin on my back stung would be a horrible understatement, but that pain was nothing compared to how my heart hurt when I saw Mel lying limp in Niben's lap.

She wasn't glowing. She wasn't flickering.

It wasn't until I stood inches away, bleeding all over my cousin and grandmother, that I saw the tiniest flash of light winking on and off across Mel's skin. She was breathing, barely.

I pulled Mel toward me, half expecting Niben to not let her go, but my grandmother collapsed forward, burying her face in her knees.

"It's too late," she croaked. "Mel can't recover from this."

I hugged Mel as tight as I could, remembering all the other times she'd hugged me, the times we'd grappled on the beach, and the times she'd restrained me from hurting myself. Sparring matches with bamboo swords. Bad jokes. Invasions of privacy. Bacon and chocolate.

We'd barely begun to fix things between us.

Mel was not going to die on me today.

I focused on all the things that made me think of Mel while teasing the hottest fire out of the energy I had taken from Hanzel. Not all the Angelic energy belonged to her. Some was Aelfric's. I put that aside. And the rest? I didn't know whom the rest belonged to or when it was stolen, but the energy was going to Mel. I drove power out through my skin, willing it to burn the psychosomatic maggots away while traveling from me to her.

She remained a dead weight in my arms.

I kept feeding her the energy until it was gone. I pulled the power that had been stolen from Niben, mixed it with my own, and poured it into Mel. I took the little bit of Aelfric's energy I had set aside and gave it to her too.

After using up all the stolen Angel fire, I focused on Hanzel's energy, which still crawled under my skin. I let slimy magic sink into my muscles, my heart, and my soul. I willed the dark to change, to morph into the fire that already lived inside me. And then I pushed it back out, adjusting it to feel more like Mel.

"Erin, that's enough!" Mel flailed, opened her swirling eyes, and pushed me away.

My body sagged. I tried to sit up, but exhaustion kept me down. I barely managed to open my eyes.

Glowing like afternoon sun, Mel offered me a hand.

I took it, thinking she was only going to help me get up.

Warmth flooded my body, bolstering my muscles until I could stand. I tried to pull away before Mel wasted any more of the energy I'd just given to her, but I was too weak, and she was too strong.

Heat pushed pieces of pavement out of my back and healed the wounds left behind. My ribs burned as bones I didn't realize were broken fused together. I doubted it was an accident that when Mel healed the self-inflicted wounds on my arm, it felt like she was cauterizing them with a hot poker.

"Never scare me that way again," I said at the same time Mel did.

Mel snorted and giggled as tears poured out of her eyes. She wasn't bright enough to hurt my eyes, but she still glowed so much more than she had this morning.

"You gave me too much. You were hurt worse than you realized. This is a better balance," she said.

"Shadowhulhu has Grandpa." I pulled away from her, stumbling with dizziness.

"Dammit." Mel slid her shoulder under my arm so I could lean some of my weight on her. She pulled me close to her. "We'll get him back. We'll find a way to get them all."

We both turned to Niben. She sat on the ground, staring at us. Her eyes were wide, and her cheeks were puffy and red. She launched herself at us, crushing both Mel and me into one hug. She let go and put a hand on Mel's cheek. "I thought we'd lost you."

Mel rested her forehead on Niben's shoulder. "Me too. I was standing in space with my dad, and I asked him if I died. He winked at me and said, 'Not if Erin has anything to do with it.' Then he was gone, and I was back."

"Hanzel had drained more than 90 percent of your life force, and then Erin drained him. Erin didn't just give you your own power back." Niben steered Mel so she could see Hanzel's body.

Mel tensed. "Erin killed him."

Niben grinned, showing her teeth. "I hope he stays dead this time."

"We should go back inside." Feeling like my ribs were a trash compactor, I slithered out of the group hug and picked Grandpa's phone up off the pavement.

5 DAYS, 18 HOURS, 58 MINUTES, 27 SECONDS.

Niben looped an arm through Mel's, and then hooked my arm with her other one. I tensed. She grabbed my bicep when I tried to pull away. "Erin, that fiend has killed and tortured hundreds, maybe thousands of people. The world is safer with him dead."

I nodded, but her words didn't make breathing hurt any less.

*

A loud thumping echoed from the house like Bessie's tail hitting something, only louder. Mel opened the door, and Mike fell onto her with his hand raised as if he was going to pound the door again.

"Amelia!" Mike slid to his knees in front of Mel and wrapped his arms around her waist. "I love you, but don't ever do that to me again."

Aunty Lucy crushed Mel with a hug. Smoke curled out of her prosthetic legs.

The smell of pancakes and chocolate wafted from the kitchen.

Bessie knocked me down so she could lick my face.

Mel, her fiancé, and her mother slid to the floor, crying.

Bessie left me to go lick Mel's tears.

I stood a few feet from the door, watching.

I'd never felt so alone.

I jumped as Niben squeezed my shoulder. "You're not alone, Erin."

I leaned against Niben. I let her put a warm arm around me and rested my head on her. "How do I carry this weight? I took another life, maybe an evil one, but still."

Niben leaned her head against mine. "You have to figure that out for yourself.

*

When I fell asleep, my dreams picked up right where they had left off.

"Tonight, we're going to have some quality sibling bonding time." Lucy grinned as she unsheathed two swords.

Bubbles interrupted the serene glistening of moonlight on a calm ocean. A white cylinder rose out of the water followed by a dozen tentacles with razor-petal flowers where an octopus would have suckers. The Kraken's shadow rose up to the sky and spread until its massive center and writhing tentacles blocked out the moonlight.

"Kneel before me and live!!!" Shadowhulhu's voice boomed over the churning water.

Aunty Lucy stuck up both her middle fingers. "Go back to Hell!"

Two walls of water rose in the shape of her hands, giving the monster the middle finger. The tips of the fingers turned to points. They froze as they rose and stabbed it.

My dad unsheathed a massive, glowing broadsword and ran forward, leaping over chunks of frozen seawater Lucy made for him until he could reach it and plunge the sword into its center.

The beach faded to a barren landscape.

The dead field transformed into a pile of rubble, which I was half buried in. My heart lurched. My throat inflated. My lungs filled with air. I climbed out of a pile of rubble, which faded into a bridge of flowers. Vincent, more swirling white flakes than solid body, stared at me.

"You know my terms," I said.

"I agree to them," he replied.

We met in the middle, and I shook his one solid hand.

"Call me Vincent," he said.

"Vincent," I repeated.

He peered over my shoulder, saw Sam, and rushed toward her. She tried to hug him but fell through him instead.

The bridge vanished.

Chapter Thirteen

Between: the space between worlds. One can enter it at one point on Earth and emerge miles away a mere minute later. Warning: however, travel is limited to where Between touches Earth, and there is no shortage of danger traveling Between. Demons use it as a way into Earth, but anyone can easily become lost in the expanse of nothingness.

—A Demon Hunters Lexicon

With shaking hands, Aelfric poured champagne into a glass that was half-full of orange juice. He had dark circles under his eyes, and dim, barely visible light radiated off his body.

"That is his third one." Niben winked at me and placed a platter of french toast on the table. "And he has only been awake fifteen minutes."

I glanced at her. I couldn't think of anything to say, so I helped myself to breakfast.

"You didn't fight off God-knows-how-many Demons, get drained by bloody Hanzel, and teleported by Jeremy." Aelfric drank half his mimosa in one gulp.

"Right. I only did two out of those three things." Niben sat down and crossed her arms. She appeared equally tired, only she didn't have a glowing aura I could use to gauge her energy levels.

"You what?" asked Aelfric as he finished the mimosa and picked up the champagne to pour another.

Bessie thwacked Aelfric in the leg with her tail with enough force to make him drop the bottle, spilling the remainder of the champagne all over the table. Bessie trotted over to me and licked my hands. She sat and stared at me, all proud of herself.

"Have you ever heard of the Bracken Bubble?" I asked before Aelfric and Niben could start arguing. Last night, she'd admitted she had no clue what it was. Lucy didn't know. Jeremy and Allen thought it sounded like something from a video game.

"The bracken what?" Aelfric had his elbows on the table and his hands cradling his head. He hadn't even bothered cleaning up the champagne.

"The Bracken Bubble," I repeated.

"Never heard of it," he said.

"Vincent might have mentioned it." Sam walked into the kitchen, yawning, and took the seat next to me. "He was born in a something bubble. Might have been the Bracken Bubble."

"Did he tell you anything about it?" I asked, praying he had.

"He did, but his voice got all garbled as soon as he said 'bubble.' I remember him trying to fight it once, but then he stopped breathing for a few seconds, and the Incubus got control." Sam stared at the floor, biting her fingernails. "He got himself back in the driver's seat quickly, but the incident was scary as fuck."

Niben's hand froze with her fork halfway to her mouth. "Driver's seat?"

Sam glared at me. "You didn't tell them, did you?"

"Tell us what?" Aunty Lucy wheeled herself out of the first-floor guest room. Her red-and-gray hair stuck up straight, and she had dark circles under her eyes.

I leaped to my feet, glaring at my aunt. "I think you also have something to tell us."

Aunty Lucy's forehead wrinkled, and her head tilted. "About what?"

"You fought Shadowhulhu before. You and my dad fought the Many-Tentacled Destroyer the night you lost your legs to the Kraken."

Color drained from her face. "No. We didn't. Not unless it was after I blacked out. I'd never heard of it until yesterday."

I walked closer to her. "No. You froze the ocean into middle fingers. You made ice stairs for my dad. He had a glowing broadsword similar to Mel's, but it was bigger and brighter."

"I don't remember." Aunty Lucy gripped the edge of her wheelchair so hard skin strained against her white knuckles.

"Stop lying to me!" I spun toward the others. "All of you!"

"Erin, I don't think she's lying, though I'd know for sure if she dropped her shields." Mel rose from the table and marched toward us.

"No. Amelia, I don't want you in my head." Tears poured out of Aunty Lucy's eyes. She covered her mouth with her hands and muttered, "Dammit, Liam, if you weren't dead, I'd—"

"What would you do?" Niben loomed behind me and glared down at her daughter.

Aunty Lucy jabbed a finger at Niben. "Did you help him do this?"

"Do what?" Niben stepped in front of me.

"Alter my memories and take some away. You have the power to do that."

"So did he." Niben sank to her knees and put her hands over Aunty Lucy's. "I swear on my soul, I never changed or removed your memories."

Aunty Lucy glared at Niben with her lip curled up.

Mel put her hand on her mother's shoulder. "Mom, Niben is telling the truth. *She* isn't shielding and is as shocked as you look."

Aunty Lucy's breath rattled. "There have always been holes in my memory from that night, but trauma can do that to a person. I never thought my own brother, my twin..."

Niben and Mel both hugged Aunty Lucy as tears drowned her words.

I stayed put. "His journals didn't say anything about this."

"Why would he write something down if he was trying so hard to keep it hidden from all you?" Aelfric stood at the counter, pouring whiskey into a cup of coffee.

"He wrote everything down." Aunty Lucy peered over Niben's shoulder. "We used a cypher when we were kids when we didn't want our parents to read our journals, and knowing him, he didn't want his secrets to die with him. He probably dreamed us having this exact conversation right now."

"Liam was always deliberate about revealing information at what he thought was the right time, and even now, I can't help but wonder if he'd still be here had he not kept so much to himself." Niben stood up, turned, and stared at me. "I also wonder what *you* haven't told us."

*

Saint Patrick's was literally the fullest I'd ever seen, and I recognized a lot of people in the crowd. Jenny Dunn and her parents shared a row with Will and his. Other families from school sat near them—José's "friends" from the soccer team and the girls who had tormented me with Jenny Dunn.

Had someone not put a Reserved sign on the front row with the extra space for a wheelchair, we would've been standing in the back, and we weren't late. Normally, the hunters took up the whole front row. Today, Lucy, Mel, Mike, Sam, and I barely filled half of it.

Sam had wanted to stay at the house, but Niben insisted on Sam coming to do research in the archives. Sam came, and Niben glamoured her enough so no one could recognize her. Sam showing up in public now would raise questions, red tape, and paperwork. We could get arrested. None of those things would help us save the world.

Aelfric could barely walk from the table to the liquor cabinet, so he'd opted to stay behind. Allen and Jeremy decided to stay with him and make sure he didn't drink himself to death in our absence. The others? They were in the Bracken Bubble, wherever the Hell that was.

Between.

Mel and I both jumped at the sound of her father's voice.

How bad were things if he answered questions we hadn't asked him, even if the answer was vague and nonsensical?

I think he means Between as in the place. Mel studied the church, trying to spot her father.

I didn't see him anywhere. Between was a start, but Between, the space between Earth, Faerie, and Hell, was bigger than those three realms combined.

The church was absolutely packed, and not only with people. Normally, there were two Angels who hung out on the altar during mass. Mel said they were Sentinels and mostly watched over humans, sharing a touch of healing energy to anyone with faith of any kind. Today, there were seven. Mel, who usually seemed to enjoy the company of the two, watched the seven as if they were a bad omen.

They are bad omens. It means they are gearing up for a possible war, and the balance is in danger, especially if Dad is here. The best-case scenario would be the Angels and the surviving humans rebuild some kind of civilization from what's left of the world.

The anxiety accompanying Mel's words made me shiver.

We won't let it come to that, I thought. I had pieces of puzzle, but how and when they fit together kept shifting. We could do this. We had to.

Piano keys sent soothing melodies through the church, playing softly while a person made the pre-mass announcements, dedicating prayers to the victims of Friday's shooting and Saturday's fire. The procession started. The back door opened, but a hot breeze blew through the church, disturbing air and energy alike.

Mel's father walked in wearing blue scrubs. His body barely contained a light that could blind me if I looked directly upon an uncontained version of it with my Sight open. Even bound as it was, his skin glowed like a sunset.

Mel squeezed my hand.

Hi, Dad. Why are you here?

To see how you are holding up.

Mel rested her forehead on her palms. *How do you think I am?*

I'm sorry, he said. *There is so much I wish I could spare you from.*

I tried to listen to the mass and not think about the fact that a powerful Angel lurked in the back of church. I had so many questions I wanted to ask him, but I doubted he'd answer any of them.

You don't know until you ask, he said.

I glanced at Mel. She shrugged.

What is the Bracken Bubble? I asked.

A pocket dimension created by one of my Fallen brethren, he said.

You're not starting an apocalypse by telling me this, right?

I could almost hear the smile in the Angel's telepathically projected words. *No. A servant of the Fallen already disclosed not only that the Bracken Bubble exists, but its creator is holding a human captive in it. To maintain the balance, I can share this information.*

So, can you tell me where it is? Hope swelled in my chest.

I don't know where in the Between the Bracken Bubble is, but you have foreseen a way to track José.

How? I very well might have and not realized whatever I was seeing was at all connected to him because my dreams were so fragmented.

The lector got through the first reading. The choir stared singing.

Does my mom know you're here? Mel asked when it became obvious her father wasn't going to answer my question.

He didn't answer that one either.

Mel squeezed my hand harder, and while she didn't project any words to my head, I sensed thoughts racing in her mind: a need for more answers, the urge to run to the back of the church and hug her father, the fear that his presence made the future I dreamed more likely, and that he was so frustrating.

Deep laughter tolled in my head. *Carry on as if I was not here.*

Michael, the Archangel, shielded his presence from us as much as he could. If I tried to concentrate on where he was, my focus slipped elsewhere, to Mel's frustration.

I hate when he does that. I'm an adult by human standards, but an infant compared to someone as ancient as him.

Niben tapped my shoulder. "Erin, stand up."

I blinked. Everyone was standing but Lucy and me.

As I stood, I realized Mel was staring at me, more confused than I was.

In her eyes, maelstroms of green and brown swirled faster than normal. *This is a disaster. He shouldn't be here. He's worried way too much about me. The balance might already be fucked, and he isn't helping.*

I put my arm around Mel and half hugged her. *It's not a disaster yet. We're going to be okay. I promise. Try to relax and recharge as you usually do here.*

She tensed. *Erin.*

Okay, that was kind of a shitty thing to think at you. I hate when people tell me to relax when I'm anxious.

Mel thoughts vanished behind a rushing waterfall. She put her arm around me and pulled me closer so she could whisper in my ear. "I'm nervous, but not to the point where I unknowingly aimed my thoughts at you."

"I only ever hear what you want me to, what you project in my head," I whispered back. Now that I wasn't so lost in Mel's head and mental conversations, I could more clearly hear the priest reading the Gospel.

"I project thoughts into Mike's and Grandpa's heads. I direct thoughts at you like I do if I want to chat with Niben, who is also a telepath," Mel whispered.

"So, what are you saying?" I asked, louder than I should've in church. Father McPherson glared at me before he began a homily by acknowledging the weekend's tragedies.

Mel raised her eyebrows. "You don't get it, do you?"

Niben laughed at the other side of the pew. *You were reading Mel's thoughts, uninvited and unintentionally, exactly like Mel does to everyone who doesn't or can't shield around her when she isn't shielding.*

I didn't hear anyone else's thoughts though. At least not that I was aware of. I also didn't try to, for fear if I succeeded, I wouldn't be able to turn it off ever.

Telepathy shuts off if you shield. Mel's waterfall went away, flooding my head with her amusement.

Shielding takes work, I thought. *This isn't funny.*

I had planned to let my mind wander as open as I could make it, to meditate, maybe even let myself fall asleep in hopes of picking up on some other vision of the past or potential future. I was too afraid I'd tap into other people's minds instead. I focused on every prayer, trying to ignore a stream of thoughts from Mel's mind, and when it came to offer people a sign of peace, I smiled and waved at Jenny, who flailed her hand in my direction.

I needed to talk to her.

"I'll meet you all downstairs," I said when mass ended.

"Good luck." Mel winked and followed everyone else down to the archives.

I stayed where I was and braced myself for Jenny Dunn. I'd been mostly ignoring her texts and calls when I had a working phone, something I didn't have at the moment. I might not be able to tell her everything, but she had the right to know José wasn't ignoring her.

I watched her get closer. She smiled, wiped tears from her eyes, and sped up. So far, so good. No accidental mind reading.

She jogged toward me, stopping a few feet away. Her eyes were red, her skin rubbed raw. Snot bubbled out of one nostril for a second before she wiped it away. "Why have you and José been ignoring my calls and texts?"

"My phone broke." My throat got tight. My hands strangled each other behind my back.

"You were on Facebook early Saturday morning," she said accusingly.

"And then I went to visit Sam, and I broke my phone." I took the melted heap of plastic out of my pocket and handed it to her. "Actually, this is the second phone this has happened to in the past three days."

She cradled the ruined device in one hand, running her fingers over the wavy plastic with the other. "You were there for the fire."

She put a hand on my back, horrified I might have lived through two nightmares in one weekend. Shit.

"Yes," I said, stepping out of her reach.

"Was José?"

"No. He—" Dammit. How could I explain this to her?

"The news listed Sam as missing," said Jenny.

"I know." I stared at Jenny's pink sandals because I was too much of a coward to make eye contact.

"Where is José?" she asked.

I didn't look up.

"Erin, he is always at church with you on Sunday. Did something happen to him?"

A swarm of anxiety buzzed from my chest down to my arms. I pressed my palms to my jeans. Telepathically asking an Angel questions about José's location felt like progress even if the answers weren't much. But this? Admitting to Jenny how Demons had stolen José?

"Erin, did he get hurt? If he is in the hospital, tell me which one so I can go see him." Jenny put a hand on my shoulder, and for a moment, movie-like images flooded my mind, alternating between a vision of him conscious in the hospital bed appearing well cared for and very bruised and unconscious, hooked up to machines.

My muscles tensed, my hands closed into fists, and my heart raced, because she was touching me *and* because I was seeing her thoughts. What was happening to me? What was I becoming? I didn't want to become a telepath.

Please don't tell me he's dead. Please don't be dead. This kid is going to need a father. Please, Erin, don't tell me he is dead, thought Jenny.

I jumped away from her, and thankfully, her thoughts vanished from my mind. "He is alive, but he isn't in a hospital, and please don't touch me."

Jenny crossed her arms. "Then, where is he?"

"I don't know." The words burned my throat.

Jenny reached out to touch me but stopped herself. She clasped her hands behind her back. "Erin, you're a psychic. You have to know."

I closed my eyes to hide my tears.

"You have to have at least seen something. You love him. In movies, emotions are tied to people's powers," she said.

"I'm not a superhero," I said, choking on tear snot.

"I'm sorry. That was—this must be hard for you too." She walked a few feet away from me to sit on the altar steps. She covered her face with her hands and started crying.

I watched her cry.

When I stopped shaking, I sat down next to her. "So, you believe I am a psychic?"

"Yes," she sniffled.

"Do you believe in other things?" I asked.

She stared up at the ceiling. "Most of the time I believe in God."

I forced myself to look into her cold blue eyes. "What about Demons and Angels?"

"I mean, I guess it's a package deal, right?" She studied the church, the Angelic busts carved into the pillars and the stained-glass window depicting the Devil tempting Jesus in the desert. For a moment, I wondered how much of those stories were real. Then I stopped myself. Of course, some of them had to be real. All religions and myths start with some truth. The real question was whether the story happened in the way the church told it. How many miracle-performing saints were hybrids like me? Was Jesus—

"The apocalypse!" Jenny stood up and glared down at me. "In the movie theater. You said the apocalypse was starting. This has something to do with that. It's really happening, isn't? Like the stuff in Revelations?"

"I haven't read enough of the Bible to answer your question." I did my best to explain the situation to Jenny.

She swayed. I worried she'd faint, but she sunk back down to the step and ran her hands through her hair. "So, have you seen any visions of him?"

Visions were the one part of the deal she accepted. I couldn't tell what she thought of the rest; at least I couldn't without attempting to read her mind.

She folded her hands in her lap. "Please, Erin, tell me you saw something."

I closed my eyes. "I dreamed about him twice. Both times, he was in a dark cell. His captors fed him, and they didn't hurt him."

We sat there for a few minutes. She sniffled while I tried not to cry. I got up to leave, but she said, "Other abilities? Like magic powers?"

I tilted my head toward the baptismal font. She followed me over to it. I reached up to a big candle and called energy from its flame. The candle went out, but a ball of orange light hovered in my palm. Jenny watched in silence as water rose out of the baptismal font and formed a transparent ice globe around the glowing light in my hand. "Don't tell anyone about this, okay? Not even Will."

Jenny's breath hitched, but she agreed.

She glanced up from the ice that hadn't melted even though it contained fire. "That night in March, the man...the thing you tackled off me. That was a Demon, wasn't it?"

I nodded.

Tension deflated from her shoulders. "I've been wanting to ask you for months. I wanted to know if my attacker was a monster, or if I told myself that because of how traumatic that night was."

"I didn't think you would've believed me if I told you."

"I might not have. But you know things. And then that." She pointed at my hands.

I closed my fist. The ice collapsed. My skin absorbed the energy as water soaked my hands.

"You can find José, right? You're going to figure out where he is and get him out alive?"

"I'm trying." I stared at the floor, at wood slathered with so many layers of polyurethane that it looked like it was encased in amber along with scratches and dents from more than a century of use.

"If there is anything I can do to help, anything, please let me know," said Jenny.

I finally turned around and made eye contact. "I have a feeling I might have to take you up on that offer, eventually. Thank you."

My hands shook as Jenny stared at me. I thought she was going to hug me.

"Hey, Erin, where is José?" asked Will, walking toward us, flanked by the twins.

On the verge of laughing and hyperventilating, I tried to smile as if this were normal banter. "A pocket dimension. You don't happen to have a spare Tardis? Or one of the magic stick things the doctor uses to find cosmic shit?"

Will's face contorted to frowns and creases. "Oh. Erin. I'm sorry."

"He's missing, not dead. Don't 'sorry' me." I turned from Will to Jenny, forming three short sentences in my mind. If Mel could project words into anyone's head, perhaps I could too. I took a couple deep breaths and hugged Jenny.

Not lying about the pocket dimension. Don't tell anyone. I'll find you when I'm ready.

Jenny's eyes widened, and she nodded.

I pulled away from her. My lungs burned.

Why did breathing always get so hard?

I backed away.

I'd kept it together. I'd told her what I needed to. I stepped through the exit near the elevator but kept going past it, darting through the sacristy to the hidden staircase.

Jenny had heard what I wanted her to. My projection worked, which was freaking terrifying. I'd spent the past two months working to develop my ability to manipulate and channel energy. My control and focus had been gradually improving. But telepathy? Empathy? That was Mel's shit.

I was changing too quickly. It was bad enough I'd killed someone. Now I considered the possibility I could use José and Jenny's unborn child to track him. What did that make me?

I got halfway down the stairs before I collapsed, crying, gasping, and choking. What was I becoming? Would I still be me when I found José? How much more damaged would he be? Was I going to be? What if I wasn't human enough?

José never wanted to be a hunter. What if being kidnapped was the last straw? What if he saw Jenny's pregnancy as a way to escape the world of hunters and truly get over me now that I openly wanted to be with him?

It was too much to think about.

Too heavy a load.

Too much.

Chapter Fourteen

It is relatively easy to trap a Demon with an energy-infused symbol. Binding a Demon, or a piece of one, to an object is harder and exponentially more dangerous. However, if done correctly, the object can bestow the hunter with powers the Demon possessed such as True Sight or the ability to steal energy from living beings.

—A Hybrid's Guide for Trapping and Warding by Louise Desjardins, 2nd edition published in 1985.

My eyes took a few minutes to adjust to the warm, yellow light of incandescent bulbs. Shelves stuffed with books, notebooks, and three-ring binders covered every wall. Mike sat at a big oak library table with three monitors facing him in a crescent. Mel sat at the same table, reading out of a huge dusty tome. Lucy had her wheelchair pulled up to a table in the far corner with a pile of journals. She glanced back and forth between them and a sheet of paper before writing things in a notebook.

Niben sat at another table with open journals and leaves of typewriter paper strewn across the top. Niben read fast, making notes in a composition book as she went.

"I want Mirabel Bearclaw's notes from 1977. Third case from the righthand corner of the rear wall, second shelf off the floor, assuming Seamus didn't rearrange this place in the past decade."

Frowning, Sam shuffled over to the shelf and pulled out the journal before strolling back and plopping it on the table. Niben flipped to a specific page in the book, compared it to another, set it aside, flipped through another, looked up, and then asked Sam for a fourth book.

"Where would something about symbols or artifacts be?" I hoped to put my effort into something someone else wasn't already working on.

"There." Niben pointed at a wall filled with academic manuscripts, encyclopedias, and annotated mythology texts. It was the one section of the archives that wasn't filled with the journals and logs of a few centuries' worth of hunters. I strode toward in that direction, looking at the titles: *Demon Hunter's Lexicon, Crawler Mutation, Effective Ways to Kill Trolls, Krakens, and Other Large Demons*, and *A Hybrid's Guide for Trapping and Warding*.

"*Trapping and Warding* might have what you are looking for," said Niben.

The damned book was heavy. "Did you spend a lot of time down here when you lived with Grandpa?"

He'd already be complaining were he here.

Chuckling, Niben looked up from the words. "This used to be a dumping ground for old books and journals. I made it a library."

I carried *A Hybrid's Guide for Trapping and Warding* over to a worn armchair and opened it. I'd been working my way through this beast on and off for a couple weekends, and based on what I'd read, I didn't think it would have the information I wanted, but I'd only scratched the book's surface.

I flipped through the pages, scanning to decide what parts I should read. The chapter titles and subheads focused on the why and how star traps worked. The passages explained a dozen different types of wards someone could make with minimal ability to tap into the energy that surrounds and connects all living things. Of course, the more someone could manipulate magic, the stronger the wards were.

The last third of the book was dedicated to storing energy in different objects to make them perform a variety of functions: one could charge knives with energy so they made Demons explode on contact or imbue two identical objects with the same energy, creating a link between the two, and one could be used to find the other. The latter information would've been useful before José got abducted.

Nothing explained why Sam's necklace gave her Sight or even referenced pentacles. However, the shape of an object only mattered because of what it meant to the user.

I flipped to the section on traps. I'd read this section, sort of. I'd glanced at the words, anyway. The text read like a cross between a magic manuscript and a physics textbook. After half an hour of looking up words and rereading, I found myself on the brink of understanding something but unable to put the pieces together. My stomach growled.

Niben had abandoned the journals she was comparing and talked to Sam while pointing at things in the three books open in front of Sam, which were all about human Witches and curses.

Lucy continued to read her brother's journals, struggling to decipher what my dad knew but didn't share.

Mike still worked at a computer.

Mel was sprawled on the floor with the same big book, staring at the ceiling instead of reading. I put my book down and walked over. Peering down at the pages, I read an account about an Angel-hybrid's soul being trapped in a glass bottle for three decades after surviving the loss of his physical body.

"Hey." I slammed the book shut and sat down next to her. "Find anything useful?"

"I sort of have a theory, but I'm too hungry to put all my thoughts together." Mel stretched her arms out, letting out a long sigh. "There's food upstairs, and I know a snack will clear my head. Want to come get one with me?"

I sighed. There was lots of food in the church hall where the parish was holding a memorial reception for all the people who had died this weekend. But there were also at least fifty people, including former classmates wondering where José was. They'd make me think about him too much. They'd want answers I couldn't give them.

"Everyone up there wants answers no one can give. Seeing people from school might be good for you," said Mel.

"What if I start hearing too many people's thoughts?"

"You know how to shield," she said.

"But time. We don't have much."

Mel rolled her eyes. "We both need a break from reading, and we're both hungry. Fifteen minutes isn't going to be a huge deal in the grand scheme of things."

"I'd go if I could," said Sam.

"I'm sorry." I'd hardly asked Sam how she was doing.

*

A multitude of misery stood between the cookies and me. People stood in clusters, many hugging each other and crying. The reception was reminiscent of a wake but worse because so many young people were being mourned. Three of the victims had been students at Saint Pat's—two freshmen and a junior. Four more had been parishioners. I shuddered as guilt swarmed me. Those people would be alive if I had only stayed home Friday night.

Thankfully, my mental shields prevented me from getting a wave of some soul-crushing emotion when the first person bumped into me on my quest to get to the cookies. Knowing that I could turn off this newly acquired telepathy was a relief, but it meant I couldn't mentally reach out to Mel.

"Erin? We've heard all kinds of rumors!" said one boy who stood next to his identical twin. One of them was James, and the other was George. Both blocked me from following Mel to the table with all the food. Whether she realized we'd been separated or not, she kept walking.

I couldn't remember which name belonged to which twin. I should've known. José had been dating James when I first moved up to Maine. José smiled a lot during that time—real smiles and not the fake ones he flaunted around his friends. Between visiting me and spending time with James, he'd hardly been home.

"Will claimed Jenny said you haven't even heard from José," said the other one. He wore a light-green polo. The other twin's shirt was orange.

"George is being an ass," said the boy in the orange shirt. James. He had the tiny scar next to his right eyebrow from slipping on rocks while making out with José on some beach. He put his arm around me. It felt like being crushed by a decaying log with ants and beetles crawling out of it.

"How are you holding up?" he asked

"I am." I slithered out from under his arm. "As long as you don't touch me."

"I'm sorry." James put his hands in his pockets.

George crossed his arms. "Jenny said when the shooting started, José tried to protect you, but then you ran toward the shooting. It stopped a few minutes later. The news says the shooter's necks were snapped. Did you...stop them?"

"You think I charged three people who had automatic rifles and survived long enough to snap their necks?" I stepped back. I couldn't allow such a rumor spread. I did not need to be dragged into the investigation around the shooters. I did not need to be labeled a hero, even a rumored one, for a tragedy that wouldn't have happened had I not been there in the first place.

George shrugged. "Jenny saw you head towards the gunfire. Andrew O'Malley saw you push someone down so a bullet passed over him."

I stared at George, waiting for a punchline, for this to be a joke, but there was no amusement in his red face and blue eyes.

"He's serious," said James. "That was the last thing Andrew saw before he got shot in the hip, and it's the only specific thing he remembered."

"Who is Andrew again?" I couldn't place him. I wanted to make sure I didn't run into him anytime soon.

"The goalie," said George. "The short one whose hair is a different color every week. He saw you heading to the shooters."

"He saw me trip mid panic attack and fall into the next aisle," I said. "I had this short-lived delusional moment where I thought I could reach them and stop them. A bullet whizzed past. The bullet didn't touch me, but just the smell, the closeness...I thought it ripped through my stomach in the same place I got shot in March. I couldn't breathe. I thought I was bleeding out all over again until one of the first responders found me, and I realized I didn't get shot. I'm not a hero."

My breaths came quicker as fear and guilt strangled my throat. My hands curled into fists. Maybe I had stopped the shooting, but it wouldn't have happened at all if I hadn't been in the theater. My skin buzzed. I needed to get away from these boys and their rumors. I needed to find Mel and the snacks and crush my emotions with food.

I brushed past the boys, wove around a circle of people laughing and crying at some funny story, ducked under the waving hands of an angry man yelling about what's wrong with the world, and crashed into Jenny Dunn, who clutched Will's hand while talking to Mel only a couple of feet away from the food.

"Erin, I'm glad you're here," said Jenny.

I took a depth breath, glaring at her and Will, but failed to unclench my fists. My nails sunk into my palm. The physical pain took the edge off the emotional agony, making words bearable. "I'm not a hero. Not even close. Don't make me sound like one when you talk to people. Don't spread rumors about me."

Jenny paled, taking a step backward. "I'm sorry."

"You too." I pointed at Will. "You gossip more than her."

"Erin, calm down. Jenny just said what she saw: you pushed José off you and went in the direction the bullets were coming from," said Mel.

I sucked in a slow breath.

My palms were damp. I bit my lip until it bled. I understood why Jenny assumed I was trying to help; she remembered me taking a bullet for her. Maybe that prior knowledge colored Will's take on my action. And they were right about me charging toward the shooters, though I had no intention of letting other people know.

They were wrong about me being a hero.

I was a monster that worse monsters wanted for themselves.

And when those monsters couldn't get me, they took José instead because they believed I'd do anything to get to him. They knew I'd go for Sam next. We burned a building down. Dozens died in that fire. All those deaths were the results of my action.

Those deaths happened because Demons are predators that eat people and their fear.

Mel?

Your shields fell apart when you did.

"Whatever I said, it was before we talked. I'm sorry." Jenny gave me a handful of tissues.

I nodded, but my throat burned. My fingers shook as I opened one fist. The muscles ached, and the air stung my palm.

"They have counselors here." Will stared at the blood on my palm.

"I need to eat." The words came out one at a time and seemed sluggish and harsh. I needed to crush my anxiety with sugar and carbs and then get back down to the archives where I wouldn't have to face the consequences of an apocalypse I was failing to stop. Anxious tension made my muscles cramp and ache. The food was within reach, but anxiety froze me.

Mel took the handful of tissues from Jenny and pressed one into my hand, then closed my fist around it. With another, she wiped tears from my face. I leaned into her, for once desperately needing a hug.

"I'm sorry," she whispered, wrapping her arms around me and pulling me close. "This isn't what I hoped would happen."

I know. You wanted me to see people coming together to support one another and to see what good might come out of this nightmare.

Warmth came over me, easing the tension in my muscles.

Mel, stop.

You're hurting.

So are you. I held my breath as the warm sliver of healing she'd given me infused with my own energy. I breathed it back to her.

She stumbled back, breathing slow. She shook her head and blinked her swirly eyes. Her glow brightened.

You're the one who said I learn quickly when I pay attention.

Mel smiled and giggled before breaking out into a laughter as musical and uplifting as church bells on Easter Sunday.

"I made you up a plate of food." Jenny held a tray filled with cheese, crackers, brownies, and at least five different kinds of cookies. "The star-shaped ones have marshmallows in them. They're heavenly."

I took one, tracing the five points with my finger. The pale-yellow cookie was dusted with flecks of white sugar, reminding me of vaporized Demon bits. A circle of white sugary goop sat in the middle.

It was a star, a container holding pieces, or a single piece, of something else. It contained marshmallow like star traps contain Demons. How Sam's necklace contained a piece of Vincent.

*

"I need a Sharpie or paint, something I can draw on the floor with." I burst into the archives with Mel on my heels. She muttered cautions and protests because I shielded, not wanting anyone to shoot down my hypothesis before I tested it.

Mike opened a drawer and grabbed a marker. "Here you go."

I grabbed Sam by the arm, pulling her away from Niben midconversation.

"What the hell?" Sam didn't fight me as I led her to the archive's back door.

"This is going to be interesting." Niben watched with her head tilted.

Hinges squealed as I opened the door, charging through a musty basement hall and into the small gym. I dropped my shields, so I could focus more on the energy in and around me, and drew a star trap on the red mat floor, focusing on imbuing each point of the seven-sided star with energy, willing the trap to not only to contain Demonic entities but hybrid energy as well.

"What is that?" asked Sam.

"A star trap." Mel watched from the doorway. "If you can trick a Demon into one, then said Demon can't get out until the energy is disrupted from the outside, or the symbol focusing the energy is damaged, which again would be from the outside because a trapped Demon can't touch the edges."

"What? You think I'm a Demon?" Sam glared at the drawing.

"Oh no. Not you. And this trap is different. I think I know why the necklace lets you see things humans can't."

I glanced at Mel. She stepped further into the room, followed by a smirking Niben.

Sam stepped into the circle.

"Take the necklace off and hold it. Next, try to move the pendant outside the circle."

Sam did as I instructed. As the necklace got closer to the edge, it stopped moving. When Sam's hand kept moving, the pentacle swung away from the edge. The muscles in Sam's arm strained as she pushed, but the necklace wouldn't move.

"Is there a Demon trapped in my necklace?" asked Sam.

"A piece of one. You were wearing that pentacle when I blew up the Incubus."

Mel shivered. "More like shattered him."

Niben shook her head. "I doubt a piece of him accidentally became bound to the necklace."

"I think I freed Vincent when I smashed the Incubus, and before I banished all the shards, he somehow got part of himself into the pentacle."

"Is that why it gives me the Sight?" Sam put the pentacle down and stepped out of the trap.

"I think so." I glanced at Niben and Mel. They both nodded, confirming my theory.

Niben tilted her head, eyes narrowed, and focused on the pendant. "I have met Witches who had developed the Sight over time, so I'm not entirely sure it would work with a regular human. Whatever amount of him is in there is activating your Sight."

She turned around and strode back toward the archives. Sam and I followed, but I paused when I saw Mel staring at the floor with her lips pressed together. Her fingers tangled in the little bit of hair she'd grown back.

"What's wrong?" I backtracked until I stood next to her.

"My mom...she left with my dad." Mel closed her eyes and took a slow breath. After a few minutes of silence, she said, "Mom read something in your dad's journal. He said she was the next one the Many-Tentacled Destroyer would take."

I frowned. "I thought he wasn't allowed to interfere."

"The balance is already tilted towards the Fallen. They have four hunters. Taking someone he knows is a target tips the scales a little more towards him." Tears dripped down Mel's cheek as she sucked in a deep breath and opened her eyes. "My dad always loved my mom even though she didn't reciprocate the feelings. The Fallen would use her against him. And against me."

Mel stepped forward and put her hands on my shoulder, staring into my eyes. "Mike is on the list too. I don't think this trap the Fallen has laid is only for you. I think it's for both of us."

I pulled my cousin into a hug. "Mel, could you have gone with your dad too?"

Her hair brushed my cheek as she shook her head. She backed away from me and stared at the ceiling. "He didn't offer to take me. Whatever the trap is, I think he wants you and me to spring it together."

I grinned. "If he wants us to spring it, then he must believe we can get out of it."

"You know, when we were little, your dad always wanted me to watch out for you." A smile tugged at Mel's lips as she shook her head. "But my dad hinted you'd be the one saving me."

"Erin! Mel! Come see this!" Niben's voice echoed from the other room.

"I got your back." I winked at Mel before jogging back to the archives.

I found my grandmother shaking her head at the pile of open journals and notes Lucy had left behind. She pointed at one, and I started reading.

Liam, you idiot! I could've helped you was scribbled next to his account of the night Lucy lost her legs and how he had made sure she didn't remember exactly what happened.

The truth was a narrative like the one I dreamed with an explanation of what Shadowhulhu might be:

> *"a creature neither Demon, Faerie, Human, nor Angel that lived between realms devouring anyone who lingered too long until it was enslaved by a Fallen Angel seeking an escape from the punishment his peers were receiving."*

Another page narrated how one of his failed attempts to break Nana's curse resulted in a Witch blowing himself up:

> *She warned me, and I didn't listen. She said it would release too much energy for a human to contain. After the curse reached a critical point, the human would combust or disintegrate. She wasn't clear on that part, but the latter is what happened.*

> *The process of breaking was so simple. The Witch only needed to grab hold of the curse and unravel its energy like a ball of yarn. Had the energy allowed me to touch it, I would have tried it myself. I might've died how Billy did, but I could've channeled the energy better than him. My mother and sister are far better than me with*

energy manipulation. Maybe together Lucy, Mom, and I could've beaten this thing.

The problem is the energy the curse releases. At first, Billy was fine. Seconds later, energy overwhelmed him. He disintegrated before he could let go, before I could try to help. I should've felt guilty, but all I thought about was trying again, about creating or finding a container the Witch could feed the excess energy to.

There are so many reasons I need to break this curse.

Pieces of it were passed onto Grace, and it is a cancer strangling the pieces of her that are Elven and Angelic. The tiniest traces linger on Erin, making their Sight inconsistent and some of their abilities unpredictable, which would be less of an issue if Amelia stopped trying to "teach" them things.

The two of them started an electrical fire in Lucy's living room because Mel thought it was a good idea to teach Erin how to heal scrapes even though Erin is barely three, and already, their power seems more suited for destruction than healing. Thankfully, Lucy extinguished the fire in seconds.

And then there is the fact that a Fallen Angel is plotting something against Earth. Michael says if he acts, there will be a major war, mostly fought on Earth, and the collateral damage will be cataclysmic. Humanity could survive and rebuild; it would be better than them becoming cattle to feed Demons and Fallen alike, but it would still be terrible. Something he never wants to be responsible for. Something he never wants his daughter to see.

The Angel tasked me with stopping this apocalypse. He said if I fail, my child and niece, Erin and Mel, will be the ones battling this Fallen Angel. They might win. They might fail. They might become monsters the world needs protecting from.

And if the Fallen kills Mel? Michael will have his revenge. Goodbye world as I know.

Helen would be an invaluable asset in my quest to stop the Fallen, especially if she can also secure the aid of her father, Phineas, the Elf who defeated a Fallen Angel in the 1940s.

And if Helen were free to travel where she wanted, then she could go to Faerie where medicine is more advanced. Were the healers able to study her in their own treatment facilities, perhaps they could more effectively help her manage her mental illness.

If I'm interpreting my dreams right, she might be able to save me.

I put the passage down, grinning despite its grim content. I knew why no one had broken the curse yet. I also knew why Sam and I were going to succeed where my father and his Witch had failed.

Chapter Fifteen

It doesn't matter what you believe in or what faith you follow as long as you wholeheartedly believe in something.

—Common Hunter Proverb

My head throbbed as I tiptoed my way down to Grandpa's basement. Each time the stairs creaked felt like a knife slicing into my brain. The skin on the tips of my fingers ached. Little blisters and burns covered my hands, courtesy of an afternoon and evening spent proving to Sam that I could hold large amounts of energy and would not let her get disintegrated while breaking the curse.

Niben and Mel, who had witnessed my fight with Hanzel, needed no such convincing. However, showing Sam I could stick a fork in an electrical outlet and hold it there for fifteen minutes, sucking up electricity like an old refrigerator, made her feel a lot better.

We'd had a weird practice loop going. I pulled energy out of an electrical socket. Niben wound it tight up into a magical yarn ball. Sam unwound and fed the energy back to me. It wasn't the same as breaking the curse, but it was the best way we could think of to practice.

Grandpa's basement seemed extra cold and dark as Mel and I snuck down even though there was no reason to sneak. Still, I kept expecting some alarm to blare. Any minute. The lights would flash, and Grandpa would be at the top of the stairs scolding us as if we were seven and eleven, not eighteen and twenty-two.

But Grandpa wasn't here. We were doing this to save him as much as we were trying to save José. I jumped when the floor creaked over my head. The ceiling shook. Bessie was probably chasing a Pixie who had something she wanted to eat. Mel moved mats away from the trap door and descended into a chamber that was and wasn't part of the house. I sat down cross-legged on the floor.

Mel joined me. "This could be dangerous."

"A little bit."

"More than you think," she said.

"So, you usually have to sleep to get there, right?"

"Yes."

"So, can we sort of meditate ourselves to sleep or lucid dream our way out there?"

"I can fall asleep now if I let myself." Mel yawned, stretched, and lay on the floor, staring up at the wood-paneled ceiling.

I lay down with my head next to hers but my feet going the other way. I closed my eyes, breathing slower each time I inhaled. As my breathing slowed, so did my perception of time. I cleared my mind. Mel did the same. Her breathing changed to something steadier than awake but not quite as rhythmic as sleep.

Sleep tugged at me, drawing us into blankness. Blurry images flashed across my vision. I pictured myself in the cockpit of a spaceship like I did when I shielded against a serious threat except I kept the shields down. I started the mental spaceship's engine and pointed the cockpit toward the sky. Before I accelerated, I pushed a button to activate the comm.

Are you coming?

I'm trying. Static crackled around Mel's voice.

I hit a button to open the cargo bay door, sensing Mel's not-quite-sleeping mind. I tugged it toward me until she materialized in the copilot's chair, wearing tight black pants and a cape with her hair gathered on her head in two oversized buns.

"This isn't what I expected to happen." Mel buckled herself into a harness.

"Is anything ever what you expect with my brain?" I closed the cargo-bay door and pushed the throttle forward. We sped toward a black sky filled with glittering stars. The twinkling dots stretched to white lines as the ship accelerated. I glanced at Mel. Her nails dug into her chair's armrests. A grin brightened her face. I winked at her before easing back on the throttle and watching the lines dissolve into a starfield.

A rainbow of gas and shimmering liquid twined around a cluster of rocks dusted with glittering specs. Tributaries branched off a polychromatic river of time, flowing out into space. My ship soared through a current of blue and purple before landing on a flat stretch of rock.

If we were physically in space, Mel and I couldn't have merely stepped out of the ship like we did, but our bodies were still in the map room. The versions of ourselves that walked onto the platform without space suits were really just projections of our minds. Even if deep-space travel were possible, one wouldn't be able to fly here. This place existed outside of time. The colors, the river we saw flowing all around us? That was time— threads of the past, present, and future.

"I'm going to follow José's thread first." I plucked out a little piece of my hair and picked up a pebble from the platform. I twined the hair around the pebble and threw it into the river, holding a memory in my mind: José staring down at me while I struggled to slow my perception of time in the movie theater on Friday night. The stream rippled, and that memory played out on the surface of the water. I blurred down toward the shooters. My own stream tugged at me, but I resisted, holding José's dark sad eyes in my mind, so I stayed with his stream.

José collapsed, curled up and sobbing.

When the gunfire ceased, Jenny shook him. "José, I think it's over."

He stood, wiped his nose, and glanced down while people hurried to the exits.

"We have to get out of here." Will grabbed Jenny's hand and pulled her past José toward the aisle where people rushed by.

Jenny tugged his sleeve. "José, come on."

He stood up on the chair and peered down at the empty floor. "The shooters are dead. Wait, so we don't get trampled."

"There's bodies," said Will.

José gripped the top edge of a seat. "I don't see Erin."

Will put a shaking hand on José's back and pushed him toward the aisle. "Maybe they're already out," said Will.

"I'll meet you outside. I'm not leaving without them." José leaped over the seat and landed next to a body in the next row. He kept going over the seats until the aisles were clear. No emergency personnel rushed in. A few people stayed behind with wounded friends. Some cried over dead bodies. Most had fled.

José stared at the dead shooters and the black rim around their necks.

"José, remember what Erin told you!" Jenny waved to him from the door.

He stared at the lower exit and then ran up the aisle. His jaw clenched as he looked at the corpses and the wounded and ignored their cries for help.

"We need to get to the Jeep," said José.

With Jenny and Will close behind, José ran into the packed hallway and lobby. A small group rushed into the theater with paper towels and first aid kids. José plowed through them, not looking back once.

He burst out of the theater with the mob and pulled ahead of them onto the dark street. Two cars stood between the Jeep and him.

A shadow blocked out the stars and moon, tentacles shooting out of the sky. José unsheathed the sword I'd given him and slashed up as the inky appendages whipped toward him. Two tentacles twined around the sword and broke it in half. They slithered around him. He shrieked, kicked, and flailed, but he couldn't get away.

He screamed as tentacles dragged him into darkness. Even as they pulled him higher and higher, he flailed and kicked, struggling to get free. Flames ignited the space below him.

He shouted, "Erin!" when he caught a glimpse of me, glowing golden like Mel in a funnel of flames. The tentacles loosened. He wriggled free. His shirt clung to his chest, and his hair whipped around as he fell toward the glow, only to be snatched back up as the tentacles began to spin. They twirled around and around, funneling in a black hole that sucked him into Between. Shadowhulhu propelled through the bleak landscape of endless purple with no discernable direction or landmarks.

"Erin! I think Shadowhulhu is *here.*"

"What?" I spun around from where I'd been watching the scene play out on the water's surface.

Mel shivered with her arms wrapped around herself. The platform hadn't been warm, cold, or any noticeable temperature when Mel and I had landed, but now? The frigid air conjured goose bumps on my skin and evoked shivers that rattled my bones.

Mel shook her head. "Why can't I wake up? Normally, I just think about waking up, and I'm back in my body."

"Get on the ship." I grabbed her hand and ran. We charged in just as a tentacle slammed onto the stone platform. The ramp closed behind us. I took the stairs to the cockpit four at a time, strapped myself in, and slammed the throttle forward. We blasted off the rock, into a storm of thrashing tentacles.

I have you now, little ones. Shadowhulhu voice slithered into my mind.

Where are José, Grandpa, Sister Marie, and Officer Karen? I questioned the beast.

My servant, the one you murdered, already told you.

The Bracken Bubble? Where is it?

Surrender. Pledge your soul to my partner, and you will find out.

No. Where is the Bracken Bubble?

You and he are not so different. You think you are better than him, but you are not. The more you fight and lie to yourself, the more lives will be lost, and the more your family will suffer.

"Erin, shield!" Mel shouted, pulling me out of my mental conversation just as its tentacles thumped against the windshield.

I fired lasers at them while reaching for the controls and putting the shields up at full power. The tentacles I'd hit retreated with smoking holes from where my lasers had landed.

"Interesting. We can hurt it here, wherever here is," said Mel.

"Go to the swivel gun in the bottom of the ship." I swerved to avoid another tentacle and hit the red button on the corner of the steering, firing a volley of lasers. Where here was didn't matter nearly as much as destroying Shadowhulhu.

Mel unbuckled and ran out of the cockpit, stumbling as I flipped the ship vertical to slide between more tentacles. One rose straight in front of us. More thrashed around the ship, trapping it in a tube. I continued to climb while Mel battered the tentacles with fire from the cannon on the saucer's belly.

I noticed the laser holes had healed, but the tentacles had shrunk. "It isn't healing itself but rearranging its mass. Keep firing."

"I wasn't planning on stopping," said Mel.

I pushed the throttle further forward. I wondered if the tentacles were infinite; would I climb forever until we ran out of fuel, or until I ran out of energy and died?

I kept firing, hoping to shrink the tentacles enough to make an opening before we hit the end of the tube they had formed. The tentacles were so close they were a breath away from my shields.

A light blinked in front of me. A gauge told me the shields were down to 95 percent capacity.

"It's getting tight down here." Mel's voice crackled through the dash comm.

"Almost out." I pushed the throttle harder.

My shields were at 80 percent.

The tentacles were closing at the top. There wasn't enough room to get by.

Now 70 percent.

"Get up here!"

I diverted power from the rear to the front deflector shield and pushed the throttle all the way forward. "Strap in!"

Mel did.

We slammed into the tentacles. The ship jerked and buckled, but never stopped. The shields dropped to 60 percent. I banked around, so the rock platform and cosmic river were behind me, and I was heading the direction I'd come from.

"A few degrees to the right," said Mel. "Punch it!"

I hit the button for hyperspeed, and the stars stretched out into lines. Shadowhulhu vanished. Mel and I sank in our respective chairs, sighing. I started laughing.

"It's not funny," she said, but then she laughed anyway.

The lines dissolved to stars. I dropped the shields. We were no longer in a disc spaceship anymore but rather lying on the floor of the secret room in Grandpa's basement, laughing our asses off as footsteps thundered down the stairs.

The door flew open.

"Erin? Amelia?" Niben rushed in with Mike and Aelfric on her heels.

"We're fine," said Mel between laughs.

"Next time I'm packing proton torpedoes," I said.

"How about we don't do this again." Mel sat up and ran her fingers through her blonde curls.

I was too tired and laughing too hard to get up.

Mike brushed past them to get to Mel. "Are you all right? Did you..."

"Amelia doesn't appear to have expended a drop of energy." Niben grinned at us with her head tilted. "Whatever they did was all Erin."

Mike glanced at me. "I guess that explains why we heard Mel scream, 'Punch it.'"

"The Force is with me," I said between raspy laughs. "And I really want pizza."

"Well, there are half-a-dozen pizzas upstairs," said Mike. He crouched down and kissed Mel on the forehead, and she snuggled against him.

Niben offered me a hand and pulled me to my feet, but as soon as I let go of her, the room spun a little. She caught me before I fell. I wrapped an arm around her for support.

"I need a lot of pizza. And water," I said.

"What did you two do?" asked Mike, helping Mel to her feet.

Mel and I explained as best we could as we walked up the stairs, but I suspected Niben got a better idea of the adventure from the memories we projected.

"At least we know our missing people are all in the same place," said Niben.

"Assuming Shadowhulhu wasn't lying," I said.

"I'm still not sure how it was there," said Mel. "I've never seen anyone or anything else there except for the three times I brought Erin."

"Usually you dream your way there. This time you projected your consciousness onto Erin who projected both of your consciousnesses outside of time in a mental-spaceship construct," said Niben.

"Not just any ship," I said.

"I know. I saw those movies when they were first in theaters." Niben held the basement door open for Mel.

Mel dove for the pizza. I sat down in one of the chairs and grabbed the closest slice, which had bacon, little bits of egg, and maple syrup. I devoured three slices of it while everyone talked, and then I had enough energy to reach over to the box with the regular cheese pizza. I ate a few more slices, took my nightly dose of medicine, and told everyone I was going upstairs. I was tired and wanted to regain as much energy as I could before heading to Nana's, which I planned to do first thing in the morning.

Everyone said good night but stayed at the table. Bessie tore herself away from the important business of begging and followed me upstairs. The din of conversation didn't fade completely with the floor between me and everyone else, but without trying too hard, I couldn't pick out individual words. There was something warm and inviting about the laughter and voices that made me want to go down, but I needed sleep and dreams that might reveal some of the information we didn't get on our interrupted trip to the confluence.

The voices began to sound more distant when I closed the door and got in bed. Bessie joined me. With her breathing in my ear, the conversation faded. I closed my eyes, and the dreams began:

José slept in the middle of a star trap. Aside from his knuckles being more scraped than the last time, and the addition of a black eye, he appeared unharmed. He stirred, as if he sensed me there, and sat up.

"Erin, at some point, you're bound to dream me. You might be watching me now. I'm okay. The food sucks, but it's not poisoned, and the water is clean. I love you. I'd tell you not to come for me, but it would be pointless, and I don't want to die. Still, don't rush in here blind. No one is hurting me, much. Some days Dad was worse than these guys. I think the person who brings my food is a slave. There are Demon guards—these scare me most, hence the star traps. I hope you are okay too. I hope you're planning carefully and not getting yourself hurt or killed."

José faded to a dark-haired, white-skinned man chopping vegetables in a rundown kitchen. He accidentally sliced his finger instead of a carrot. He hissed in pain, but there was no blood, only a trickle of brownish lubricant and a partially exposed wire.

"Vincent, how long until dinner is done?" called Sam from another room.

The kitchen dissolved to Crawlers rampaging across the Portland waterfront, breaking glass, chasing tourists from shops, and eating anyone who couldn't outrun them. A Troll strode into a packed bar and bit a man's head off.

Light flared, erasing the violent scene and replacing it with a young Aunty Lucy, sitting on a porch, belly swollen and glowing, yelling at Michael the Archangel with her arms flailing.

"I am *not* raising a child only to watch her slowly kill herself. How do I make sure Liam's visions never come to pass? Are there any hybrids that live to old age? You warned me of so much but not that."

"The information is there for you to read in your archives. I only warned you of things you wouldn't be able to discover for yourself," whispered Michael.

"Do any of them live full lives?"

"Ask your father about his favorite drinking buddy," said Michael, and he was gone.

The scene morphed into Nana's room. A black cord unraveled faster and faster, releasing more and more energy as Sam pulled it. I caught it as it came, white light and blue fire.

The wards are failing.

Can you hold them off a few more minutes?

"You're almost there. Keep going," said Nana.

Sam hesitated. "What happens to you when it's gone?"

Nana laughed. "I'm finally free of this hell."

Darkness consumed the nursing home. When the vision lightened, I was in the receiving line at a wake. José held my hand. Nana was in the casket.

Chapter Sixteen

I don't think the war between the Angels and the Fallen every truly ended. It simply changed to something akin to the Cold War between the United States and Russia, but instead of building nuclear bombs and spaceships, they're making hybrids and influencing humanity in the most subtle of ways.

—A letter from Aelfric MacKay to Niben of the Summer Elves, confined to the archives in May of 2018.

Nana's room hadn't changed in the past decade. The bed was still against the wall. Flowers, watered by the staff, sat on a windowsill Nana couldn't reach. There was one dresser and a nightstand. A cross hung above the bed, and a collage of saints' faces was taped over the closet door.

"It's about time. Sit down and close the door." Nana's hair was wispy white cobwebs occasionally flickering to platinum blonde. Her eyes swirled deep blue and white, though they were more a cloudy white than blue. I knew that with my Sight closed her skin was as wrinkly as skin got. With my Sight fully open, it was a lot smoother. But right now, my vision was flickering between mundane and magic.

While I closed the door, Nana stared at the little statue on her nightstand: Michael the Archangel stepped on a snake that was supposed to represent Lucifer.

I laugh every time I look at that thing. I know the snake is a symbol, but that combined with the Roman armor...it's too much. Mel chuckled in my head.

"A piece of humor in a bleak place is comforting," said Nana.

"How much do you know about what is going on?" I asked.

Nana cackled. "About the fascist taking over the country? It's hard to tell what's real and what is chatter only I can hear. The staff agrees the president is not so secretly a fascist, but they don't seem to think my TV actually picks up CIA spy signals." Nana paused, shaking her head. "Of course, are you speaking of the End you are trying to stop? The Fallen Angel and its pet beast have been abducting people you know and people you love. There is a composition book in the righthand corner of my top drawer. You will find its contents quite useful."

"You didn't mention that the last few times I came here." I got up and located the white notebook with purple symbols scribbled all over the cover. "This one?"

"That one, yes, but it was not yet the right time to pass that knowledge on. You had not the ability to make use of it. Amelia, go check to make sure the wards are not compromised."

I put the notebook in my cargo pants' pocket.

"I'll try to reinforce them so if we do get attacked the way we did in your dream, we don't have to worry about them being overwhelmed. I won't be far." Mel slipped out the door, leaving behind a cloud of awkward silence that lasted thirty seconds.

"Are we going to sit around all day chitchatting or are you going to do what you came here to do?" asked Nana.

I opened my mouth, but no words came out. I guess there was no reason to procrastinate further aside from the nagging feeling something was going to go horribly wrong. A horde of Demons could show up any minute. There was a chance Nana might not survive this. But if she died, what would be the point? What was I missing?

"So, I'm going to latch onto the curse and start unraveling," Sam said to Nana.

"The last one died how I imagine a supernova becomes a black hole. The energy consumed him." Nana's face remained neutral while she spoke. "I'm assuming you found a way to protect yourself?"

"Erin is going to catch and channel the excess energy like a ground rod in a lightning storm," said Sam.

"But what is Erin grounded to?" asked Nana.

"Should I be grounded to something?" I hadn't been in my dream.

Grinning, Nana shook her head. *Perhaps the piece isn't missing at all. You just don't want to admit you are willing to do what you must.*

"I'm going to start." A spark of energy flared as Sam tugged at the curse.

The released energy resembled a sparkler moving up a vine with enormous thorns. Sam carefully pulled at it, twining power into a circle. When the sparks were nearly touching Sam, I reached out and closed my hand around them. Energy sunk into my skin, infusing it with buzzing heat.

I only had to hold my hand near Sam's, and power split off the curse and went to me. Niben had said the released power wasn't just part of the curse, but pieces of

Nana's energy trapped between its layers that had been accumulating for nearly sixty years. The curse also had energy stolen with every attempt to break it. Hopefully, I'd be able to return some to Nana at the end.

Nana laughed.

Shit, thought Mel. *I don't want to feel another death. There has been too much the past few days.*

What's happening? I asked.

Crawlers in the parking lot ramming the wards. So far, they're just disintegrating themselves, but if any people come through...

"Ouch!" Sam jumped back as a spark hit her hand. I snatched it away before she lost her grip on the curse.

"You only get one chance. Fail now, and I die." Nana grinned as if that was an appealing outcome. She winked at me. "You of all people should understand."

Did I? It hadn't been long since I'd wanted to die, but lately, as much I thought some people would be better off without me, I'd been determined to live.

The curse's energy brightened as Sam continued pulling. It was a thorny cocoon tangled around the energy Nana projected.

Do we need to switch?

No. I'm fine. Aside from pins and needles in my fingertips, I hardly feel like I'm holding excess energy.

That in and of itself is concerning, thought Mel.

The building shook, and the lights flickered.

How many of them are there?

Too many.

The ball of briars at Sam's feet collapsed and compressed.

As Sam reached the vines closest to Nana, tingling traveled from my fingertips to my shoulders and face. Sweat slicked my skin, and static charged my hair.

There is a freaking Troll...no, two Trolls! Mel screeched in my head. *Dammit. There is a car.*

An image of the Troll picking it up and smashing it flashed in my mind. And that made other people rush out, and a small portion of the Demons not occupied by vaporizing themselves on the wards took interest.

I need to help them. The wards should hold.

Mel—

Destruction requires far less energy than creation.

That meant the victims were dead. Mel had a big sword and wasn't as depleted as she'd been. She sought to avenge people, not heal them. She'd be fine. And once this was done, I could help. The power was still on. Electricity coursed through the overhead wires. Mel just had to keep them from killing more people until Sam and I finished undoing this curse.

The fact that Mel wasn't electrocuting the Demons reaffirmed my choice to stay here and have her on watch/defense. I thought manipulating raw energy wasn't Mel's thing.

That's an understatement. Damn does it feel good to swing a sword at something other than you.

Keeping the excess energy off Sam hardly required much focus now. As long as I stayed where I was, energy surged at me as if I was standing in a raging river. Two layers remained. Yellow sparks turned into blue-and-white flames. It was comparable to sucking energy from high-tension wires. The lights went out with my hope of electrically frying the Demons. The walls barely muted the echoes of shouts and crunched metal. The building shook. Thumps were accompanied by growls and snarls.

The wards are failing, thought Mel.

"You're almost there; keep going," said Nana. "This is going to be glorious. Freedom for me and power for you."

All was gone but one strand twined around Nana's arms, legs, and chest.

Sam hesitated. "What happens to you when it's gone?"

Nana laughed.

I feared I'd combust as the curse unwrapped from around her legs, bathing me in white-hot energy. I barely stayed standing as Nana's arms came free.

"I think there's going to be one more burst of energy when I snap it," said Sam.

Nana grinned.

Sam held the last inch of cursed vine with one hand and a cord of glowing light in the other. "Are you ready?"

"Get it over with," I said through clenched teeth.

Sam took a deep breath. Her hands shook. She stretched them apart, and Nana grabbed her wrists, adjusting them ever so slightly so a little light extended past the hand closest to Nana. "If you leave even the tiniest piece of curse, then it will consume what's left of me."

"But Niben said if I snap too much of your light, you die spectacularly."

"I prefer to bequeath my soul's power to Erin than let this curse consume another molecule. Better to go out in a blaze of glory Erin can use to save their family. They've already avenged my death. But Hanzel was thorough, weaving a curse to outlive him."

Nana made eye contact with me. "Do you see it now?"

Knots churned in my stomach. Somewhere inside, a monster cheered me on, hungry for more power. But another part of me knew this was wrong.

Nana never intended to live. She didn't want to help me save José and fight the Fallen. She wanted me to sacrifice her and take her power for myself.

Tears leaked out of my eyes and evaporated. Nana was old by human standards, but she wasn't human. Elves and Angels lived for *thousands* of years.

Yet most Angel-hybrids burnt out at a much younger age than me.

The building quaked. I stumbled closer to white-hot sparks.

"I know if I snap it there, you will die. I can see the border between your life force and the curse. It is here." Sam slid her hands back to the spot. "I am going to snap it here. The curse will be gone, and you will live."

Nana grabbed Sam's hands and held them further down. Sam tried to hug her hands back, but Nana held them fast.

People screamed.

I pushed against the tide of energy. Every molecule in my body was moving so fast I thought I was going to come apart.

Sam screamed as Nana pulled her hands closer until Sam's hands were blistering.

Whimpering, Sam watched me. She was drenched in sweat. Her pale skin reflected the glow I radiated. Her eyes were wide and scared. "Erin, help."

"Snap the cord," hissed Nana.

"You'll die," cried Sam.

"Do it, Sam," I said, standing right beside her. "I can't hold this much longer."

Sam shook her head and tugged her hands, but Nana was stronger. The more Sam tried to pull back, the more Nana drew her closer.

Moving seemed impossible, but I had to do something. Mustering as much strength as I could, I lurched forward. My eyes locked with Nana's, and I made a decision I feared would haunt me for the rest of my life. I put my hands over Sam's. I used her hands to snap the cord.

The cursed yarn ball melted to a shadow as white flames exploded from Nana. I caught them in a net of the energy and pushed them back toward her.

You know that won't work. Nana's telepathically projected words were followed by cackling echoing through my mind.

I burned up from the inside out and vibrated like a guitar string, but I still pushed.

She sat up. For a moment, she was young with smooth skin and hair glowing with white light. Her eyes were sky blue; tiny traces of wispy white swirled through them. She smiled as if she could float away.

I've been dead for years, Erin, trapped and sustained by the magic that killed me.

What does that mean?

It means I'm at peace. I am free to go to whatever lies beyond Earth for my kind. Thank you!

But—

The answers you seek are in the notebook.

Nana shoved the energy back toward me as she floated out of her body.

Spinning white energy formed a funnel and drilled into my chest.

I was fire. A live wire. Melting. Barely holding my atoms together. I might live if my electrons stopped trying to trade each other off and my DNA stopped unraveling and recombining over and over again.

"What did you do? She's not breathing." Sam sounded miles away, but she was right beside me.

"*Erin!*" Mel's scream echoed in my head and out loud. "*What happened?*"

I killed her. I helped her kill herself. I sacrificed her for power. I don't know, Mel. I don't know. What am I? Who am I?

I felt Mel's muscles burn as she got closer and closer. Snarling icebergs with snapping teeth were hot on her tail.

You're my cousin. Mel's voice was a tired whisper in my mind. *Nothing you do will change that.*

Pain seared my calf, but nothing had touched it. My knee stung, but I hadn't fallen. *Mel, am I feeling what you are?*

Yes. She screeched, but she didn't slow down. *Erin, I need you to help me save lives. I need you to pull yourself together. Literally.*

She was right.

I was Erin. I had a hot temper and a chemically imbalanced brain. I wasn't exactly good, but I wasn't evil either. I punched things worse than me with fists and sometimes with lightning. I needed to destroy the Demons that were chasing my cousin and eating innocent people. I needed to save José and Grandpa. I had an apocalypse to stop.

My body solidified, or at least my perception of it did. I'm not sure it had ever been as liquid as it felt.

Panting my name, Mel skidded into the room

"Get down!" I stood and lunged toward the window.

Mel dove.

I pushed out the energy my body could hardly contain. Shattered glass, drywall, and brick exploded outward. Bolts of lightning flew from my fingers even though there was no electricity for miles around.

A glancing blow disintegrated a dozen Crawlers.

Chapter Seventeen

To an extent, Mike had always believed in the supernatural, but he never believed it was as magical as the stories made it sound. He knew the realm of possible was bigger than what modern science had discovered, but even after he met me and was drawn into the family business of Demon hunting, he questioned how much of it was really magic and how much was science he had yet to understand.

—An entry from Amelia Evanstars's personal journal, written in 2015.

Blowing out a wall and disintegrating a dozen Crawlers didn't release any of the pressure building under my skin. I itched, burned, and buzzed. I wanted to claw at my scalp, yank at my hair, and rip flesh off my arms, but I couldn't move.

"Erin?" *Erin?* Mel leaped to her feet, peering at me with her head tilted. Her light had dulled. She had a scratch on her cheek. Blood pooled under a gash on both her right arm and left leg.

She put her hands on my shoulder, then yanked them back. "What happened?"

"They used my hands to kill their grandmother and take her power," said Sam.

Mel inched closer and waved her hand in front of my face. "Erin, we need to move. There's still one Troll and at least a dozen Crawlers at large. Come on."

"You seem unfazed by the fact that Erin killed their grandmother." Sam backed out of the room.

Mel jogged after Sam. *Erin, please. Too many are dead already. Please help.*

I took a step. Pins and needles shot through my leg. I took another step. Knives stabbed me from the inside out. Mel moved farther away from me toward a mass of frigid Demonic energy. I turned around, taking a few painful steps past Nana's body toward the hole in the wall.

A car slammed into a grinning Troll.

The Troll raised its hand. I lifted mine.

Mel charged out the nursing-home door, sword pointed at the Troll.

Lightning forked from my palm to the Troll, vaporizing it as Mel launched herself at it. She landed in a pile of snowy Demon bits.

A man rushed out of his car toward Mel.

"I'm fine," said Mel. "You just missed me."

"Are you sure? Something hit the glass. I saw you fall." The man glanced back and forth between Mel and his shattered windshield.

Mel pointed to the roof. "Did you feel the earthquake?"

"Are those bricks from the chimney?" The man observed something I couldn't. Mel must have crafted an illusion.

Help me get the Crawlers before they eat anyone else.

In the distance, someone screamed.

The scream cut off abruptly.

Mel bolted down the street in the direction it came from as more shrieks and shouts erupted.

I stepped closer to the window and picked up a piece of broken glass. The window had shattered so easily, but I couldn't get myself to move more than a few steps. I had killed for the second time in a few days, but this time, it wasn't someone who was trying to kill me. It was Nana. And it hadn't been panic-induced rage that drove me to kill her, but sane, rational decision-making.

I was the monster I always knew I was.

I had snapped the cord where she wanted me to.

I had told myself I might be able to save her anyway.

I had been full of shit.

I squeezed my hand into a fist around the shard of broken glass, but I felt nothing as I clutched it harder. I raked the glass up my arm, but it hardly touched the itching buzz under my skin. I squeezed the shard until it shattered in my hand.

My hand burned. My hand glowed. The wounds closed.

Erin! Help!

I stumbled back like a rhino had tackled me.

Teeth sunk into my calf. No. That was Mel's calf.

Get your ass down here!

Air rushed out of my lungs as something pinned Mel to the ground. Our hands burned as she tried to hold its jaws off of her body.

I dove out the window, flipping through the air and planning to land in a crouch like a superhero. I over-rotated, and the ground rushed toward my face. I pushed a little energy forward, a buffer, and I hit an invisible wall, bounced backward, and landed on my ass.

I gagged. Something strangled Mel. I slowed my perception of time and broke the sound barrier as I ran the two blocks to Mel where I tackled a Troll so hard we flew across the street right through the wood-clapboard siding of someone's house, eliciting a cacophony of screams and barking.

A spark of lightning leaped from my finger, vaporizing the Troll.

I backed out of the hole toward Mel with her bleeding wounds and crushed bones.

She tried to get up.

The edges of her wounds glowed, but if she expended any more energy to heal herself, she'd be flickering again.

I knelt beside her, folding my hands around hers. *Mel, I'm tangled in power lines. Use me to heal yourself. Please.*

She filled my mind with an image of cells dividing and growing along specific genetic code.

Can you make my cells do what I showed you?

I have no clue what you showed me. I sent a trickle of power to Mel when I could, afraid any more would burn her. *Use me as a puppet.*

She blanketed my mind with hers, directing energy from me to a slice on her cheek—the shallowest of her wounds. She used my stolen power to knit muscle and skin together on her calf, thigh, and arm. She fused hairline fractures closed and kneaded sprained muscles back to their normal state.

The buzzing under my skin didn't slow.

Mel took another pull of energy, bathing her brain with it to heal a concussion, and channeled it through her skin, reinforcing weak areas and replacing scar tissue with new tissue. Mel eradicated any hint of injury on or in her body before she let go of my consciousness and ceded control back to me.

She was still drained. I was still overloaded.

"Thank you," she whispered. "Do you know how much that would've taken out of me just to heal myself, let alone heal someone else?"

"Too much." I remembered the time I saw Mel heal Grandpa when he was dying in the hospital.

I hugged her, pouring more energy into her the same way I had two nights ago.

"Erin, I don't need this."

"But you do, and I'll hurt less."

Mel didn't protest again. I fed her light until she glowed so bright looking at her was akin to looking at the sun. I blinked a few times and rubbed my eyes. Her aura was twice as blinding and big as it had been the first time I saw her glow.

Sharing the energy took the edge off the pins and needles writhing under my skin, so now I felt like I was taking power from regular electrical wires instead of high tension.

Mel shook her head and started circling around me. "Erin, I've seldom given myself enough time to recharge, to...be this way." Mel grabbed my arm, and we were running supersonic toward a pack of Crawlers and panicked running humans.

I vaporized the Crawlers.

What are people going to think happened here? I inquired.

I have no clue. This way. Mel took my hand, and we ran more.

She had one goal: save as many people as possible.

As long as I was helping with that goal, she could put off thinking about what I may or may not have done. Maybe I could too.

We charged into a quaint New England downtown turned scene from a horror movie where people ran from monsters.

The Demons want to be seen. There are Siphons here, feeding off the terror emanating from the survivors, she told me.

I closed my eyes, drowning out the screams and snarls, just feeling the cold while pushing energy out of my fingertips, sending it to the cold like reverse heat-seeking missiles that were actually lightning bolts. Demons shattered to dust ten by ten as lightning danced further and further away from me, vaporizing Crawlers, Trolls, Spikes, Siphons, and...

Is that...? I stopped the lightning before it hit Vincent.

*

In ten minutes, all the Demons in the area were dust.

On the edge of my awareness, I sensed Vincent trying to pull enough particles together to materialize.

Mel and I walked through the chaos: broken cars, smashed buildings, and dazed people. When we came across injured humans, Mel used me to heal them. She said without me she would've passed out halfway through the first person with a shredded thigh and a fractured spine.

Some people thought we were Angels. Others whispered about aliens.

The sharp, stabbing buzz had subsided, but veins still felt as if they were filled with electric eels, and my skin still screamed to be ripped open just to let the excess out. I considered how I'd lived with the urge to cut before, and back then, I hadn't healed how a comic book mutant would. I could handle this.

Mel arched her eyebrows.

I felt my DNA change.

Mel ignored me, and my speculation faded to the back of my mind fairly quick when we got to one of the things that made Shelburne Falls a tourist attraction. The Bridge of Flowers.

Sam was the only person on it, and she was trying to talk to a vaguely person-shaped cloud of white flakes and sparkling dust. Vincent.

Mel froze and grabbed my wrist. *I'd rather die than wind up like that.*

"You won't," I told her. "Trust me. Help me convince Vincent to help us."

Mel took a few deep breaths. "I hope you were right about how those two dreams related."

"Me too." Hand in hand, we walked the rest of the way to the bridge.

*

"Is there anything I can do?" Sam stared up at Vincent.

The head-shaped cloud turned from left to right, and a faint "No" whispered on the wind.

"Is there?" repeated Sam.

Mel let go of my hand.

I took a couple more steps forward. "He said no. But maybe there is something I can do."

"Please," murmured a creepy wind-like voice with hints of a bullfrog talking over a bad cell connection. "Burn...pieces of Demon...bind me together."

"I'll need something in return," I said. "If I help you solidify, you help me find José."

"Information...all...can give...just information."

"If I give you a strand of power to help you reform, you will tell me everything that might help me find him and the others—Seamus Evanstar, Officer Karen Malloy, Sister Marie Daly—that were taken. You will not lie. You will tell the whole truth and not omit pieces of it. You will truthfully answer any questions I ask you."

"I...agree." His whisper was a cold breeze.

I pictured his face from a vision of the future, not a memory, and sent a thread of energy toward him, willing it to destroy what was left of the Incubus and bind the rest. Some of the floating pieces evaporated, but three-quarters of them moved together into something relatively person-shaped. Even after I let go of the strand, it sped around, shaping the collected particles.

"Vincent?" Sam ran toward him—a torso, one arm, and a head—with her arms open to hug him. She fell right through him.

"Thank you." His voice was a whisper, but it was clearer.

"I'm sorry," he said to Sam. "I'm here more, but still a mere shade."

"You and Sam can have a reunion later. I'm on a deadline, and he promised me information in exchange for this." I gestured at his form.

"Yes, I imagine my father has moved on to plan B," said Vincent.

Sam lunged towards me with a snarl. "First, you sacrificed your grandmother. Now you're extorting him. I thought we were okay. I thought you cared about me. But this whole time, you were using me. Now you're using him!"

"Samantha, stop." Vincent placed an incorporeal hand on her back.

She shivered.

Vincent said, "Had Erin not destroyed the Incubus, I'd still be imprisoned in it. They took nothing from me, yet granted me freedom."

Sam's face scrunched up. "You wanted Erin to do that?"

Vincent nodded. "I'd hoped to secure their help, but my father's bonds would not allow it. Instigating Erin to obliterate the Incubus was the next best option."

"What is your father? What are you?" I asked even though the pieces were starting to click together in my mind.

"My father is a Fallen Angel. I am what remains left of the child he made with a human-Elf woman," said Vincent.

Mel inched closer to me and squeezed my hand. She stared at Vincent. "How did you end up this way?"

"One of his kin found a way to Earth. My father is bound to the realm he created for himself. If he leaves or dies, the Bracken Bubble collapses. He asked me to go to Earth to aid his brother. So, I went, but aid his brother I did not. For the first time, I lived life for myself, how I wanted to live. I transitioned myself to male as best I could in those days. The Elves could've helped, but I feared them.

"Humanity was beautiful and messy. Monstrous yet full of grace. I couldn't be part of a plot to deprive them of the freedom that made them marvelous catastrophes.

"Unaware that Elves and hunters were biding their time before moving against him, I took him on alone and lost. He destroyed the parts of me he saw as human, bound me to an Incubus, and sent me back to my father. I am not sure if it was mercy or cruelty that led him to trap me in a male Demon, but still, I was prisoner in a strange body, watching a monster commit atrocity after atrocity until after decades, I grappled with it for control, never quite winning, never quite losing.

"My father thought it a fitting punishment to put my jailer and prison in charge of a new plot to enslave humanity as food for Demons, to defeat Angels, and take Earth for the Fallen. I saw it as an opportunity, especially when he sent me after the beings that destroyed his brother and their offspring."

Hope inflated my chest. "So, where is this Bracken Bubble, and how do I get there?"

"I don't know," he said.

My hands clenched into fists.

"The Bracken Bubble moves," said Vincent. "I knew where it was the night you destroyed my prison. I know not where it is now."

"If I found a way to track José, to determine his exact location, how could I get in the Bracken Bubble?"

"Even if you located it in the Between, survived, and defeated the Many-Tentacled Destroyer, you wouldn't be able to enter unaided unless he allowed it."

"Unaided?"

Vincent studied his ghostly hands. "I can open a door and bring you through. Part of me is still of him, and he cannot prevent the Bracken Bubble from responding to me without destroying and rebuilding it."

"If I can get us there, you can let me in."

"I can."

"Will you?"

Vincent watched Sam. They gazed into each other's eyes.

He finally tore his gaze from Sam. "Our bargain was for information. If I am going to risk what little freedom I have received, I need something greater. A body. I'd give anything to be a man again."

"I can't make you human," I said, thinking of Mike's reaction when I described a certain vision. I'd never seen him so excited. It had been like Mike had won the lottery or a Nobel Prize.

Vincent narrowed his eyes. "Can't or won't?"

Mel stepped in front of me. "Erin is like a step-up transformer and a battery. They store, alter, and amplify energy. They can bind fragments of you together, but they cannot transform you into a human. No being with the power to do that could perform that miracle without triggering the war you want to avoid."

Vincent clasped his ghostly hands behind his back and closed his eyes. "You give me a taste of freedom, even if it is freedom as a ghost, and expect me to throw it away so you can get something I will never be able to experience?"

Sam reached out to him, but her hand went through him.

I took a depth breath. "I said I can't make you *human*. What if I could bind you in a human-like form?"

"You mean to imprison me within another being the way my father did?"

I shook my head.

"I'll not force another living being out of control of their body simply so I can live," he said.

I smirked. "Good, because if you would, I'd blast you out the 'verse right now."

"What are you proposing?" he asked.

"I dreamed of an android chopping carrots in a kitchen. Mel's fiancé has built fully functional prosthetic legs. What if he could make a whole prosthetic body that I could transfer your energy and consciousness too?"

"That isn't an 'if' statement." Mel turned her phone so the screen was facing Vincent. It displayed a humanoid machine. "This is a prototype of a biomechanical replica of a human body. It doesn't eat, but its sensors mimic a human nervous system. In theory, it should move, feel, and speak like a human, though Mike has yet to develop an artificial intelligence sophisticated enough to control all its functions."

"If you bring me to the Bracken Bubble, and we successfully return home with him unharmed, I will do everything I can to try to hook you up to a body like this one. Only an improved, more realistic version," I said.

Mel said, "We will try three times to build a new machine, each time trying material."

"You guarantee nothing," said Vincent.

I stepped closer to him, feeding him another thread of energy. "It's more hope than you have now."

"Hope is not enough," hissed Vincent. "I want revenge. When you face my father, you will not kill him. I want him trapped and helpless where he can neither upset the balance nor harm humanity."

"I will *not* torture him for you," said Mel. *Don't be a monster, Erin.*

Could we kill him if we wanted to?

You might be able to.

Mel took a step toward Vincent. "Erin and I will trap him as effectively as we can, but I will not torture him."

"He deserves suffering," said Vincent.

I crossed my arms. "You can stay a ghost forever if that's what you want, and if you don't help me, then your father will win."

After a long stretch of silence and glaring, he swore an oath three times agreeing to Mel's and my terms.

We shook hands.

Today was a two for one: I murdered someone, and I made a deal with a devil.

Not a devil, thought Mel. *Genetically, Fallen Angels are still Angels. Vincent's father was Fallen. But Vincent? He is more like me. Like us.*

Chapter Eighteen

I asked Michael why there is a half-Angel child for every half-Demon child and not just for children of the Fallen. At first, he didn't answer. I stayed quiet, letting the silence drag on until finally, he said, "There are many kinds of Angels, as there are many kinds of Demons. Have you ever seen a Sentinel and a Siphon in the same room?" I had not. I asked him if that meant all Demons were Angels once. He smiled and said, "I can neither confirm nor deny that theory." I asked him if he'd been reading my comics. He smirked and vanished.

—From the hunting log of Lucy Evanstar, written some time in 1996, confined to the archives shortly after the birth of Amelia Evanstar.

Mel paced around the street, holding her phone to her ear. Sam sat on the curb with her arms crossed. The white cloud of Vincent hovered behind her. My left hand balled into a fist. My right clutched a bent lug wrench. Claw marks marred the Jeep's hood. Two cracked rusty lug nuts lay on the pavement next to the Jeep's shredded front driver's side tire. The rear window was smashed. My skin buzzed, and my blood was electric. My hands twitched. The sound of glass shattering would be cathartic, but breaking a window wouldn't help me get home.

"I am going to start smashing things if no one answers their damned phones. They can't just *text* me saying they're responding to a Demon sighting and then not answer." Mel's knuckles turned white as she squeezed her phone.

Sam glared at me. "You've done murder and extortion. Why not add grand-theft auto to the list of your crimes?"

Tears dripped from Mel's eyes to her phone screen. "We wouldn't save anyone if we got caught."

Sam crossed her arms. "Can't you make the car invisible?"

Mel wiped tears off of her cheek. "I'm so worried I couldn't focus enough to glamour the car and be aware of enough of other drivers' thoughts to make sure they didn't hit us while we were invisible. It's dangerous enough when I am completely focused."

The bent wrench clattered to the ground. "You'd know if they got hurt or died."

Mel shook her head. "I'd know if Mike died. But from this far away? I might not sense an injury. For all I know, Shadowhulhu could have him, and we still don't know where in the Between this stupid Bracken Bubble is. We might have the power to get there and take on our enemy, but what good is that if we can't find the damned thing?"

I hugged Mel. "I've been there in my dreams. We'll find it."

She threw her arms around me and squeezed me so tight I thought my ribs might crack. Her tears soaked my shirt. A sharp corner poked my legs. "Mel, Nana said the answers were in her notebook. It's in my pocket."

I dug the journal out of my pocket and handed it to Mel. She'd be able to make sense of it quicker than me.

She flipped through the pages but didn't read out loud. Somewhere in the middle, a grin lit up her tear-soaked face. "She wasn't lying when she said she knew how to find José, and you were right about needing Jenny Dunn."

"What does Jenny have to do with this?" Sam got up and walked toward us. Vincent ghosted behind her.

"Jenny is pregnant with José's kid, and this is a ritual for using someone's offspring to track them. The younger the child, the more accurate the tracking." Mel passed the book to Sam.

Sam's harsh laughter echoed down the empty street. She read aloud from the book: "The newly conceived will lead to the most accurate results, though for most of my adult life, we have used this ritual to narrow my father's location into a thirty-three-mile radius. As I age, the accuracy wanes."

Sam shoved the book toward me. "This ritual requires a Witch. You need me to pull this off."

Vincent's dust formed a hand, which he rested on Sam's shoulder. "Help them. Please. If they can incapacitate and trap my father, this world will be safer for it."

I took the book back. "There is more at stake here than my family. Vincent's father is trying to invade Earth with an army of monsters that feed off humans. So far, me and the other hunters have been reacting to what he is doing. This is a chance to finally do something."

Tears trickled out of Sam's eyes as she glanced up at Vincent. "Now that you're free, tell me what really happens if your father wins?"

Vincent's face became clearer as he floated toward Sam. "His kind feeds off human energy. Many of his Demons eat human bodies. You're cattle to him. He'll thin the 'herd' enough so the planet can support the population but leave enough humans alive so they can reproduce and be a sustainable food supply."

"Are you saying we're all fucked if I don't help Erin even though you weren't going to help if they didn't promise you a body?"

Vincent shifted his gaze toward me. "Everything has a cost."

Mel's phone rang.

"Mike? Are you okay?" Mel tensed. Her hands closed into fists.

My palms stung as her nails dug into hers. Knots formed in my shoulders. Earlier, when I'd felt Mel's pain, I'd thought it was because she wanted me to know what was happening to her, but when I let my mind drift toward hers, I could tell she wasn't doing it on purpose. Panic radiated off her. The conversation consumed her attention. I closed my eyes and focused on listening. Garbled words came through the phone.

"Waterfront overrun with...going to detonate...not sure...love you."

The call cut out. Mel stared at the phone. Her eyes fluttered shut as she took deep breaths. "Get your weapons and food. We needed to be back twenty minutes ago."

My stomach churned as I opened the hatch and took out the two katanas I'd brought, then strapped them crisscross on my back. I fastened a belt of knives to my waist and clipped a third sword to that belt. I put on a baggy hoodie and stuffed a short sword and a few grenades into a backpack.

My eyes stung as I slammed the hatch shut. I rested a hand on the corner of my Jeep and petted it as I would a dog. This car had been my father's. I didn't know what would happen if I left it, but people might die if I didn't. I reached for the passenger side door and grabbed Sam's shoulder.

She startled, then turned around holding my cooler and snack bag. "I guess your cousin decided grand-theft auto was an option."

An engine roared. Mel peeled out of someone's driveway in a Mustang that had to be at least twice as old as me. "Get in."

"You couldn't have picked a more conspicuous car?" The front door creaked as I opened it. I climbed in and sat on a stiff vinyl seat.

"Please don't kill us." Sam slid into the back.

Vincent flowed in after her.

"We're not going far." Mel slammed her foot on the gas, and the Mustang shot down the street.

*

Mel pulled over onto the grass as an ambulance sped by. She shut the car off and rushed out the door. "Follow me."

I let my perception of time return to normal as I stepped out of the car. Tall grass tickled my legs. The land sloped down to a wall of thorny shrubs and skinny maples.

The drive over must have been terrifying for Sam. I'd had to slow my perception of time to match Mel's so I didn't freak out with her passing cars on roads with solid yellow lines and then barely making it back to the right lane in time.

"I am never getting in a car with you again." Sam staggered from the car. "Where are we?"

"We're taking a shortcut." Mel rushed through the tree line, ignoring the thorns that snagged on her jeans.

She stopped abruptly, closed her eyes, and appeared to feel the air with her hands.

Vincent floated to her side. "Are you sure this is wise? Like me, the Many-Tentacled Destroyer is stronger in the Between than on Earth."

"This is the quickest way back. Erin, give me your phone." Mel set a timer on her phone before putting it in her pocket.

I charged through the brush and handed her my phone. She set a timer for three minutes and thirty-three seconds. She grabbed the air and tore it apart, opening a person-sized gash between Earth and the Between.

"Erin, you go through first," Mel directed.

I unsheathed my sword and stepped from the scraggly woods into a dim world of purple and shadow. My sword reflected my aura's orange light and white sparks. I held it out like a flashlight, illuminating as much gloom as I could. I saw nothing. I'd heard stories about the Between in which my dad, Aunty Lucy, and Niben followed paths through it when they needed to get somewhere quick. I'd read accounts of its dangers and uses in the archives, and I'd dreamed of it, but I'd never been in it before.

Because Niben and Grandpa are afraid of what you might do here.

"What the fuck is this?" Sam stumbled in behind me.

"Between is the vast emptiness that fills the gaps between Faerie, Earth, Heaven, and Hell," said Vincent. Purple goop swirled around his ghostly form, mingling with his shimmering particles until it formed a solid body clothed in black leather pants, a tight gray shirt, and a black trench coat. His pale skin and dark hair had a purplish tint, but he was solid enough to catch Sam as she tripped over nothing.

Sam smiled as she put a hand on Vincent's face. "Okay, but why are we here? And why couldn't we have just popped into this Between back where the Jeep was?"

"Time and reality are malleable." White light chased the gloom as Mel leaped through the tear, which sealed behind her. Her shoulders relaxed, and the creases faded from her forehead. "No matter how long we are here, we'll exit three minutes after we left, assuming we don't lose either of the phones with the timers. We couldn't enter on the other street because that area touches Faerie, so there is no Between there. Had we gone through Faerie, we would've trekked through thirty miles of forest and a dozen villages that aren't very welcoming to human visitors."

"Are you aware there is no path here?" Vincent glanced around while still holding Sam.

"I don't need one." Mel scooped up a ball of the same goop Vincent had built a body out of and threw it to me. "Make something."

I caught the ball with one hand and sheathed my sword with the other. Cold purple slime slipped between my fingers. If what I'd heard and read was true, I could shape this goop into whatever I wanted. It warmed and buzzed when I fed it a spark of energy. I closed my eyes, envisioning a hilt, then willed the buzzing sludge to take that form, which began to cool and solidify. When I opened my eyes, I held a black cylinder. Grinning, I channeled more energy through the tube until a thrumming beam of red shot two feet out of it.

"That was a lot easier than I expected." I grinned.

"I imagine that is precisely why your family hesitated to bring you here. It is one thing to let you discover the limits of possible on Earth, but here, it is easy to lose yourself in the lack of impossibility." Vincent spun Sam so her back was against him. He strung goop around her neck, which turned to glittering amethysts upon touching her skin.

Sam traced the gemstones with her fingers. "Can I keep this when we leave?"

"It will revert to goop and evaporate as soon as we return to Earth. Come close and stop talking." Mel closed her eyes and knelt, burying her hands in the goop.

I turned my lightsaber off and walked to within a couple inches of Mel. Sam and Vincent stood next to me. A grayish-purple chair rose under my ass. I grinned as a joystick with a trigger appeared in front of me. Glowing purple formed a dome around us. Chairs grew under Sam and Vincent, then glided the two in position so they were behind Mel and me.

The ground under our feet became metallic. A dash, complete with a fuel and shield gauges, a targeting system, and a navigation computer materialized in front of Mel and me. She'd used the between goop to build a ship around us.

I grinned at her. "Our grandparents were worried about what *I'd* do here?"

Mel pushed a lever forward and the g-force slammed me back in my chair. "If you see a Demon, vaporize it with your energy, not mine."

Vincent whooped.

I swiveled my chair around.

Sam clung to her chair with her jaw clenched and her eyes closed. "I know only three minutes will pass in the real word, but how long is it going to feel like in here?"

"Don't ask. Thinking too much of how time feels here can interfere with how much time passes," said Vincent.

"Can you tell us more about this Bracken Bubble while we are here?" I asked.

Vincent's smile faded. "What do you want to know?"

"Everything," I said. "What is the landscape like? Can people breathe? Who inhabits it? Is there food and water that's safe to eat if we get stuck there longer than we want to be? Do you have any ideas specifically where José might be and how to get into that building?"

He took a few deep breaths. Each time he inhaled, a smile tugged at his lips like he was savoring simply being able to breathe. "The air is similar to Earth's so the humans my father raises to feed his Demons do not perish. Most of the humans' food is grown in container gardens with artificial sunlight and is safe to eat. Regarding José's location, I'm sure if you have a way to track the bubble through him that will also work to find him once you are inside."

I scratched the back of my neck, struggling to focus on asking the right questions. "When we get into the bubble, how long will we have before your father sets his Shadowhulhu squid minion after us?"

Vincent shrugged. "That depends on how long he wants to drag things out. He enjoys toying with his prey as much as you enjoy creating false names for your enemies."

Mel grimaced. "How does he sense whoever enters the bubble? How much does he sense about them?"

A broad grin revealed Vincent's purple-tinted teeth. "Now you are asking the right kind of questions."

*

Cold goop oozed through my fingers as I held open a gap between Earth and the Between. Sam plopped out of the gash, stumbled through a puddle, and puked.

Vincent stood in the opening but didn't move through. "I will see you tomorrow at dusk."

Mel put her hand on his shoulder, sending a flash of light through his body. "Don't get eaten by anything before then."

"Wait!" Sam stood, wiping her face. She ran toward Vincent, but Mel stepped out of the opening and pulled me with her, so I crashed into Sam.

The door sealed behind us.

"Vincent is stronger in there than he is out here, and if you asked him to stay with you, he would've," Mel explained as she jogged past Sam toward the alley's exit.

I raised my sword in case a horde of Demons materialized. Wide raindrops pelted us as we turned out of the alley onto a surprisingly empty street. Dented and clawed cars sat in most of the parking spots. Displays were pressed against store doors and windows, though they didn't fully obscure the people hiding inside. Blood was smeared over the pavement, but there were no corpses. Mel skidded to a halt in front of a small storefront with a tiny sign that said Hemp and Forge.

"You'll be safe in there." She grabbed Sam by the arm and pulled her up the stairs. A man with dreadlocks, dark skin, and sunglasses opened the door, nodded in Mel's direction, and led Sam inside.

Thunder rumbled.

Mel and I slowed our perception of time and ran.

Down at the waterfront, steaming Demon flakes covered the street like fresh snow. Smoke curled from the shattered windows and flames licked at others. Some cars were flipped over. Lightning danced between streetlights like one of those electricity exhibits at the science museum.

Mel's pace slowed to a walk. She studied the destruction with wide eyes. "Mike, what on earth did you do? Where are you?"

"You think he did this?" I called the stray volts to me and regretted it as they amplified the hot buzzing under my skin.

She scooped up a handful of Demon dust and let it fall through her fingers. "There must have been hundreds of Demons."

"What kind of weapon did this?" I pulled more stray electricity from the lampposts just in case any people were to walk through the area.

A lazy rumble shook the air. Lightning struck half a mile in front of us. Mel grabbed my hand. "I think Niben is controlling the storm. Come on."

The Demon flakes got deeper as we sprinted. The sky boomed, and lightning flashed, attacking tentacles writhing in and out of the storm clouds. Niben stood on top of a two-level tour boat with her hands in the air. She snapped her fingers. Thunder shook my bones as forks of lightning danced across Shadowhulhu's tentacles. They shrunk into swirling clouds.

"Can you sense where Mike is?" I slowed to a jog, searching for a way onto the ship.

Her forehead crinkled as she stared at the boat. "He's close."

We kept moving toward the boat. Aelfric was sprawled out on the boarding ramp, bleeding from more wounds than I could count. Mel and I knelt beside him. We dropped our shields.

Mel squeezed my hand. *You feel like a volcano or power plant. I can't gauge how much energy you've used.*

Not enough. It's building up again.

Mel put her other hand on Aelfric. I pushed a steady stream of energy to her. She mixed it with her own light and poured it into Aelfric's wounds. Muscle knit back together and new skin grew. Bones cracked into their right places and fused together. Energy filled his brain, brought the swelling down, and revived freshly damaged tissue.

Electric eels still squirmed under my skin. We poured more energy into him, refilling some of his reserves. He jolted awake. I ducked to avoid his flailing arms.

Mel let go of him and stood up. "Where is Mike?"

Aelfric blinked and used his hand to shade his eyes. "In the ship with Niben."

"Niben is *on top* of the ship," I said, looking up.

Mel sprinted down the ramp and onto the ship.

On the top deck, Niben fell to her hands and knees, panting. Mike popped up from the stairs and crawled over to her.

Two tentacles whipped out of the sky. One knocked Niben off the boat, and the other snatched Mike up to the sky. Mel burst onto the deck, screaming, but Shadowhulhu and Mike were gone.

Chapter Nineteen

I can never decide whether hunting with Mel and Mike is safer or more dangerous than hunting with Seamus or Sister Marie. Mel can heal me if things go wrong. When they work how they're supposed to, Mike's inventions are good at killing demons. His car even has weapons built into it. However, his weapons don't always work right...sometimes they blow up.

—From the hunting log of José Estrella, written in April of 2017, confined to the archives later that year.

Casco Bay was the kind of cold where, on a normal day, my feet would've gotten numb after standing in it for a few minutes. Diving in now was pure bliss. It cooled my too-hot skin and slowed the pins and needles that had ceaselessly poked me since I'd absorbed Nana's power.

My sparky hair and glowing skin lit up the water around me as I swam toward the stormy energy that belonged to Niben, who floated just below the surface of the water. I kicked toward her. Even though my lungs were starting to burn, I didn't surface until I had her in my arms.

Niben was unconscious, but my shields were still down, and I could sense Mel moving through the ship like a zombie. My throat was raw because hers was raw from screaming. A mantra of *This is my fault. All my fault. I started this, and now Mike is paying for it* played over and over in her head, but she never actually thought of whatever action she claimed started it.

By the time I got to the pier, Mel was sitting with her feet dangling down while tears leaked out of her swirling, unblinking eyes. I didn't see a ladder nearby, so I froze the water under my feet and built a staircase of ice that I carried Niben up. She was taller than me and solid muscle, so I thought she'd be heavy, but either Elves weighed less than humans, or I'd gotten very strong.

When I got to the top, I handed her off to Aelfric, who was once again too bright to look directly at without blinking a million times. He held her facedown. His light enveloped her until she was on her hands and knees, vomiting seawater.

I crouched down beside Niben. "What happened?"

Niben coughed and wiped her mouth with her sleeve. "There were thousands of demons. I don't think I've ever seen so many all at once."

"Did you use the storm to get rid of them?"

Niben nodded as she pushed off the ground and sat with her legs crossed. "The storm and the DeLorean. I struck it with a lightning bolt, overloading its energy core, and then Aelfric and I directed the energy from the blast towards the Demons."

A sob squeaked out of Mel's mouth, followed by a louder one. Her body heaved. She cried so hard I feared she would fall off the edge into the bay. I scooted over to her, wrapped an arm around her tense shoulders, and pulled her toward me.

I glanced at Niben. "What do you mean energy core?"

"Mel can explain it better." Niben stood, limped over to us, and sat on the other side of Mel, who was still crying too hard to speak.

Niben took a deep breath and attempted an explanation. "There are unstable elements in Faerie that generate large amounts of energy but do not generate the same kind of harmful radiation that some Earth elements do. After a few years of experimentation, Mike found a way to harness this energy to power human devices like his car, and more recently, the weapons he's been building. By hitting it with enough electricity, we overloaded and blew the reactor, generating enough power to take out the horde of Demons."

Had they lost control of that energy, they would've blown up the whole waterfront. Mel's thoughts were accompanied by an overwhelming wave of anxiety and rage.

"Thankfully, we didn't lose control of blast." Niben stared up at the dark clouds that were still assaulting us with rain. Thunder rumbled. "But that storm is a different story. I imagine the National Weather Service will be issuing a tornado warning soon."

Mel took deep, fast breaths, never seeming to get enough air. Her lungs were burning, and so were mine. I put a hand on Mel's shoulder and said, "Tomorrow night, we are going to go get everyone Shadowhulhu took and wreak some havoc in the Bracken Bubble while we're there. And once everyone else is home, we will make the Fallen pay."

Sobs wracked Mel's body. She collapsed on me as rage, fear, and incoherent murderous thoughts crashed over me. For the first time, I understood what it had been like for her all the times she'd consoled me.

*

By the time we got to Hemp and Forge, Mel had shielded so she didn't feel the thoughts and fear of the people who had sheltered in the shops. Despite having my shields up, I could still sense her waiting outside with Aelfric while Niben and I went in to get Sam and a few supplies we needed for the tracking ritual.

This particular shop was the safest place people could have hidden. The owner, Andre, was a smith and retired hunter.

A bell rang on the glass door as it slammed shut behind Niben. "Andre, the attack is over."

"Niben? I haven't heard your voice in years. Mike didn't tell me you were here." Andre's voice had a forced pleasant tone.

I'd never seen more than one or two people in Hemp and Forge at a time, but today I counted at least twenty packed between displays of candles, jewelry, and T-shirts. The good stuff–the swords, knives, and staffs—were on the rear wall in glass display cases hanging from the ceiling.

Andre's voice boomed through the small space. "It's safe to go back outside now if you want to brave this storm, though I don't recommend heading south until it passes. There are tornado warnings for South Portland and Cape Elizabeth."

At first, everyone stayed where they were, but one woman inched toward the window. "There's people outside!"

She put the hood from her coat on and rushed out of the shop to her car, which, aside from a broken passenger side window, was undamaged. More filed out after her;

soon people were pouring onto the streets from other shops.

When most of the humans were gone, Andre inched closer to the counter. He grabbed onto its edges. "How bad was it?"

"That was the largest horde I've seen on Earth, and there were only three of us left to fight and hold it off. It was over by the time Erin and Mel arrived." Niben put Nana's journal on the counter in front of Andre.

His hands scooted toward the journal before he traced the carvings on its cover. "The other hunters. Are they dead?"

"Captured, but we have a plan to rescue them and need some supplies to make it work." Niben opened the journal to the page with the ritual. She read off the items we needed, like the seven-sided-star pendants we needed as well as the candles and herbs.

I peeked at what was left of the weapons on the back display. Only two quarterstaffs remained in the corner. The swords I was wearing were the last of the katanas from Grandpa's supply, and while I could use other blades, those were what I was most comfortable with.

An orange sword I'd been eyeing a couple of months ago was still there. I took the sleek blade off the shelf, slid it into its orange sheathe, and slung it over my back. Next, I grabbed a simple oak staff. Its only decoration was a seven-sided star carved into each end.

I browsed the other swords in case there were any others I wanted. They might not be here next time I came in if I came back.

"Do you need anything else?" Andre placed a stack of copper pendants on the counter beside a bag of sage and fourteen candles.

"I'll purchase the weapons Erin wants." Niben glanced toward me and winked.

A hilt shaped to resemble a lightsaber's caught my eye. I grinned. The sleek blue blade extended two feet from the handle, ending in a sharp point. I picked it up and pressed the red button on the hilt. LEDs projected green light on to the blade. I hit the button again and the lights turned blue.

"You're paying with..."

"Cash? My credit cards expired years ago, and I've been too busy trying to stop the apocalypse to renew them since I've been allowed back on Earth. If there is something specific you want to trade, it may have to wait. I'm short on time."

"How likely is it that there will be a world left for me to spend cash in?" asked Andre.

The third time I hit the button, LEDs bathed that blade in red. I swung the mock lightsaber, testing the weight. It wasn't nearly as awkward as I pictured—different than the katana, but it was functional and leaving the store with me.

"It depends on if the person humming Darth Vader's theme song while swinging a lightsaber around the back of your shop can survive infiltrating the Fallen Angel's pocket dimension, rescue four people, return through uncharted Between space, and in the process, hopefully collect enough intel for us to create a plan to take said Fallen Angel out before he gets his invasion fully underway."

"So, we're fucked."

"Not at all." Niben's laugh was music, a summer breeze drowning out reports of a waterspout off Crescent Beach.

Chapter Twenty

I'd invited Erin over to game with me, Will, and the twins because my father had gone up to Beals to pay a debt to the mermaids and always spends the night when he goes there. Will took George home around ten. James was spending the night, and I was looking forward to being alone with him. Except at midnight, Erin was still there, and Dad stumbled into the house, shouting incoherently. I ran downstairs to shut him up. I told Erin to wait with James, but they both followed me anyway.

Dad didn't see them right behind me. He yelled something at me and swung his fist, but the blow never landed. Erin had gotten between us and grabbed his fist. Erin bared their teeth at him.

"If I see you hit him again, I will kill you."

A vein pulsed in his forehead. His other hand curled into a fist. For a second, I thought he was going to hit Erin, but he backed off.

My father may be a monster, but he isn't stupid. He knew he didn't stand a chance against Erin.

—From the hunting log of José Estrella, written in October of 2016, confined to the archives later that year.

The lights were all on at Grandpa's when we pulled down the driveway. The TV's glare tinted the front windows blue. Bessie appeared at the door barking. Allen opened the door and squinted. "Your auras are bright, but your faces are gloomy. What happened?"

Bessie, forgetting her size, tried to run between his legs. She knocked him over and bounced on her hind legs. Her snout bashed my nose before she pulled back and licked my face.

Mel sniffled, and Bessie ditched me for her as she sunk to Bessie's level. Mel wrapped her arms around Bessie's shoulders while the pup lapped up her lingering tears.

Allen glanced back and forth between Mel and me. "That thing with the tentacles took Mike, didn't it?"

I nodded. My shields were at full capacity, but Mel's anguish and guilt gnawed at my chest like my own conviction that I was a monster. She believed this was her fault the same way she had blamed herself for José's asshole father's betrayal and death.

"Right. I'm going to go check on Jeremy." Allen backed toward the house.

I rushed past him and went straight to the bathroom. I needed a moment alone as much as I needed the toilet. When I was done with the necessary stuff, I leaned against the wall, closed my eyes, and breathed in deeply, trying to focus on unwinding the knots in my chest. In a minute, I'd resume doing for Mel what she did for me. I'd hug her, bring her snacks, and drop my shields so we could talk without words. I'd get her focused on planning a rescue and remind her that by tomorrow night, we'd either be dead or reunited with everyone Shadowhulhu had taken.

You could be reunited at any moment. The words were a distant, hissing whisper. I opened my eyes. The mirror over the sink was dark blue. Black tentacles swirled through it. *Surrender. The boy will be yours forever.*

I retreated into my mind, the cockpit of a starship, and realized my shields were still up. I diverted more power to them, not returning my attention to the world outside my skull until I knew my mind was shielded to the max.

Wondering if what I was seeing was real, I stepped closer. Had I fallen into some half-awake/half-asleep trance? Was my subconscious trying to process something and showing me what it thought I knew, but my conscious mind still couldn't figure it out? Was this a dream? I raised a finger to the mirror.

A shadow tentacle shot out at me.

I jumped backward, screeching.

My rear end crashed into the wood door, which gave out behind me. It slammed down onto the pine floor with me atop it. I leaped to my feet, ready to attack with my bare hands or make an ice knife from the toilet water, but the mirror was back to normal—no sign of Shadowhulhu.

Variations of "What happened?" and "Are you okay?" rang through the air as I ignored everyone and stared at the mirror, seeing only my reflection: translucent skin stretched thin over blood like molten lava, emitting a red-orange glow. Searing green eyes with flecks of gold, orange, and brown swirling through them. Ears with points like knives poking up through fiery-red hair. Literal sparks leaped off my curls like an electrical outlet about to catch fire.

What the hell had I become?

"They're shielding like they're facing the Death Star," I heard Mel say. "Even when I play into the weird, space-opera reality they've created in their mind, and I hail them like I'm another ship, they ignore me."

Mel inched closer. She unclenched her hand from Mike's phone. Her fingers dug into my shoulder. I lowered my shields just enough for Mel's consciousness to slip past them, and I closed them around us.

What have I done? I asked her. *Will José even recognize me?*

Without Sight, you'll be the same pasty freckled redhead you've always been. But his Elf stone will reveal you in all your fiery glory. Mel wrapped her arms around my shoulders, squished me close, and rested her quivering chin on my shoulder. *This is about more than you seeing how you've changed.*

I closed my eyes and dropped my shields, replaying the memory of what had happened in the bathroom, broadcasting it loud enough for Niben and Aelfric to hear.

"That was not a vision. The Destroyer can't actually get us here, but it can use mirrors to taunt us." Aelfric took a bottle of scotch out of a half-empty liquor cabinet, scowled, put it back, and slammed the door.

Mel pulled me over to the table. She placed the phone she'd been holding down beside the four others spread out across the table, all with identical countdowns.

3 DAYS. 19 HOURS. 21 MINUTES. 18 SECONDS.

"The Fallen aren't only after Erin." Aelfric filled a glass with water from the kitchen sink. "They've left just enough of us to do the ritual from Helen's book and mount a rescue. Niben, Sam, Jeremy, and Allen perform it. Erin, Mel, and I go to the bubble. A Fallen gets two

Angel-hybrids to enter its layer willingly. It will be able to use as leverage against the Archangels along with Erin, who, as far as I am concerned, is a nuclear arsenal. It's a trap."

I stood up straight and glared into Aelfric's swirling green-and-blue eyes. "Admiral Ackbar said the same thing, but the rebels blew up the Death Star anyway."

"Only one half Angel is going." Mel's eyes were wide. Her lips pressed together. I couldn't tell if she was going to scream or laugh or punch something. "There is going to be a big gaping hole open to the Between while that ritual is ongoing. Aelfric is going to stay here and guard it."

He shook his head. "As Michael's daughter, you are the more valuable hostage, so you should be the one to stay back."

"Erin and I are more powerful together. If they go, I go." Mel leaned back in a chair and put her feet on the table, a smile forming on her face. She was settling in for a good argument.

*

Hot water poured over my skin, washing bits of sand, stray Demon particles, mud, and my own dried blood off my body. The rushing spray of the shower and the constant whoosh of the fan drowned out the noise of people arguing downstairs.

Much to Jeremy's dismay, Mel had asked me to keep my shields down because she was too scared to be alone in her own mind. She could barely contain her rage, ready to flip the kitchen table at Niben and Aelfric who still insisted Mel stay behind in case the Fallen's end game was to provoke Michael to attack.

I stayed under the running water until my skin felt shriveled and hot enough that I could pretend I hardly noticed the heat buzzing under my skin. I'd run out of things to wash long ago and simply enjoyed the moment of feeling human.

Eventually, I forced my hand to turn the water off. With my Sight closed as much as possible, I stepped out of the shower, grabbed a towel, and scrubbed myself dry, letting the friction briefly extend the time without the buzzy skin feeling.

A towel with a star trap painted on it covered the bathroom mirror as a precaution to make sure Shadowhulhu couldn't use the reflective surface to taunt me again.

Wrapped in a towel, I sprinted down the hall to my room where Bessie sprawled out over the bed, warming up my pajamas. She rolled over and tapped my face with her paw as I pulled them out from under her. It reminded me of putting on clothes fresh out of the dryer, except they smelled of dog instead of laundry detergent.

I lay down, telling myself I'd only rest for a minute. But one became two. When Bessie moved, I stretched out, slithering under the quilt. I planned to listen to the conversation through my bond with Mel, and pick the right moment to reenter. Bessie plopped down and rested her head on my stomach. I closed my eyes and focused on what Mel was hearing and saying, ignoring her mental commentary as much as I could.

"The ritual beam will get you to the Bracken Bubble, but I don't know how long we can maintain it. I doubt there will be a path home," said Niben.

"I don't need a path," said Mel.

There was silence for a whole three heartbeats.

"I required decades of practice to learn," said Aelfric. "When did you first try? When did you last succeed?"

"Mike got kidnapped after hacking something he shouldn't have. I didn't have a passport or the money for a plane ticket, so I went through Between. The most recent trip was today," said Mel.

"Tell me about another," said Aelfric.

"José got 'lost' when he and Pedro were helping the Bearclaws hunt Trolls up near Stowe, Vermont. The two of them got separated, and that ass didn't bother searching for his son. I found José unconscious just before a blizzard blew."

That would've been a good moment to go downstairs and support Mel, but I was paralyzed by fresh rage conjured by the story of José's father leaving him to die. If Pedro Estrella weren't already dead, I'd murder him right now.

I almost killed him then. Mel's voice was loud in my head, drowning out Aelfric and Niben's responses. *I dragged him into the Between and left him far away from any path. I'd never seen my father as angry as he was when he talked me into returning for Pedro because there would be consequences if I didn't.* A wave of stifling shame rushed over Mel's words, making it hard for both of us to breathe.

I wasn't kidding when I told you his treachery was my fault. I'm almost certain Pedro struck a deal with the Fallen while he was there. I should've told someone the night he died, but I just couldn't think about it, let alone say it out loud. I'm not as good as everyone thinks. I'm every bit the monster you claim to be.

Then we'll be monsters together, I assured Mel.

I'm going to take a walk outside. Can you stay awake until I get back?

Sure.

I'll be back in ten minutes. Mel retreated from my mind.

I yawned and thought about getting up sooner than in ten minutes to make sure I didn't fall asleep on Mel. Bessie stretched, resting her snout on my stomach.

I closed my eyes just to rest them. I wasn't going to fall asleep.

But shitty cousin that I was, I did fall asleep.

José's Elf stone glowed on his forehead as his fist slammed into my jaw. He snatched a knife off my belt and slashed it across my stomach as he bolted past me and crouched in a corner. His hand shook, but he didn't lower the knife.

"I saw Erin die. The Destroyer snapped their neck. Erin hit the wall outside that gap, dead."

That scene faded, and my dreams turned to the past.

"Liam, we need to leave, now," hissed Pedro Estrella.

"We're exactly where we need to be," said Liam. "Stay with me, and we'll both be okay. Be brave, my friend."

"You told me we were hunting a Yeti," said Pedro.

"We were when I told you that." Liam unsheathed a katana that gleamed in the moonlight. Pedro unsheathed a rapier.

A Demon, one with a knife-shaped torso and legs moving so fast they blurred, zoomed out from behind a tree. The edge of its thin body would've cut my dad in half had he not blocked it with his sword. While my dad struggled to hold the Demon back, Pedro dropped his sword and bolted like a rabbit.

Liam frowned. A Crawler leaped at him from a tree. He swung his sword without looking, and it blew up. Three of the tall blade Demons shouted at him. He blurred, and they were in pieces.

Tears slid down Liam's cheeks. "Damn you, Pedro Estrella! I'm not ready to die."

The violence scene dissolved to something calmer.

I lay on a beach, soaking up sunlight, trying not to think about what my cells were doing with it. Two sunblock-lathered kids threw sand at me.

"Daddy, Erin is being mean again!" screeched the one with hair that blended into the sand and skin a shade darker.

"Erin is always a meanie pants," said the kid with darker hair and pale, faintly glowing skin. "They never want to play."

"Erin is supposed to be watching you two," said José, water dripping off his hair and bare scarred chest.

The scene faded. I stood beside Mel's dad, in space, and he was too bright to look at.

"Erin, isn't *your* future worth fighting for?"

"It is." I gazed at the stars glittering millions of years in front of me. Wings made entirely of blinding white light lazily flapped behind Michael. My hands glowed like embers. "What am I?"

"The one being on Earth who can save my daughter. A magnificent anomaly not accounted for in the rules of a game I've refereed for an eternity past and will referee for an eternity yet to come." Michael the Archangel's glow pulled away from him and hovered above us before shining light us on us like a spotlight. He strode toward me. The buzzing under my skin frenzied as he placed a heavy hand on my shoulder. "I can't lose Amelia. I can't watch her burn out or shatter when she's hardly had a chance to live. If you want to prevent a way, you need to protect Mel. Don't let her burn out or sacrifice herself for anyone. Don't fall asleep when she needs you."

I cringed. "And what if I sacrifice myself for someone? Who protects her then?"

"If you try, I suspect you'll find true death does not come easy for you."

I waited for him to elaborate.

"Think of Amelia as batteries hooked up to solar panels. She can hold vast amounts of energy, but once it's gone, it takes a long time to recharge. You are a super-efficient generator. Given the right fuel, you exponentially produce energy. Together, the two of you will be unstoppable."

"I'm as much your creation as she is, aren't I?" I stared at him now that I could. He was back in the scrubs he wore in his human guise.

"Are you accusing me of arranging circumstances, so the right people met each other at the right time? Of influencing which genes you inherited from which parents?" Galaxies of cosmic mischief twinkled in Michael's eyes.

I crossed my arms, digging my nails into my biceps. "How much did that mess with your precious balance?"

He let go of me and gazed at the star field. "The balance has been disturbed for decades. Thus far, I've refused to let the Fallen provoke me into an attack, but if they persist, I will act. Humanity needs their own guardian, one who can stand up to Heaven and Hell alike. A counterweight to zero the scale when it tips too far in either direction."

"A counterweight. That was what Vincent called me."

"Redemption is not beyond his reach. Remember that."

"Was he the one I needed to forgive?"

The Angel laughed. "You are the one you need to forgive."

Chapter Twenty-One

In fiction, Faerie is often depicted as having monarchs, gentry, and courts. While some parts of Faerie are that way, the one I interact with the most is more socialist. Healthcare, and enough food to survive off, is provided to everyone who lives in the realm. No one owns the land. Some fields permit Elves to farm. Some forests provide shelter while others eat trespassers. The Matriarch is a monarch who rarely uses her political power, allowing most laws to be decided by democratic voting.

—An entry from the journal of Seamus Evanstar. Written in May of 2014, confined to the archives later that year.

I shuffled into the kitchen, guilt slowing my steps as I saw Mel slumped over the table, hair hiding her face and a few frustrated tears.

"You should make some bacon since you slept so much," Mel yawned as she picked her head up, appearing very young and very human.

"I'm sorry I fell asleep." I opened the fridge and took out the remaining bacon.

Mel slumped over the table, resting her forehead on her arms. *Please tell me you dreamed something useful like us successfully rescuing everyone.*

"José isn't going to recognize me when I find him." I slashed the bacon open with a paring knife, tempted to slash my hand and see if it would still automatically heal itself.

Mel got up and snatched the knife out of my hand. "What else?"

I took a pan out of the dishwasher and put it on the stove while I told her about the others.

That last one broke the gloom on Mel's face. She didn't fully smile, but her lips twitched upward. "At least there was some hope."

"Hope is a good thing." Niben came up from the basement and plopped a notebook on the table in front of us, opened to a list:

> Candles made from pure beeswax and nothing else.
>
> Neither Flower extract
>
> Dried sage
>
> A "delvhaniun" blade
>
> Copper wire
>
> Rocks
>
> A seven-pointed stars made from conducting material.
>
> Collect Jenny Dunn
>
> Teach Erin how to open doors to Between and Faerie.
>
> Set up ritual
>
> Check and organize weapons

Sort through Mike's tech. See if Amelia can figure out how any of it works and if anything will be of use.

Feed my grandchildren

"That is a relatively short list for you anyway." Aelfric pulled up a chair at the table. "Who is doing what?"

"You are going to find an open hardware store. Amelia, Sam, Jeremy, and Allen are going to stay here and prep for the ritual and make sure all the necessary weapons are functional. Erin and I are going to Faerie and then collecting Jenny Dunn."

*

Niben knocked, even though my bedroom door was open, and waited on the threshold carrying a full trash bag.

"Come in," I said, guessing the bag was filled with clothing.

"It was Liam and Lucy's, what they wore when I took them to Faerie from when they were in their late teens to their early twenties." She put the bag down on my bed and fought with the knot for a few minutes. I would've torn the bag open, but she carefully undid the knot.

"At least for the Summer Elves, clothing and gender have no correlation, so don't make assumptions about which pieces belonged to whom. I don't think there is an item in here that Liam and Lucy didn't share."

"Why can't I wear my own clothing?" I sorted through tunics and leggings with a few shorter shirts and flowing skirts mixed in. They were colors of summer: leaf greens, bark browns, sunflower yellow, lupine purple, hydrangea blue, and marigold orange.

Niben sat down on the edge of the bed. "I want you to appear as if you belong there. I hope we can be quick and not run into anyone else, but I suspect my mother will want to meet you. I fear she'd be insulted were you to visit her realm in human garb."

I studied a short-sleeved marigold tunic that was mostly solid in color save faint outlines mimicking veins running through petals and leaves. "Should I be afraid of your mother?"

Niben ran her hands through the hair on the back of her head. "Are you afraid of Mel's father?"

"He's annoying and makes my head hurt. I'm afraid of what he'd do if Mel died, but I don't fear him even though I probably should." I put the tunic on the bed with a pair of leggings and returned the rest of the clothing to the bag.

"My mother is not much younger than him, but she is twice as manipulative and possesses ten times his hubris. As she grows older, I fear she forgets the multiverse existed before her. I'll see you downstairs in ten minutes. If you feel the need to bring a weapon, carry a staff. Leave your swords here. Don't bother with shoes." Niben's skirt swished behind her as she left without giving me a chance to ask questions about her mother. My great-grandmother sounded as she could be quite terrifying and extremely useful.

*

Cold wet mud squished under my feet as Niben and I walked from Grandpa's yard into the forest. After a few yards, we stopped where three old maples formed the points of a triangle. Niben had changed from her brown cotton leggings and green tunic into a knee-length halter dress that was green on the bottom and purple on top. One brown satchel was slung over her shoulder.

"Open your Sight and your mind and your senses." Niben brushed the air with her hand, searching for the seam. "Find the place where the air feels warmer and the molecules buzz at a different frequency. Find the seam between that air and this air. Slowly pull it apart."

I watched and felt Niben do exactly as she had told me until the air shimmered and parted. Warm air radiated out of the tear. On the other side, the trees were bigger and the underbrush thinner with abundant flower blossoms.

Niben pulled her hands together and closed the door she'd opened. "Now you try."

"Okay." Niben made opening the way seem easy, but when Niben and I switched places, I couldn't find anything to grab onto.

I closed my eyes and focused on breathing. Maybe if I changed how I perceived time and everything seemed slower to me, I'd be able to sense where some places were different. My hands fumbled through the air and found a spot where the molecules bounced quicker. Grabbing it was a different story. Matter slipped through my fingers every time.

I focused on those molecules as if I was trying to make an ice knife, but I didn't pull anything from them. I let them consume my attention. I imagined them as pieces of the plastic bags used for picking up dog poop, one that had just come off a roll and wouldn't open. Instead of licking my fingers, I pulled a little moisture from the air so they were damp, and then I grabbed the buzzy corner where this world touched Faerie and slowly pulled it apart, revealing the same forest Niben had shown me.

"Good. Now close the way and reopen it."

I lost count of how many times Niben had me open and close the door. With each repetition, she ordered me to bring my perception of time closer to normal until I could do without slowing it at all. Only then did she let me step through. And once we were through, I had to do the same thing from the Faerie side.

"Very good," Niben muttered before striding down a path. Without speaking, she led me past trees as wide as an eight-person kitchen table. Orange and yellow flowers marked the edge of a soft, mossy path.

She stopped abruptly and stepped off the trail.

I followed her, careful not to tread on any flowers, mushrooms, or sharp rocks, trying to memorize the landscape so I could find my way back to the trail if Niben decided to test me.

Niben stopped under a weeping willow with deep-brown, purple-tinted bark and blackish-purple flowers instead of leaves.

"This is Neither Flower." Niben plucked three strands of flowers and put them in her satchel. "We can make the extract if I don't have any in storage."

We returned to the path the same way we had come from and continued down it just a little more until it split. She wiped her eyes with her sleeve before we bore right.

A hint of anxiety fluttered in my chest. The only other time I'd seen Niben cry had been the night Mel had almost died and when Grandpa had been taken.

The trees thinned, giving way to a familiar field of tall grass and lupines.

"You recognize it?" A smile tugged at the right side of Niben's mouth, but brimming tears made her eyes appear greener like how rain brightens lawns and leaves.

I hoped her tears were benign and not because she knew something bad was about to happen that I wasn't aware of.

"I remember being here with Grandpa and Dad when I was very small. I ran around chasing Pixies. Grandpa carried me around and called me Sunshine. It's hard to separate what I actually remember and what I forgot but then dreamed."

Her smile grew. "Do you remember the way to my house?"

I shook my head. "So far, this field is the only familiar thing."

"It's something. At least you remembered something." Niben walked through the tall grass, brushing the tips of it with her fingers.

We climbed up to a tree wider than Grandpa's house. Closer inspection revealed the structure was three trees twined together with windows and balconies growing out of its side. It split after three stories into thick trunks and branches. Many of the sturdier limbs held mini houses, each filled with Pixie nests.

I had déjà vu. I'd been here before but couldn't pull a specific memory together in my head as I followed Niben down the hill to where an asymmetrical door provided entrance to the house. Niben placed her palm on it, and the door swung open to a kitchen. The table had a barky trunk for legs and a smooth varnished surface. The counters were the same polished wood. More bark covered the cabinets. In the middle of the room, a water-filled moat surrounded the hearth.

"Oaklyn hates fire, but she will tolerate me cooking inside if there is plenty of water around the flames." Niben hung her satchel on a vine growing out of the wall near the door, then removed the Neither Flower and spread that across the table.

Past the kitchen, a spiral staircase growing out of twisted wood provided access to the areas above and below. Beyond, a larger table long enough to fit twenty people filled the room. The empty walls were pockmarked with divots where the wood was a tiny bit lighter. Had pictures hung there once?

I like seeing her sad less than I like fire. Her human family made her happy. I do not understand why she took their images down, so I do not let her forget where they once were in case she changes her mind.

I searched with my eyes and mind, trying to figure out who was in my head. I didn't sense another being in the house, but the walls, furniture, floor, and every other piece of this tree radiated as much energy as Niben did.

I am Oaklyn, the spirit of this home.

Niben sat on a stool by a counter. "Oaklyn is a nosey, interfering spirit, and I've told her I will put those pictures up next time I am here for more than a few hours of sleep."

Oaklyn laughed, causing the whole structure to shake. A vase inched close to the edge of a vibrating shelf.

"If you break that..."

The laughter slowed to a purr. The angle of the shelf tilted slightly, and the vibration eased the vase closer to the wall.

What has my Niben so agitated?

Niben closed her eyes and took a deep breath. *Our enemy abducted Seamus. We need to rescue him.*

Ah. From the presence of the Neither Flower, I infer that he is being held in the Between. I remind you that you do have already-made extract in your stores since you often fail to hold your inventory in your mind.

I leaned against the counter next to Niben. "So, you live in a sentient tree house with a sense of humor?"

"Welcome to Faerie." Niben shook her head, pushed herself off the stool, and strode down the stairs to the lower level.

I followed her.

Tables, benches, shelves, counters, and cabinets filled an expansive basement. Vials containing a rainbow of liquids, solids, and things in between lined the shelves. Each was labeled with characters that were not from any human language. Many had an English translation in parenthesis, including two canning jars of Neither Flower extract.

Niben moved them to a table in the middle of the room. "This should be plenty. Oaklyn, please move the fresh plant to the chilled storage unit."

"Do you have the knife we need here too?" I hoped we didn't have to make too many stops. If we weren't ready for dusk, we'd need to wait another twenty-four hours.

"Yes. And I promise we'll be back in time." Niben's voice was steady, but her posture was stiff, her fingers fidgeting.

I followed her past bookcases laden with manuscripts bound by leaf and leather, open-faced cupboards filled with bowls and utensils for mixing and mashing. Hammers and wrenches hung from a wall that stretched to the far end of the room where the curve of the tree trunk was loaded with swords, knives, bows, arrows, shields, chain mail, plated armor, and even a few battle-axes.

"Impressive." I stepped forward, tracing the vine pattern on the smooth hilt of a broadsword.

"Mmhmm." Niben picked up a cutlass, cradling the blade like a baby. "I used to keep some of these at

Seamus's house. He whined when I took them back here as if they meant more than him to me."

Her face went blank. Her lips pursed together as if she was trying to crush invisible walnuts. Her fingers quivered when she belted the sword to her hip. She chewed on her lip as she studied a selection of chain-mail vests. When she picked one up, it shook in her hands. The little rings chimed. "This fit Liam and Lucy when they were your age."

The mail quieted when I took it and held it out over my chest. "Am I borrowing this?"

"I'm giving it to you. The material is slightly conductive and very hard to heat, safer for you than the steel mail you can purchase on Earth." Niben picked up a sheathed dagger, slid the knife halfway out, shoved it back in, and added it to her belt. "Delvhaniun, on the other hand, is a superconductor I'm afraid to let you touch."

She kept her hand on the hilt as she bowed her head and closed her eyes. Her breathing was jagged as if with each inhale her ribs stabbed her heart.

My chest tensed. I took a deep breath and hugged my grandmother. She was as solid as a tree trunk. Her scent reminded me of a forest drenched in summer rain.

She wrapped her arms around me and squeezed. "I'm sorry I haven't been here for you. I never wanted to miss so much of your life."

I pulled away but didn't fully let go of her. "But you agreed to."

Niben's cheeks were reddened from tears. She sniffled as much as any crying human. "I agreed to stay in Faerie and not contact you until you discovered the supernatural for yourself. I never imagined it would take fifteen years for you to do that, not with how much time you spent with Lucy and Amelia." Niben slowly filled her lungs with air and exhaled. "If we survive the night, please let me stay part of your life."

"I've seen you several times a week for the past three months. Why would that change unless one of us doesn't survive?"

"I don't mean as a trainer or sparring partner. I'm a harsh teacher. I don't want that to be the whole of our relationship. Let me be your grandmother." Niben squeezed her eyes shut and shook her head. "I want to watch movies with you, go kayaking, and play games. I want to show you my favorite places in your world and mine. I want to know who you are when you aren't trying to save the world."

I let go of her. "I'm no one good. No one you really want to know."

Her frown hardened into snarl. "Erin, don't do this to me. Not now."

I crossed my arms. "Do what?"

"The same self-deprecating nonsense you do to José and Mel. How do you expect to survive long enough to save your family if you don't value your own life?" Niben closed her eyes and clutched the hilt of her dagger. "Please tell me saving them isn't a suicide mission."

I turned my back to her and stared at the ceiling where dozens of roots twined together. "I've not dreamed of a future where I stay dead."

*

"Guard your thoughts, but do not shield. I'm certain she has information that can help us, but she will not give it up for free." Niben sprinkled water on her face from a pool gathered in a bowl that had grown out of a wall.

"Does she speak English?" I knew the Elves had their own languages, but Niben was the only one I had met.

"My mother is fluent in more languages than most humans know exist, yet she acts as if speaking aloud in *any* language is a burden." Niben dried her face on a towel, squared her shoulders, and turned around. "Do I appear as if I've been crying?"

"No." The red had faded from her cheeks, and her gaze returned to feline indifference.

Niben took a deep breath. "All right. When you meet my mother, just be yourself."

"Really?" That was the most cliché piece of advice a parent or grandparent could give.

A half smile brightened Niben's face as she walked by me toward the stairs. "You may not like who you are, but my mother will find you amusing at the worst."

"And what is the best-case scenario?" I jogged up the stairs behind Niben.

She paused halfway up and studied me with sad eyes. "There is no best where she is concerned. The most useful outcome will be if she sees your stubborn power more than your youth and seeks to make you her ally."

"I assume your mother enjoys alliances with monsters?" I asked, hoping she didn't notice me raise my shields.

Niben rolled her eyes like she was thirteen, not three hundred, and kept walking. We turned the final bend and stepped into the living room, meeting a person with skin like fertile soil, eyes like July sunset, and verdant hair that might have been grass growing out of the top of her head. Her clothing was green with pants the texture of stems and a shirt veined like a leaf. Tangible energy radiated off her like heat off a granite mountainside in the summer, and even though there were no wrinkles on her rough skin, I knew she was ancient. Niben was a child next to her, and me? An infant? An embryo?

"I'd rather be offended by honest thoughts than not know what the offspring of my daughter's son is thinking." The ancient ruler of the Summer Elves had a voice like pine trees creaking in the wind.

"I told you not to shield," said Niben through gritted teeth.

I did not drop my shields. "Will you promise not to mess with my thoughts?"

The ancient Elf winked at Niben and turned to me. "Your mind is safe in my presence."

I dropped my shields. *How should I address you?*

I have many names, but today, you may call me Great-Grandmother Chelonia. Use she/her/hers pronouns. How may I address you?

Just call me Erin. My pronouns are they/them/theirs.

My great-grandmother's head tilted. *Interesting. Faerie nonbinary beings use ne/ner/nis. I presume humans have not yet settled on a gender-neutral pronoun?*

There are more than I can keep track of, but nothing universal, at least in English. I'd rather adapt they than get people to agree on something completely new.

Understandable. Mortal pronouns are fascinating, but I am more curious why Niben has decided to bring you here now, collecting Neither Flower of all things.

Niben stood with her shoulders straight and her hands clasped tight in front of her. *Erin has found a way to track the missing mortals taken by the Many-Tentacled Destroyer. It requires Neither Flower.*

Humans are so fragile. Perhaps the one you can't let go of will perish, and you'll care for your own kind again.

My hands curled into fists itching to punch something.

There is more to this than rescuing lost lovers. Niben closed her eyes and inhaled slowly.

I was surprised Great-Grandmother Chelonia's face didn't creak when she grinned. *Michael still thinks he can avoid a war by having Elves and hybrids do his dirty work. I cannot determine if this is because time has worn him soft and complacent or because he is lazy. Once, he was the fiercest of warriors.*

I forced my fists to unclench and let my hands hang loosely at my side as I inched closer to my great-grandmother. *I don't give a shit what his motive is as long as it doesn't result in everyone dying.*

The ancient Elf glowered at Niben, who lowered her head. Her bottom lip quivered. The air between the two of them was hot and humid as it is in summer just before a thunderstorm rolls in. If they were talking, they'd shielded the conversation from me. Either way, the only thing this meeting was accomplishing was making me frustrated.

I stepped between the two of them and looked directly at my great-grandmother's volcanic eyes. *Do you know anything about the Bracken Bubble?*

Flames writhed where most beings had pupils. The orange turned to yellow, then white. *How do you know of that place?*

The Many-Tentacled Destroyer took the "mortals" there. I killed one of its minions getting that information. The minion could've been lying, but the Many-Tentacled Destroyer confirmed the information when I fought it at the Confluence.

Great-Grandmother Chelonia's breath was a pine tree screeching in a storm. *Show me memories of your battles.*

I will if you offer information about the Bracken Bubble and the Fallen who inhabits it.

Great-Grandmother Chelonia narrowed her blazing eyes. *You will show me three memories in exchange for three parcels of relevant information.*

I glanced at Niben. She nodded.

I accept those terms.

I focused on my battles with Shadowhulhu. First, I replayed the battle at the movie theater. Second, I showed her the fight during which Grandpa got abducted. Third, I projected the space battle at the Confluence. When I was done, Great-Grandmother Chelonia's black feline pupils returned, smoldering like hot coals.

The ancient Elf hissed. *Gareth. You must not let him breach Earth.*

You know him? Niben unclasped her hands and took a step closer to her mother. *No one else has spoken his name, not even Michael.*

I do not dare speak his true name, though I am not afraid to use the common alias of that toxic scum. Great-Grandmother paced circles around Niben and me. *Ages ago, when I was young, Gareth tried to conquer Faerie. It wasn't long after the First Fall, the Great War of the Angels. He and a handful of other Fallen had escaped Michael's forces. They invaded Faerie, killing thousands of Elves, including my parents and elder siblings. Michael refused to aid us, fearing it would undo the accords he had in place to keep the Fallen away from Earth. We rallied and defeated Gareth's forces. His Fallen allies were killed or captured, but he retreated to*

Between where he built his own pocket world—the Bracken Bubble.

I clasped my hands behind my back. *So, fact number one is that Gareth the Fallen might be after both Faerie and Earth. Does Gareth have any weakness that might help me extract my friends and family from his realm?*

Great-Grandmother stared at the ground as if her memories were hidden in Oaklyn's roots. *Most of his power is tied up in the Bracken Bubble. His will holds it together. It is both his stronghold and his weakness. He can bend and shape pieces of the bubble as weapons, but if he puts too much effort into battle, it will collapse.*

In order to gain access to the bubble, I vowed to weaken and imprison him instead of killing him. How can I contain him? I pushed the memory of making a deal with Vincent to the top of my mind.

Great-Grandmother's toothless grin was a fault line rending soil in an earthquake. *You cannot, but there are places under my control that could imprison him for eternity.*

Niben bared her teeth in a predatory smile. *And what will you give us for facilitating your revenge?*

Great-Grandmother's laugh conjured tremors deep from the ground that rattled Oaklyn from her roots to her highest branches. *What will you give me for aid in rescuing your partner?*

Niben narrowed her eyes. *I am not rescuing anyone.*

Holding my head high, I thought, *I am going in to extract my family with Vincent's help. He didn't give me a deadline for binding his father. I'll find a way eventually.*

I didn't flinch under my great-grandmother's stormy gaze, weathering her silent contemplation even though fire ants crawled through my blood and across my nervous system.

Three stakes appeared in the ancient Elf's hand, each a different material: silvery metal, gnarled wood, and blood-red crystal. *Plant these in the Bracken Bubble. Tell no one you have them or what you plan to do with them. One will allow me to track the bubble. The second will grant me access should I choose to invade. The third will grant me limited control over the material once I am inside.*

What do I get if I do this?

Material for Vincent's body so you can uphold that part of your bargain.

I didn't ask for that. Why offer it instead of binding Gareth?

Planting three stakes on a rescue mission takes far less effort than imprisoning a Fallen Angel. If you succeed tonight, both at rescuing the prisoners and planting my stakes, then we can negotiate the capture of Gareth. This is a trial. Do you accept?

I do, I thought without checking for Niben's approval. I'd tarried here long enough, and planting stakes seemed a simple enough task.

You must plant them without *Gareth noticing.* Great-Grandmother vanished in a blur of sunset and oak-leaf light.

Chapter Twenty-Two

I've made some terrible decisions lately, some of which have almost got me killed. Getting drunk at parties is a horrible idea when I could get called away from said party to go hunt Demons. It's almost as stupid as sleeping with Jenny Dunn to make Erin jealous. They didn't care about any of the boys I screwed around with. Why would they react differently to me fucking a girl? Sometimes I wish my father would just get carried away with his beatings and kill me before I end up killing myself, or someone else, with bad decisions.

—An entry from the hunting log of José Estrella, written on March 3, 2018, after getting lectured by Mel about hunting drunk. Confined to the archives at the end of the month.

"Do you recognize where you are?" asked Niben.

I stood in a patch of forest where the trees were mere saplings compared to the ones in Faerie. The soggy ground was overgrown with thorn bushes that after ten feet gave way to a yard with more mud than grass.

"Mom's house," I said.

"You can change into human clothes and grab a snack before Jenny arrives." Niben carefully stepped over brambles.

I opened my mouth to make a comment about not having a car, but then I remembered that Mom's was here. The car keys were in the house, but I didn't have a house key. Niben took Grandpa's key ring out of her satchel and unlocked the back door.

Not being immediately greeted by Bessie felt strange. The house was too quiet. Empty. Every step on the floor made creaks that sounded like desperate cries for company. When I turned on the tap in the bathroom, water gushed through pipes, causing them to jangle.

I texted Jenny, letting her know I was at the house. I jogged up to my room where I threw on a pair of cargo pants, a clean binder tank, and a T-shirt. I shoved the Elf clothes in a backpack with a bunch of underwear, shirts, and pants. I tried to not look in the mirror, at the unmade bed, or at anything else before running downstairs to the cookies. I stuffed my face with junk food until Jenny knocked on the door.

"You know where he is?" asked Jenny as soon as she saw my face. Her blonde hair was done in one neat braid. She wore black knee-high boots that had flat, practical soles, gray leggings, and a loose purple tunic with unicorns on it.

"That's not what I told you on the phone," I said, letting her into the house.

"You know a way to find him. You said something about a tracking ritual." She took a few steps before stopping to touch the rain jacket on the coat rack: José's rain jacket.

I grabbed the coat and tied it to the outside of my pack. "Things are going to get weird, but this should work."

"As long as it gets him back, I don't care how strange it gets. This isn't about me. It's about our child having a father." Jenny's voice cracked, but she puffed her chest out and held her shoulders straight.

I crossed my arms. My nails speared my skin. Jenny was coming regardless of her answer, but there was one thing I wanted to know before we left. "Do you actually care about José?"

"Why do you think I hated you so much? I knew he loved you," she squeaked with way less meanness than I hoped. She walked around so she was facing me, reached out to put her hands on my shoulders, and then stopped herself. "I'm not doing this to steal him away from you if that's what you think."

"That isn't an answer." I stepped back, putting a more comfortable distance between us.

Jenny closed her eyes and took a deep breath. "Sometimes I like the idea of being his friend. Sometimes I think I'm in love with him. Other times I want to punch him in the face."

"No punching him." I stalked across the room, stuffed the remaining cookies in my backpack, and slung it across my shoulder.

"How often did his dad beat him?" Jenny's feet made the floor creak.

I froze. "He told you about that?"

Jenny stopped and stood next to me. "No, but he made up the stupidest excuses for his bruises every time he took his clothes off."

I glanced out the window, noting how the sunbathed the yard in golden light.

A couple months ago, I might've punched her for saying that, but for once in my life, I couldn't muster the energy to be angry.

"We should go." Niben came out of the living room with her satchel weighted down by dog food and DVDs.

*

Mud and leafy branches were bathed in afternoon light from the sun as my mom's car trundled down Grandpa's driveway. Niben slowed the car to a crawl at every big bump. I'd have bottomed the sedan out half a dozen times by the time we got all the way to the house.

The car stopped. Bessie barking greeted me after I opened the door. I was halfway to the door when Aelfric let her out. She charged to me, leaned against my leg, and wiggled on me, slapping me with her tail.

Aelfric lumbered out of the house. "You made it back in one piece!"

Niben rolled her eyes. "We wouldn't have if you were driving."

"It's not my fault Americans drive on the wrong side of the road."

Trying to block out Niben and Aelfric's bickering, I edge closer to Jenny. "There is one thing I didn't tell you."

She jumped back. "What?"

"Sam is helping us find José. You need to play nice with her."

Jenny paled. "Erin, she tried to shoot me."

I crossed my arms. "With a gun she took from you."

Jenny stared at me with her mouth hanging open but didn't flinch away when I grabbed her hand so I could hear what she was thinking. *When did Sam tell them? Is Erin going to kill me? Was this all a ruse to lure me here? I've been trying so hard to make amends.*

"I've known since a few seconds after I got shot. It was one of the last things I heard before my heart stopped beating. And no, I'm not going to hurt you. This isn't a ruse. Sam isn't going to hurt you either." I let go of her and walked the rest of the way into the house.

"You can read my mind?" Jenny stumbled forward.

"Psychic, remember?" I tapped my temple. I didn't tell her that with anyone other than Mel, my telepathy was new, sporadic, and only worked when I touched people.

Jenny followed me up to the porch and peered into the house before stepping over the threshold. She jumped behind me when she noticed Sam sunk into an armchair, watching more bad news about fires and mass shootings stream across the TV.

"You two have to tolerate each other," I said to Sam and Jenny.

"The next five hours are going to be so much fun." Mel emerged from the stairs half covered in dust. "We are all going to cook food, eat it, and explain what you all need to do while Erin takes a nap.

Jenny grabbed my wrist. "Why does Erin need a nap?"

"So I can see the future one more time before I charge off into the unknown." I yanked my wrist back.

"We all have a stake in this, and I'm willing to bet there is a lot Erin didn't tell you." Sam got up, walked toward Jenny, and extended a hand. "Truce?"

Jenny backed away from her, staring at the front door.

"You can't back out now," I said to Jenny. "We can't do this without Sam."

Jenny inched toward the door.

I got between it and her literally in the blink of an eye. She leaped backward.

"If you want your kid to grow up in a dystopian future where humans are treated like cattle, then by all means, walk out that door." I wouldn't let her leave. I'd knock her out and tie her up for the duration of the ritual if I had to.

Jenny stared at me.

"I could use some help making meatballs if you are done having a staring contest with my cousin," said Mel from the kitchen.

Jenny backed away from me.

"You were at the graduation. You made Erin leave so José and I could talk, and then you calmed Erin down at the memorial on Sunday," Jenny said when she was closer to Mel than me.

Mel shook Jenny's hand. "I'm Mel, Erin's older, nicer cousin."

A chilly, forced giggle crawled out of Jenny's mouth. Before Jenny could respond, Mel introduced her to Jeremy and Allen, who started giving her tasks to do. The busier Jenny was, the more her shoulders relaxed and the less terrified she appeared.

"I'm going to go see if Niben needs help with anything before I also get recruited for kitchen duty." Sam walked to the porch where Niben and Aelfric were laughing. They hardly seemed to notice me when they came inside and started working to get things set up for the ritual. They tried one last time to talk Mel out of going, but no one questioned whether I was going. Maybe Grandpa would if he were here. Or perhaps he'd see the weapon I'd become.

I should've been happy no one was trying to stop me.

*

Mel hadn't been kidding when she'd said I should take a nap before we started.

"Who knows when the next time we get to sleep is?" She put her hands on my shoulders and steered me upstairs.

It was six o'clock. The sun didn't set for a couple more hours. Everything for the ritual was in place. The people performing it were practicing, but Mel and I weren't part of it. We went through the door it opened.

Mel had gone through the mismatch of tech Mike had left at Grandpa's before he'd disappeared. We'd found functional ear buds, which were essentially magic two-way radios capable of encrypting and transmitting speech in someplace like Between or Faerie. We hoped they'd work in the bubble so we could stay in contact after we split up.

She also found an infrared sensor with a screen that not only displayed heat signatures, but also marked Demon, Elf, Angel and hybrid energy signatures. It was a handheld version of the system Mike used to monitor Demon and hunter activity. We loaded that and the last of the lightning grenades into a backpack along with other weapons and supplies.

We found pieces of an automated mini defibrillator Mike had been building for me in case my visions stopped my heart again, but it was only half assembled. Mel put it together, but she didn't know how to program it.

There was nothing more we could prepare.

"Except steal a glimpse at more futures," said Mel.

"What makes you think I could fall asleep if I wanted to?" I asked.

"I can make you sleep. And you do want to sleep because you want one more peek at the future before you charge off into it."

"Will I still dream if you make me sleep?" I had the sinking feeling she had done this to me before without me knowing.

Mel didn't deny it.

I should've been mad at her, but I couldn't muster the energy for anger.

I'm sorry, she squeaked in my head.

I plopped down on my bead. "Just make me sleep long enough to dream and hopefully see something useful but not so long that I miss our window to leave."

Mel put her hands on my temples.

The room vanished.

Tentacles writhed around me as I ran, dove, and slashed.

Sun glistened on tranquil ocean water.

While I dove through a hole from the Between to Grandpa's basement, a tentacle shot past me and snapped Sam's neck.

"Where is Erin?!" shouted José before his fist hit my jaw.

Blue light slammed into Mel, and she shattered into a million pieces. The scene rewound. The same blue light hit me, and I felt like I was going to break apart into a million pieces, but I didn't shatter. I took another hit and another until I was just a bunch of supercharged electrons held together by sheer stubbornness facing down a storm of shadow and fractured light.

Lightning cackled out of my fingertips.

Chapter Twenty-Three

The futures I see where humanity has a fighting chance are the ones in which the people I love suffer the most. What kind of father is willing to set in motion a time stream in which he knows his child will attempt suicide, become addicted to cutting their own flesh, and eventually, find themselves in a state of being where they won't be able kill themself no matter how bad they want to die? Where do I draw the line? What have I become?

—From the hunting log of Liam Evanstar. An encrypted version was confined to the archives after his death and was decoded fifteen years later by his sister, Lucile Evanstar.

Clad in canvas work pants, a flannel shirt, chain mail, and a down vest more appropriate for a brisk November hike than a summer evening, I was sweating in the cramped basement room. I hoped Vincent wasn't lying about the Bracken Bubble being cold.

Niben, Allen, Jeremy, and Sam were in position over the seven-sided star, which had been carved into the floor and filled with Neither Flower extract. An identical one was carved on the wall where the portal to Between would open. The one on the floor was also traced with electrical wire, but the wire just circled in the center of the one on the wall. The wire was stripped in two one-inch sections where each participant stood.

Even though I couldn't see them, I knew every Pixie outside the house was on high alert. It was unlikely that something hostile would get past the wards, but if it did, the Pixies were the only other thing standing between it and the ritual participants.

"They can be flying piranhas when they need to fight," said Mel.

I'd never seen them in action, but I believed it. The larger threat was the hole that would be open between the map room and Between. It was Aelfric's job to guard that.

Jenny stood in the middle of the circle, wearing one of three copper seven-sided-star necklaces. Niben handed two to Mel and me.

"Can you carry any more weapons?" Sam glared at the two swords strapped to my back and the assortment of knives belted to my hip.

I ignored the sarcasm. "I have room on the belt for a gun holster, but I'm a horrible shot."

Sam rolled her eyes.

I didn't mention that there were guns and grenades in the backpack.

"Erin and Mel, you two are going to stand in the center on either side of Jenny, but you are not going to touch her. You also should not touch any of the wires or lines," said Niben.

We both got in the middle, careful not to touch anyone or anything.

Niben made eye contact with each member of the group: Allen, Jeremy, Aelfric, Sam, and Jenny. "Once we start, we need to stay here in position as long as we can so they can find José and not get lost on the way back."

Mel glanced at Niben. "I won't get lost."

"But Erin might if something happens to you." Niben closed her eyes and took a deep breath before addressing the rest of the group. "Any questions before we start?"

No one did.

The word "ritual" conjured images of chanting and handholding, but what happened was not so showy. Jeremy grabbed his section of stripped wire and channeled energy into it, followed by Niben, Allen, and Sam. The star lit up. Jenny grabbed onto the wire. After thirty seconds, energy flowed out to the wall, spiraling through the wires in the middle, to the stripped ends, and a circle opened in the wall, leading out to Between.

I clasped my hands together to stop them from shaking as Mel and I stepped out of the star, careful not to touch anything, and dove through the open portal into the blackish-purple Between. A faint green beam shot out of the map room. Aelfric was waiting for us, armed to the teeth, illuminating the gloom. He nodded but didn't engage in conversation. Vincent waited a little away from him, looking exactly as he had when we'd left him the previous day.

"This will go quicker if we're not walking." Mel paused, closed her eyes, and gathered Between goop around us. A soft, fleecy chair formed under me as a cockpit materialized around me.

I was in the copilot's seat with weapon controls. Mel was driving, just like on our trip home from Western Massachusetts, except this time, we were much more likely to be attacked.

A door hissed open, and Vincent came in, taking a seat behind us. "You've definitely got style."

The door closed. Mel pushed the throttle forward, and the construct sped toward the green line. We reviewed the plan we'd made based on the information Vincent had provided and on the details I'd seen in my dreams.

Had we not shielded, I would've spammed Mel's mind with worries or meaningless small talk about comic books and movies, and I wasn't in the mood to chat out loud, especially not with Vincent there. Sure, there was plenty I could have asked him about his past, but I didn't want to know. I didn't want to like or hate or pity him. I just wanted him to play his part and get us into the Bracken Bubble. If he died, I didn't want him to be another person I could miss.

I replayed my dreams over and over in my head, making sure I'd memorized every detail I could about where José was being held. I watched the clock on the dashboard. It never moved from 7:57 p.m.

Sometimes I only saw a seemingly infinite expanse of blackish-purple space. Other times, pieces of other worlds stretched into vast emptiness. We sped by an elbow of a white frozen realm. Later, we passed an arch of lush green forest shrouded in mist.

After what felt like an eternity of anxiety-inducing nothing, we saw reached our destination. The Bracken Bubble was a cross between a tumor and one of those sticky seeds that get stuck all over Bessie's fur in the fall. The green beam shot straight into it.

The ship shrunk. Mel switched the controls over to me so she could focus on cloaking. I didn't see Shadowhulhu anywhere. In my dreams, he had been inside the bubble, not outside it. Mel stared straight ahead, eyes narrowed but not blinking. Vincent had his arm around himself. His leg shook. I would've been clawing myself somewhere if my hands weren't squeezing the steering wheel.

"Veer to the right of the beam and dive down so you're halfway between where it hits and the bottom," said Vincent. "My father is focused on the area right around his prisoners, so if you go in too close, the ruse might not work."

I resisted the urge to barrel straight through, blowing up everything in my path. The goal was to go undetected for as long as possible and inhibit Gareth's ability to determine who had entered his realm.

When I reached the spot Vincent thought Gareth wasn't focused on, the ship's roof fell away along with the chairs and controls until we were just on a floating platform, cloaked in Between goop as we approached the Bracken Bubble.

Mel squeezed my arm. "You ready?"

I nodded. For a second, we both dropped our shields, minds colliding as we threw the shields back up, mine encompassing both of our consciousnesses. If I closed my eyes and retreated in my head, it was like we were standing in the same spaceship cockpit. When I opened my hands, a reddish-green haze was superimposed over everything I saw.

"Shields are up," I told Vincent.

He dug his hands into the bubble, disappearing into its side. Was he going in without us? Betraying us?

Just wait. Even as Mel told me to be patient, her mind was twitchy with impatience too.

The side of the bubble parted. Vincent held open a hole barely big enough for Mel and me to slither through. Rough rock scraped against my skin, snapping shut as the last inch of my foot passed through, sending me headfirst onto the dusty, rocky, green-tinted gray ground. I tucked just in time and rolled to my feet on a barren stretch of cratered land where the purplish soil had a nuclear-green glow.

"Stay close." Mel grabbed my hand just before I got out of range of our combined shields. "The longer we stay together, the longer it will be before he figures out exactly which two beings snuck into the bubble."

The green line veered to the left and up a steep hill. I had no clue how far we had to walk

This place isn't as big as it appears from the outside, thought Mel. *Vincent wasn't lying when he said you could cross it in a day.*

I scooted over to my side of the cockpit, keeping as many of my thoughts as I could behind a mental privacy screen. Mel could still hear them if she chose to, and I could hear hers if I focused a little on her instead of myself. Then, in the physical world, I turned to Vincent. "Do you have any idea how long it will take to get up to the beam?"

"It should not take more than an hour to reach that level. The Bracken Bubble is not large."

Regardless of the Bracken Bubble's size, time was still lost to me. There were three green orbs up in the "sky," but I couldn't tell if they were supposed to be suns, moons, or big lamps. They were what gave the land its greenish radioactive tint. But could I use them to tell time?

Ask Vincent.

I did.

He glanced up and smirked. "They move. One represents the sun, one Earth, and the other the moon. They represent time passing on Earth and all the years my father has been unable to conquer it."

I took out a device that was a combination handheld version of the technology we used to track Demon and hunter activity and an infrared scanner. No life-forms registered on it unless I pointed it at Mel, Vincent, or myself.

We walked.

The craters shrunk as we ventured further in, and the land sloped up. There were some boulders and random rock formations but not very much cover if we needed it. The slope got steeper and leveled out.

Vincent paused. "Mel, you might want to hide us."

Ahead, a collection of purplish domes lined the perimeter of a fenced-in area on a stretch of relatively flat land. Figures moved around within, but they were few compared to the number of domes.

I pointed the scanner at the village. It showed human-shaped heat signatures and Demon energy. Staying close enough so our arms were touching, Mel and I followed Vincent forward. She bent light around us, so we blended in with the landscape.

A handful of humans wove fabric with an old-fashioned loom while a couple of Spikes glowered at them. At the center of the village, there was a greenhouse with lamps shining white light from the ceiling, powered by a group of humans pedaling bikes while more Spikes watched them. A couple Crawlers lazed a few feet outside it. One of them gnawed on something.

A human femur. A cringe crossed the mental screen with Mel's voice. A wave of her rage washed over me.

I squeezed her hand. "Not yet."

The rage wave receded.

Vincent had told us there were numerous little compounds with human slaves. Eventually, Mel would create a diversion by rampaging around, slaying demons and freeing humans.

We passed this one without being noticed, and part of me wondered if we actually went undetected or if the Demon guards, who could potentially see through Mel's glamour, had been ordered to ignore us.

Chapter Twenty-Four

I can find very few records of hybrids mixed with more than three species and fewer records of hybrids of four species. Those with equal distribution of Angel, Demon, Elf, and human are rare and powerful, but their might is surpassed by beings who are even more mixed. Most who have met such beings agree this is for the best, yet Michael and his siblings want more of those beings to walk the Earth. I believe one of the reasons Hanzel cursed you was to prevent you and your progeny from having more children who could potentially create super hybrids.

—An excerpt from a letter from Phineas of the Winter Elves to his daughter, Helen. Confined to the archives after Helen's death in 2018.

We climbed three slopes and crossed three plateaus. Every time we passed a compound, the inhabitants ignored us. We scanned each one, but there was no sign of Officer Karen or Sister Marie. We knew José wasn't there because the beam wasn't. Infrared scans confirmed all the humans were out in the open. We didn't recognize any of them.

As we hiked up the fourth hill, Vincent said, "Unless they moved him since we entered, José should be on this level."

Shadows loomed in the distance. The first thing we saw when we crested the top was a village crammed with people. More Spikes and Crawlers than I could count prowled the perimeter. Two Puppet Masters towered over everything and waved their hands, directing a wave of humans armed with crude clubs at us. Beyond that loomed a round dome that was as wide as a football stadium and a half as long. The green beam shot into the bottom level of it.

Time to split? Mel's rage spilled over our privacy screen, mingling with my simmering anger and uncertainty. I itched to take my sword out and go cut the Puppet Masters up. But that was Mel's job. Mine was to keep going while Mel made a lot of noise and, hopefully, didn't get caught in a trap I feared was laid out for her.

I hugged her. *Maybe we should stay together.*

Mel pulled away. *No. We are going to spring this trap and smash it to pieces.*

Please don't get yourself killed. This is extraction and recon. We'll return and end this place when we have more support.

How? It's going to move.

Trust me. I dropped my shields for a split second and put them back up without Mel in them.

"See you at the rendezvous." Mel unsheathed a broadsword as she jogged off toward the Puppet Masters.

Before I could further second-guess my plan, I ran toward the green beam. Vincent kept up with me, floating more than running.

"Erin," hissed Vincent, coming up beside me. "Don't forget this place is mostly Between matter held together by my father's will. Altering it is the quickest way to alert him to your presence."

The big dome, the one I'd been dreaming, the one José was imprisoned in, stood ahead of me. Demons filled the space between the dome and me.

"Did you hear me?" Vincent tapped my shoulder with a buzzy, semisolid hand.

"Yes. He made this out of Between. If I mess with it, then he knows I'm here. If he dies, this place dissolves." Crawlers paced around, snarling and snapping their teeth. Behind them, an army of Spikes formed a blockade. Shadowhulhu hadn't shown itself yet. If the time stream hadn't changed, it would attack after I got through the Spikes.

"Think about it," he said.

"Can you sense your father?" I asked Vincent.

"He's close."

"Get ready." I unsheathed my two swords and inhaled slowly while running until my perception of time slowed. Crawlers couldn't speed up too much, so to me, they lumbered in slow motion. I flicked the switch on the katana with the lightsaber handle, giving the blade a red glow. My energy mingled with the light and infused the steel with power.

The first Crawler I hit exploded into white confetti. Two more came in range of my blades: one to the right and the other two to the left. I jabbed at one with the charged blade.

Poof! Demon turned to snow.

I decapitated the other.

Four circled me, mustering more speed than the others, but they were still much slower than me. I channeled a little energy into the second sword until the runes glowed and the blade had the same Demon-exploding effect as the saber.

No more Crawlers came. Those that were still alive skulked away. I'd never seen a Crawler be anything but a frenzied, suicidal, human-eating beast. Did something about Earth make them berserk? Or were these well-fed where the ones that attacked on Earth had been starving in Hell for God knows how long? If they were well-fed, then Vincent was right about the humans in the villages being livestock.

If the Fallen and Demons invaded Earth, the surviving humans would be cattle. I'd known that in theory, but seeing evidence enraged me. Stolen energy buzzed under my skin. It woke the monster slumbering inside me. That monster roared; it twisted my guts and pounded my head, demanding violence.

I tightened my grip on my swords and bared my teeth. If I survived today, I'd return to free the humans. I'd avenge the ones I was too late for.

Blocks of Spikes marched toward me as if a formation was going to do anything but keep them in neat rows while I hacked them to pieces. I sent a little more energy into each blade, spinning them, testing the weight to make sure the energy didn't hinder their ability to move.

I further slowed my sense of time and sprinted toward the Spikes. Ten exploded as I broke their ranks.

Spikes were smarter than Crawlers, able to move faster. I needed a direct hit to obliterate a Spike, but they were proficient in swordplay. When they parried my strikes, their swords steamed on contact with mine. Thankfully, after three or four hits, their blades, clubs, maces, and axes melted, leaving them defenseless against my supercharged blades.

The sheer numbers nearly overwhelmed me, but I stayed fast, always moving, dancing out of reach when the

Demons got too close. Occasionally, I felt a blow on my shoulder or sharpness in an arm even though nothing had hit me. I didn't have time to ponder why I was feeling Mel's injuries. Thankfully, her wounds seemed relatively minor.

The dome was half a mile away if my sense of direction was to be trusted. The Spikes surrounded me, but with my two blades, I fended off most of their attacks. A club snuck through my guard, smashing into my leg behind my knee, sending me to the ground. Heat surged in that area of my body, burning as bone fused together. The healing hurt worse than the bone breaking.

I gritted my teeth, using the pain-sparked rage to keep blocking and to swing harder. I stepped up and propelled myself through the air, coming down on a Spike hard enough to split it in two. I spun around with my blades out, chopping through four more before they could form that circle again.

My skin crawled like it was infested with fire ants as if healing a bone had fully awoken dormant energy. I could work with that. I poured energy into my blades until lightning forked out of them, dancing across Spike after Spike, decimating the horde.

Twentysomething remained when the dust settled.

They charged at me.

I swung, stabbed, chopped, dodged, parried, and blocked.

Two, four, six, ten went up in plumes of snow.

A mace slammed into my back, shoving air out of my lungs but not penetrating the chain mail. I rolled out of the way of a club, slicing two pairs of legs and obliterating the Spikes they were attached to. Four more came at me, but with a spin, my blades burned through their midsections. They fell apart, but they didn't fully disintegrate. I channeled power through the blades, sending bolts out to vaporize the rest.

Panting, I slowed my perception of time. My heart raced as I fumbled the sensor out of my backpack and scanned the dome. It confirmed Sister Marie and Officer Karen were inside along with a handful of human heat signatures.

There was no sign of Vincent or his father.

I put the sensor away, stood up, strode forward, and stopped shy of crashing into Shadowhulhu as tentacles materialized in front of me. They snapped around my wrists, arms, legs, and neck. I pushed energy out, and the tentacles retreated long enough for me to slice at them with charged swords. Smoked curled where blade and tentacle met.

"You can still surrender," boomed the beast's deep voice. "My master is merciful. He'll forgive you for obliterating his army if you help piece them back together."

I closed my eyes, breathing slow, speeding up my perception of time despite the pressure growing in my head. The duration during which I could maintain this had grown exponentially in the past two months, but my endurance wasn't infinite. The faster I moved, the less time I could sustain it for.

I charged the blades, aware that the buzzing under my skin was the slowest and quietest it had been since I took all that power released when Nana died.

"Even if you get to him, you will never make it out alive. Surrender, now."

Inhale. Exhale. Inhale. Exhale.

Heat seeped from the swords through all my layers. Tentacles snaked closer. They brushed my skin, then snapped around me. I released my energy, lightning forking from my blades as I lashed out, slashing the tentacles into little wiggling pieces, working my way closer and closer to what I hoped was the center of the beast.

I hadn't killed Shadowhulhu in the dream where it snapped my neck. In another dream that may or may not have been part of the same time stream, it followed me back and killed Sam. I needed to try to destroy it or, failing that, wound it badly enough that I could outrun it on the way back and close the gap before it killed anyone.

I marched forward as the monster condensed and reformed. The air had the viscosity of molasses. More tentacles fell victim to my blade. Some dropped to the ground, wiggled a little, and then went still while others dissolved or exploded into confetti like the Crawlers did.

"Stupid, arrogant child!" boomed Shadowhulhu.

I sent a more concentrated burst of power, ripping tentacles from the monsters. Rocks flew off the ground, battering the dome, creating gaps big enough for a prisoner to see through but not fit through.

A few more tentacles came at me, and I sliced them, struggling to stay focused on the beast and not watch the holes for a glimpse of José, to make sure some piece of debris had not wounded or killed him.

For the first time, I saw where the tentacles stemmed from.

"Do you know what you've done?" said a mouth filled with purple teeth.

Only thirty-three remained attached to a blob of something that resembled a giant, three-dimensional bruise.

"Erin? Is that you?" called José from a hole in the dome's wall.

My heart sped up. Warmth filled my chest.

"José, stay back!" I adjusted the grip on my blades.

"Erin, no. You shouldn't have come. They'll hurt me. They'll make you swear an oath you can't break or kill us both. Run!"

I ran but not in the direction he wanted me to run. Sparks dancing across my body, I charged Shadowhulhu. Tentacles whipped toward me. One, two, three fell victim to my blades. The fourth got my ankle, writhing under the surge of my electricity. I kicked it off. Two more shot toward me, snaking around my wrist. They snared my other leg, my torso, and my wrist. They disintegrated on the edges but kept twining tighter and tighter, drawing me closer and closer to the beast's main body.

"You were supposed to surrender!" it bellowed.

"Erin never surrenders," croaked Vincent.

"Vincent," I hissed, forcing air up my constricted throat. "Do your job."

"My master preferred I take you alive but would rather me live than you." Tentacles crushed my throat and whipped my body toward the gray dome.

Chapter Twenty-Five

Together, Erin and Mel could be a near-unstoppable force. It's terrifying. I didn't mean to upset Mel, but when I saw them making their Buzz Lightyear action figures glow and thought of the things I dreamed about them, I just snapped. I wish I could explain this to Lucy, but discussing their futures splits them into more possibilities.

—From the hunting log of Liam Evanstar. An encrypted version was confined to the archives after his death and was decoded by his sister fifteen years later.

Darkness. I swam in an ocean of it. I was a bioluminescent jellyfish in the deep sea, except I wasn't as jelly as I felt. I still had my arms and legs. I still had my body, but it was strange, wobbly, and not so solid.

I'd been here before. The day I'd gotten shot. The first time my heart stopped beating.

Liquid current swirled around me, tugging me up, down, right, and left. Fearing those currents would take me places I couldn't go back from, I swam in circles, waiting for my body to heal itself so I could wake up. I couldn't die now. Not so close to rescuing José. Not when I'd seen myself live past this point in so many time streams.

Cardiac arrest. I'd gone out with my perception of time still slowed, so the time it might take for my body to heal might just seem longer. My skin had still been buzzing when I'd blacked out. My crushed throat, broken, bones, and concussed brain had to heal before I woke.

I counted to a hundred and twenty.

I did it again. And again.

Shit.

When I'd gotten shot, I'd stayed here even after my heart had resumed beating. Days had passed until I'd woken up for real. Being out for days here would be the end. Mel couldn't take Gareth alone. He'd either shatter her, use me as leverage to get her to surrender, or torture her until Michael started a war to save her. I could wake up captured. Gareth could torture me or force me to watch while he tortured José until I agreed to serve him. Maybe he'd just make sure I stayed dead.

My days of wanting to be dead were over.

I needed to survive.

The currents got stronger. I treaded harder. I couldn't die. Not yet. I closed my eyes, mentally grasping for any energy I could sense. No matter how far outward I reached, there was nothing but cold. I pulled my awareness inside myself, delving down into the core of my consciousness. I remembered what it felt like outside the movie theater seconds before I lost consciousness. I searched not for the buzzing that lingered under my skin, but the fire at the core of my being. It was there somewhere. It had to be.

I spun, spiraling further into myself until my limbs seemed heavier, more solid, and I sensed something warm. I called it to me as I continued drilling my consciousness back toward my soul.

I jolted. A spark hit me. The black flickered.

I focused on closing the gap between that warmth and me.

Lightning forked over me. I blinked back and forth between a pile of rubble and the black limbo between life and death.

A stronger bolt seared my body, quaking every limb, scoring every nerve. I opened my mouth, gasping as my burning throat expanded. Buzzing energy soared through my spine, fusing a fracture back together, sending pins-and-needles-type energy to my limbs.

Mel screamed in my earpiece. It wasn't words, but a raw, keening battle cry. Razor-sharp pain and cold assaulted my arms, legs, and stomach as she recklessly charged through a horde of Demons to avenge my death. I threw my shields up before Gareth noticed I was alive, then touched my earpiece and yelled, "Mel, I'm fine. Put your damned shields back up!"

Pain pulsed in the back of my head.

"And stop letting things hit you! Focus!"

"Erin?" Mel's hoarse voice cracked in my ear. "You died: I felt you die."

"You've said that before." I pushed a log-size chunk of rock off my stomach, ribs burning as they snapped back together, allowing more oxygen into my body. "Did you find Mike?"

"He's close, I can feel him, but—" Mel screeched at something.

"Just focus on staying alive and finding him." I reached into my pocket and took out the silvery stake my great-grandmother had given me.

"Let me know if you find the others." There was a click. The earbud went silent.

A secondhand blow jostled my right shoulder, and then I felt nothing but a vague awareness of Mel and a burning in my muscles that could just as easily be mine as hers.

I rolled toward my sword, which lay a few feet away from me in a pile of rubble. I stabbed the ground with the sword at the same time I shoved the spike in. I used the sword to get to my feet. Dust, rubble, and pockmarked land surrounded me. The dome towered over me. Shadowhulhu was gone.

The orange sword had been snapped in half. I pulled the lightsaber replica out of the ground and sheathed it. My backpack was still on my back. I swung it off one shoulder and unzipped it. The food was all squished, but the weapons appeared intact. I took out the scanner and aimed it at the dome.

A heat signature blinked a mere fifteen feet away. In the distance, I thought I heard yelling, hacking, and growling, but the noise could've been my stomach growling and blood rushing through my veins.

My head hurt. Everything hurt. I was exhausted but alive. My skin didn't buzz anymore. I almost felt normal— a tired, somewhat-human Erin who didn't have someone else's power effervescing under their skin. Almost. There was still a faint, feverish heat humming quietly and contentedly, telling me it was never truly going away.

"José?" I called, taking deep breath after deep breath.

He didn't answer.

If I had survived my throat getting crushed only to have killed José with a piece of debris from my body hitting the wall, I wasn't leaving without first destroying this place. I peeked in the smaller hole José had poked his head out of, but I didn't see him. I closed my eyes and focused on listening to what was behind that wall: uneven breaths, gasps, shaking, and partially stifled tears.

"José? Are you hurt?"

No answer.

Approximately twelve feet up the wall, there was a gash big enough for me to fit through. I climbed piles of rubble that got me a little closer, but I still couldn't reach. Breathing deeply, I slowed my perception of time once more despite the throbbing of my head. I crouched and sprang toward the hole in the wall. My stomach and knees scraped against purplish concrete before I belly flopped through the floor. I caught the edges with my hands, so I dangled into José's cell. I relaxed my body, letting my sense of time return to normal, then dropped down.

"José? Are you in here?" I called as my eyes adjusted to the dark.

I heard him trying to quiet shaking breaths as if he was hiding from a monster who'd come to kill him.

He was hiding from me.

"José, it's Erin," I said.

"Erin died."

José charged me. His Elf stone glowed on his forehead. His Sight was open.

I let his fist smack into my jaw and crack it. A monster, at least one that was out to get him, would've grabbed his hand and snapped his wrist before it hit my cheek. The monster that loved him took the blow without flinching.

He snatched a knife off my belt and slashed it across my stomach as he bolted past me, crouched, and waited to see what I did. The knife tore my shirt, but it didn't scratch the chain mail. I stood as still as possible while searing heat mended the fracture he had made in my jaw.

"It's me, Erin. I might look different in your Sight, but I'm still me. I love you." I held my hands up over my head like he was a cop and I a surrendering criminal.

His dark eyes squinted, and his forehead creased. He held the knife steady, pointed at me. Dark circles made him resemble a raccoon. His lip was split and swollen. Torn clothing revealed bruises and scratches.

"José, you sent me a message in my dreams. You said they didn't hurt you much. You said you were okay, but you're not."

His hand shook, but he didn't lower the knife.

"I saw Erin die. The Many-Tentacled Destroyer snapped their neck. Erin hit the wall right outside that gap, dead."

"Yes, but I didn't stay dead." My raised hands shook. "It's me. Ask me something only I would know."

Sniffling, José shook his head and bared his teeth. "If you're something possessing Erin's corpse, you'd have access to their memories. I can see your energy all over the body, whatever you are."

"I'm Erin. You're seeing my energy, which isn't the same as it used to be."

José darted at me, a knife aimed at my throat.

I grabbed the blade end of the knife with my bare hand, grinning at how the released blood all but silenced the residual hum of stolen energy.

I yanked it out of his hand.

He swung at me.

I jumped out of his reach, slashed my own face with the knife, and threw the knife on the ground between us.

"José. It's me. We're not in a galaxy far, far away anymore. This is more of a comic book turned movie. I did something brilliantly stupid, and I'm one of those mutants that just doesn't die."

He froze a foot away from the knife. His mouth hung open as he watched a fiery glow fill the slices on my hand and face.

I took a step toward him. "Mel can't deny I'm a mutant now."

"Erin?" His shoulders softened from rock to jelly. Somewhere between laughing and hyperventilating, he stumbled forward and hugged me as tight as he could. "Dammit, Erin, don't die in front of me again."

"Mel's been saying that to me a lot." I cupped his face with my freshly healed hand.

He trailed his fingers across the area of my cheek that I'd cut. "When you bled, the wound glowed like Mel. Now, there isn't even a scar."

"Did you forget I'm a little Angel too?"

José's face inched closer to mine. "Can I kiss you?"

"Please."

His lips collided with mine. I kissed him like I needed to breathe him in to live. The hot buzzing that coursed through my body had nothing to do with stolen power. It was crazed hormones making me feel the most human I'd felt since he disappeared, and I wanted to linger in it forever.

I pulled away, pushing every scrap of emotion I felt into a dark corner of my mind. I still had to get the others, meet back up with Mel, and get us all out of here alive.

I touched the seven-sided star clipped to my ear. "Mel? Can you hear me?"

José watched with his head cocked and a crooked smile on his lips.

"Yeah. I got Mike, but he's—did you get attacked again? I felt your face get cut up."

A chill surged through me. José and Mike—the one person I cared most about rescuing and the one Mel cared most about rescuing—had been separate. Taking me alive became optional once Mel was in Gareth's reach.

"José didn't recognize me. I'm going to search for the others." I touched the spot where his knife had torn my shirt and twined a stray string around my finger. "I think they're nearby."

"I'll see you at the rendezvous."

"You're not alone." José let go of my waist and squeezed one of my hands.

"You think Mel would let me come here alone?" I glanced at the hole I'd fallen through. I studied the warped cell door. "Step back."

"Do they have Mike?" José asked.

"Mike, Grandpa, Sister Marie, and Officer Karen." I took a few steps back, ran at the door, and kicked it open.

José picked up the knife he'd dropped. "Is it just you and Mel?"

"Have you seen any other prisoners?" There wasn't time to explain Vincent.

José clutched at my arm. "No. Erin, they said this place was impenetrable; you couldn't get here unless you..."

"I found another way." I looked right and left and saw nothing but empty hall. For the moment, we were alone. I slung the backpack off my shoulder, opened it, grabbed the gun, and handed it to him.

"I doubt I killed all the Demons in this Bubble of Bullshit."

He took the gun, checked the safety and the number of rounds in it, and peered into the bag.

"Are those grenades? Do you even know how to use a grenade?"

"Pull the pin." I took a granola bar out of the pack, tore it open, and shoved it in my mouth. While I chewed, I took out the scanner and handed José the pack. I swallowed my food and grinned. "It goes boom. Direct the fire to Demons that need incinerating. The shiny ones are the lightning kind."

José's hands closed around the straps, but his dark eyes were fixated on me. "Last I remember, you just were practicing pulling energy from candles. How long have I been here?"

"Four very long days." I turned the scanner on. There was a heat signature above me.

José stroked the air an inch above my hair like he wanted to touch me but was afraid he'd get burned.

"What happened to you in those four days?"

I studied the gray hall. "You should ask, 'What did you do?' but I think you'd rather me not answer that one. Are there any stairs in this place?"

His hand dropped the few inches to my hair and slid down my neck to my shoulder.

"You didn't make a deal with that monster or the Fallen, right? Please tell me you didn't."

"I am a monster. I didn't need to make a deal with one to save you." And that was the truth. Vincent was a victim, not a monster.

José gripped my shoulder with quivering fingers. "How did you get here?"

My shoulder tensed. "I found another way, but we need to hurry."

I strode forward.

José kept up but didn't let go. "This kind of power has a price."

"I've paid, believe me." I pointed my scanner at each door as I went by them. No heat signatures.

"Is it permanent?" José's clutched my shoulder like it was a handhold on a cliff he was dangling off.

"I think so." Some cells contained hybrids, but they weren't the two I was searching for. The scanner could name Sister Marie and Officer Karen. If I stopped to free every prisoner, I'd never make it.

I clenched my teeth and stomped on. The longer we were here, the bigger the chance of Mel getting captured; she was bait for a much bigger fish than me.

"Are you okay?" José's dropped his hand to my hip.

"Are you?" I didn't slow down. I didn't give in to the urge to cuddle up and lose time in the rhythm of his heart.

He walked so close I thought he might trip me. "I've had just enough to eat and drink to stay functional. At first, they didn't touch me. Then they were working their way up from my-dad-a-little-mad but never quite made it to my-dad-raging-drunk-after-a-botched-hunt."

One of my hands balled into a fist. The other cracked the scanner's plastic handle.

"Erin, stop. Look." José pointed at my cracked screen. A black-and-white badge hovered on the left of the screen.

I banged on her cell door. "Officer Karen?"

"Erin? Don't tell me—" Officer Karen's anxious voice began before I cut her off.

"Step back. Breaching in five, four, three, two, one!" I hit the door with the same running kick I'd opened José's with.

"I'll take that as a no," Officer Karen replied as she pushed herself up on shaking feet. What skin wasn't covered with bruises was paler than I'd ever seen it.

José took a step back. "They're starving you."

"Yes, but I'm still in control. For now. But don't touch me. Just in case." Karen's breaths were labored as she hobbled toward us.

José retreated from her overdilated eyes.

Demon-human hybrids didn't *need* to feed off human energy like an Incubus, but if they were deprived of actual food, or if something else siphoned energy from them, then they could lose control and kill someone for their energy.

Sister Marie hobbled out of the cell behind Karen, not looking much better.

"That twisted, ass of a monster," I hissed.

"You know, this isn't the first time someone has tried to make her kill me." Sister Marie hugged me. "I assume you wouldn't be kicking doors down had you signed your soul over to the Fallen."

"Give me your hand," I said to Karen before Sister Marie asked how I had ended up here.

Karen stared at me.

"Do you prefer me to zap you? I've vaporized more than a hundred Demons, got strangled, and healed myself, and I still have excess energy crawling under my skin." I focused on pushing some of it out through the palm of my hand until the energy morphed into a fist-sized piece of popcorn.

Karen flinched at the ball of energy, chucking nervously. Reaching out like a zombie, she touched it with a shaking fingertip, which sucked at the energy like a straw. The tremors went away. Her hand steadied. Her pupils shrunk.

"Thank you."

"I'd rather you not seem like you're going to pass out when the big bad realizes I'm not actually dead, and then we have to fight the rest of the way out." I kept walking in the direction I'd been going before I broke her cell down.

I tapped my earpiece. "Mel? I got Marie and Karen."

Static burst through the star-shaped earbud before Mel's voice crackled through. "Vincent's compromised. I can't find Grandpa."

"I'll get him. You and Mike need to get out."

Something screeched through the earpiece.

I jogged up the gradual incline, scanning door after door. Grandpa wasn't hybrid enough to register on the scanner, and I wasn't seeing any human heat signatures. What if he was in a different building? What if he was too fragile to survive here?

A heat signature glowed on the edge of my scanner. Finally. I banged on the door. "Grandpa? Are you in there??"

"Erin? It's a trap!" Grandpa yelled, voice muffled by the door.

"Is your cell rigged?" I was in position to kick the door down.

"Not my cell. But this whole place."

"I know that. Get away from the door." I kicked it down.

Grandpa hobbled over the fallen door with a scowl like he was mad at me for coming to save him. He pulled me into a gruff hug before examining Officer Karen. "I thought you'd be worse."

Officer Karen hugged him. "I was until the Energizer Bunny here threatened to *zap* me if I didn't take the power they offered."

Grandpa glanced at José. "Do I want to know what that means?"

He shook his head.

I tapped my earpiece. "Mel? I have Grandpa."

I only heard static. My heart raced. I'd have felt it if she'd gotten hurt. I'd know if she died.

"José's pack has weapons, food, and medical supplies. Try to keep up. This will help you find me if we get separated." I gave Grandpa the scanner and jogged in the direction we'd just come from, trying not to go faster than they could.

Sweat slicked my palms, and my heart beat faster than it had during the battle with Shadowhulhu. I wanted to drop my shields, find Mel, and speed toward her, but I couldn't abandon the others. They didn't know where the rendezvous was and were too tired, beaten, and poorly armed to stand a chance if they got caught.

Grandpa's breaths were shallow and wheezy, but he managed to jog beside me. "Why in God's name did you bring Mel to the lair of a Fallen Angel? Do you know what he will do to her?"

I coughed as air rushed out of my lungs. I stumbled and fell flat on my face.

Chapter Twenty-Six

When two beings' souls mingle, they form a bond so intense they can feel each other's pain from miles away. This is common between lovers but has been known to happen with siblings and cousins who exchange energy in less intimate ways, such as frequently healing each other's life-threatening injuries.

—The History of Hybrids, 3rd edition, published in 1984 by Amena Nasser

José was at my side in an instant. "Erin? What happened?"

"Erin? Talk to me." Grandpa crouched at my other side.

"Mel's hurt. We need to hurry." I stood up, letting her pain wash over me and fill me with rage.

The cell across from me was empty. I slowed my perception of time and kicked the door, pushing it straight through the exterior wall on the other side of the cell. I pulled a wood stake out of my pocket and drove it into the ground as I crash-landed with the chunks of wall and let my perception of time return to its normal state.

Officer Karen took the pack from José and climbed down from the second level. She stepped into the V-shaped dent that went halfway to the first floor, crouched, and then grabbed the edge and lowered herself before dropping the last few feet. Grandpa and Sister Marie followed a bit less gracefully but still managing.

José wiped the sweat off his forehead, gritted his teeth, and started downward. He made it to the *V* and froze. Whatever injuries he was hiding—probably broken ribs—had finally caught up to him. I considered the pieces of rubble. How long would it take to pile them up as steps? Were there enough?

I jumped as the skin around my ankle seared like a tendril of fire had wrapped around it. I was on my feet, but rocks cut into my knee. My cheek stung. My ribs ached as Gareth continued to beat the shit out of Mel.

I closed my eyes and dropped my shields. The secondhand pain intensified to the point where I growled out loud. Gareth was going to suffer tenfold whatever he dished out to her. I gritted my teeth and focused on the wall in front of me. It looked and felt like concrete, but it was made from the same goop Mel had used to make our ship. Bands of old energy hummed at a low frequency, binding it together. It was a guitar string that never stopped vibrating. I pulled energy out of myself and bathed my hand in it, tweaking it until it hummed the same frequency as the energy holding the wall together.

I sent that energy forward. A disembodied hand grabbed the wall, molding what felt like old Play-Dough with barely enough moisture left to form a rudimentary staircase.

"Hurry. I can't hold it long," I told José.

The strands were already starting to resist. He clambered down as fast as he safely could.

I let go of the stairs when his feet hit the ground. Hairs stood up on my arm. I shivered as something ancient and cold shifted its focus to me.

Did you think your pet squid could kill me? I thought at Gareth, the Fallen Angel.

A voice reminiscent of groaning earth whispered in my mind. *If you care for your cousin so much, surrender to me. It will make things so much easier.*

Will you let her go free and promise to never contact, harm, or be near her in any manner, direct or indirect? If you care about capturing me, you need to guarantee the safety of everyone I love, especially *Mel.*

Croaking laughter quaked my brain. *Your arrogance is almost endearing. Despite my Destroyer having killed you, you still think this about* you.

Pressure built around my temples as the Fallen's consciousness twined around mine like a snake.

I pictured myself in my mind's cockpit and fired.

The pressure let up.

Something massive flew toward me. I fired a volley of lasers at it. Singed feathers flew at my windshield. Wind buffeted the ship as something screeched outside. I fired another volley and threw my shields back up.

Officer Karen's face was an inch away from mine. Her hand pointed toward the disintegrating staircase. "How did you do that?"

"I'm a damned mutant. Come on." Resisting the urge to sprint full speed, I jogged in the direction I had sensed Mel. The pain dulled when I shielded, and I didn't feel any new blows land. Hopefully, that meant my mental skirmish with Gareth had provided enough of a distraction for her to get away.

The air was cold and dusty. The green light that had led me to José was still on him and connected to the group holding the portal open back home. The point where the green exited the dome was where I was supposed to meet everyone.

Rocky landscape stretched out ahead where the beam shone toward a gray wall. Behind us, smoke rose from the place I had last seen Mel, but based on what I'd sensed when my shields were down, she'd made progress toward the rendezvous.

Domes similar to the one José had been in blocked most of my view to the left and the right. I slowed as we approached the edge of the right dome. I didn't see Shadowhulhu or any armies of Demons.

I kissed José on the forehead. "I'm going ahead. Use the scanner if you lose sight of me."

I slowed my perception of time, and I sped off. As soon as I cleared the building, I saw a blur of dim light dashing toward the spot where the beam hit the end of the bubble. As I got closer, I saw Mike running beside Mel. Vincent was a few feet behind him.

If Mel got caught again, she was toast.

Gareth pursued her from only a few yards behind. He was taller than a human with twisted gray wings jutting out of his back. A long cloak hid the rest of his body. I couldn't tell how much was shadow versus actual fabric.

I had to get to her before he did, but my brain throbbed. If I pushed myself any harder, I might not be able to help.

A bolt of blue light shot out of Gareth's hand. I growled. The blue bolt shattered a rock an inch away from Mel's right foot. The force threw her forward.

Pain shot through my calves and back as slivers of rock cut Mel. Gareth caught up to Mel. I coughed as his foot cracked her ribs. The movement jostled my aching brain. Blood tricked out of my nose.

I was merely yards away, so I let time return to normal.

"I thought Michael's daughter would be tougher." Gareth's voice was dry and gravelly in a way that made me shiver. He kicked Mel so hard that she soared across a few yards of dusty purple land. "Call your father!"

I strode forward, powered by pain-fueled rage.

Mel doubled over, curling up. He kicked her again and again. "Just cry his name and he'll charge in here with his legions."

I was going to rip Gareth's tongue out of his throat and break his teeth.

Gareth raised his fist, a blue ball of energy within. "Call out to him. He'll come save you."

"I wouldn't be so sure about that." I was close, but not close enough to get between the energy ball and Mel before it hit her. "Michael's an asshole."

His hand still in the air, Gareth turned in my direction. "You know I speak of Michael the Archangel, leader of Heaven's legions."

"More like arch asshat, shitty father of my favorite cousin." I slowed my run to a strut, pulling my lips up in what I hoped was an arrogant grin.

Mel's body heaved, and I couldn't tell how much of it was crying or laughing.

The hairs on my arms stood, gravitating toward the raw energy crackling in Gareth's hands. I wanted that power.

It dissipated as Gareth stepped toward me. "So, you know being an Angel doesn't make a being good."

Mel got up on her hands and knees. Out of the corner of my eye, I saw José duck behind a big boulder to my left. Grandpa was right behind him.

"Good? What is this, first grade? Nothing is as simple as good and evil." I told myself that a pair of broken wings didn't make Gareth any worse than Shadowhulhu or the Incubus Vincent had been trapped inside. He was merely another monster trying to kill my family and me.

"Yet you're here opposing me despite your obvious disapproval of my enemy. What have I done to make you hate me more than him?"

"Let's see. You kidnapped my partner, orchestrated a mass shooting, unleashed starved Demons in areas filled with humans, and you tortured Mel." I strode closer to Gareth as Mel slowly got to her feet.

Gareth spun around and kicked her in the face. Her dim light flickered.

Gunshots rang out as Grandpa emptied an entire clip into the Fallen before ducking back behind the rock.

Laughing, Gareth stomped on Mel's spine.

The space between each sputter of light grew.

My confused nerves were firing so many pain signals my brain didn't know what to do with it all, and much to my horror, I was laughing as maniacally as Gareth.

I unsheathed a knife, hastily infusing it with energy, and threw it. Gareth raised his fist to catch it, but the blade sailed past his hand and sunk into his shoulder. He screeched as smoke poured out of the wound.

Backpack in hand, Grandpa sprinted from his hiding spot to one closer to Mel.

"Michael may be a jerk, but he doesn't do this kind of shit." I pulled my sword from its scabbard, infusing it with a fresh wave of energy so the blade glowed red.

Gareth pulled the knife out of his shoulder and threw it down at Mel, who rolled out of the way just in time.

"Leave Mel alone," I said, stalking toward Gareth.

Appearing barely conscious, Mel reached for the knife.

"If she calls out to her father, I will." He stomped on her hands, digging his heel in hard. Mel screeched.

She passed out.

My fingers twitched.

I charged forward with a blow that could've decapitated Gareth had a gleaming blade not materialized in his hand. I swung at his midsection, and his blade parried mine.

"Erin Evanstar, you think you have any hope of defeating me?"

I slashed at his face. He blocked. I pressed my blade against his, letting my perception of time slow down as sparks flew. "I am going to destroy you."

"Doubtful." He swung at my side. I parried just in time and went for his neck, which, of course, he blocked.

I challenged his confidence with my blade, not words. He matched every move, getting inside my guard more than once, tearing through my vest to my chain mail and opening a gash on my left hip. Even if I hardly noticed the pain of my skin getting slashed open and searing itself shut, I wasn't going to beat him at swordplay. His blade sliced the back of my thighs. Blood tickled my calves for a second, followed by the burn of my body healing itself. Not knowing the limits of my regeneration ability didn't mean it was inexhaustible.

Something blurred behind him. Mel's feet disappeared behind the rock that had concealed Grandpa.

I slashed and parried. I kicked between Gareth's legs, striking home even though it meant his blade slashed through my shirtsleeve to my bicep. I kicked him in the face. He stumbled backward. Lunging forward, I swung my sword at his neck, singeing his shoulder.

He regained his balance and bombarded me with a flurry of fresh attacks that I barely blocked as he beat me back to a rock.

Officer Karen left a grenade by my feet, slashed at Gareth with a knife, and then ran. I tackled him into it as it exploded, pulling some raw energy into me and pushing the rest into a beam focused on him.

"This is fruitless," he growled, holding most of the energy at bay with some kind of shield that deflected it back at me.

Screams echoed across the bleak landscape; all but one came from behind the same rock.

Officer Karen yowled like a feral cat as she stood, raised a twitching arm, and lobbed one of the silver lightning grenades at me. She swayed and dove behind a rectangular stone the size of my Jeep.

I called the lightning toward me as it forked out of the orb, obscuring myself with a wall of cracking energy as I ran toward my family.

"Shield failure!" Vincent spun out from behind a different rock, drawn to his father by an invisible force.

Pulling the electricity into myself, I leaped over a rock, landing between Mel and José. José clutched his head. Mel was unconscious.

With Officer Karen and Sister Marie holding him back, Mike's eyes rolled back in his head as his fists swung toward Mel.

Blackish-red blood dripped out of Officer Karen's nose and ears.

Grandpa was kneeling beside Mel frozen with a hand halfway to her. The other clutched a metallic leaf pendant so hard it sliced deep into his hand.

I retreated into my mental cockpit, firing telepathic lasers at the purple tentacles that assaulted everyone's mind. The tentacles, a mental projection of Gareth's, retreated with smoking holes. I dropped my port and starboard shields, pulling in José's confused mess of a mind, which was being assaulted. Mel let fragments of a shattering hull crumble as she stumbled in too.

Holy hell. Unfiltered, her pain, fear, and sheer exhaustion nearly paralyzed me.

The smoking tentacles transformed into a dragon.

"Full power forward shields!" I shouted, needing the words to focus with so many presences in my mind.

Fire danced across the shields but didn't go through. I grabbed Grandpa with my right hand, mentally tugging on a vine that smelled like a summer storm, like my grandmother.

I slammed those side shields up and hailed Officer Karen.

Her voice was too garbled to understand.

"Airlock open," I said, picturing them open as fire bloomed across my forward shield. "Get inside."

A World War II bomber with SWAT armor hovered alongside my airlock, vanishing as Officer Karen and Sister Marie dragged Mike on board. I slammed the airlock shut, spreading the shields evenly around the ship just as Gareth's dragon swung around and breathed fire on the rear.

José blinked rapidly, turning in circles.

I stood, adjusting my focus so I saw my mental cockpit superimposed over reality.

In the physical world, I crouched behind a rock. José sat with his back to it and eyes closed, passed out for all intents and purposes. Mel lay in a heap on my other side; her fading light flickered.

"Med bay, now!" I ordered the Mel in my head–the version with the two big side buns and tattered orange flight suit.

"Erin, this isn't—"

"Now! Get your ass to the med bay." In the physical world, I dug the last Elven stake out of my pocket, the crystalline one, and held it tight.

Mental Mel studied her injured hand, looked back at me, and left the cockpit. I tracked her dying energy downstairs to a hall where she brushed past Karen and Sister Marie and crashed into Mike, who was gazing around completely dazed. He gathered her into a hug and kissed her on the forehead.

"Did we die? Is this Heaven?"

"Our consciousnesses are in Erin's brain," she said, squeezing him as hard as she could.

"Mel. Med bay. Now!" I moved an imaginary door so it opened under her feet, and she fell into a tank of water. An air mask that was tethered to the ship by a tube snapped around her face, not only feeding her air but a trickle of my energy. Karen yanked Mike away from the spot Mel had just vacated.

"José and Grandpa, you fire guns." I pointed at the two joysticks in front of them.

Grandpa gazed up at me like he'd never seen me before. "This is the type of thing Niben and Aelfric did during the war, but it was B-52s and aircraft carriers, not spaceships."

"Strap in. This is going to be a rough ride." I fired the engines, raising the ship above the flames.

In the physical world, I shoved the crystal into the ground and stood. Mel slumped into the space I'd vacated. I counted a whole thirty seconds between flickers.

Grandpa hadn't moved. Mike was passed out in Karen's lap. She nodded—the only one still awake.

In my mind's eye, the dragon flapped its wings and grew six arms, each with clawed hands.

"Fire at will!"

José and Grandpa pummeled the beast with lasers, adjusting their aim every time it moved. Each of their bolts hit home.

In the physical world, Gareth stood facing me with blue energy balls formed around his fists. His grip on Vincent must have been loosening because Vincent wasn't going toward him anymore but past him to the place where the green light passed through the bubble wall.

While José and Grandpa kept the dragon busy, I dropped the rear shields a sliver, calling electricity to me from every electronic device in the backpack. It wasn't much, but a ball the size of a snowball sparked in my hands. I stretched it out and threw it at Gareth. He stumbled as it hit him in the chest. His dragon faltered, realizing how many laser burns it had accrued.

José and Grandpa kept firing.

Holes opened in the dragon's wings. Bolts vaporized a hand. I blew off an arm from the elbow up.

My knees wobbled.

Electricity stopped arcing over Gareth's chest.

The blue balls in his hands grew.

"Is that all you got? A dragon and a couple of sparking gloves?" I shouted, glad the rock was hiding my shaking legs so he wouldn't realize I had neared the end of my reserves. "You're going to die, Gareth. You and this shitty dystopia you've built for yourself are going to be space dust scattered across the multiverse!"

He wound up like a baseball pitcher, hurling the first blue orb at me, the kind that had shattered Mel in my dreams.

My heart palpated as it hit me square in the chest.

Lights flickered in my mental spaceship.

I stumbled back half a step and caught myself as I dispersed the energy through my body.

"Did the shields go down?" asked José.

"No. That was a power surge." I braced myself.

When the next ball hit, I was ready and didn't stumble as the energy flowed through my now-warmed-up nervous system.

"That tickled!" I shouted.

Gareth laughed. "You think you can channel my power? It will consume you from the inside out."

He lobbed two more balls at me.

Physical-world José jolted awake as my foot twitched into him.

"This is weird. Erin, watch out!"

He started to stand, but I pushed him down as another ball hit me.

Grandpa cringed. "Erin, he's a Fallen Angel. He's evil, and you're eating up his power like—"

"Electrified bacon," I supplied. "Energy is energy."

And even if Gareth's energy was different, it was simply a matter of wavelengths and frequencies. I was a reactor, but I also functioned as a power converter. My body automatically adjusted the energy to something I could use. With slightly more focus, I converted the stolen power to a spectrum of evenly distributed wavelengths, to light that matched Mel's. I bathed her in that light.

In the physical world, she jolted awake, eyes wide, hands flying to the ground and digging in.

"Tell me when it's too much," I said.

I thought Mel nodded, but it might have just been her shaking from the sudden influx of energy that made her glow brighter and brighter every second.

Another ball grew in Gareth's hands. I slowed my perception of time down a little and dropped my shields a hair, feeling him pouring energy into the ball. When he threw it, I leaped forward, catching it midair before his energy had completely been severed from it. I latched onto that thin thread and pulled energy from him as if he were an electrical outlet.

Fire and hornets raged under my skin. My molecules were fast and molten like they had been when Nana first died, but I was Erin, and out of sheer stubbornness, I stopped my DNA from mutating again.

"Impossible," said Gareth, swords materializing in his hands.

He sliced the cord between us.

"Possible," I said, grinning as I telekinetically summoned my abandoned sword. The air thrummed around it as the metal blade transmuted to a red laser.

"Let me out," said Mel through gritted teeth.

The med bay door opened. Mel yanked the mask off and charged back up to the cockpit. "I can't decide if I want to deck you or hug you."

A wicked grin bloomed on my face. "I deserve both."

In the physical world, Mel stood, glowing with an eye-searing aura seven times her size. "I hope I'm allowed to take this energy, that I don't get a terrifying lecture from my dad about messing with the balance by being charged up on a Fallen's power."

I squeezed her hand. "I'm following your father's cryptic advice."

Gareth charged us with swords out. I waited for him to get to me. His blades melted on contact with mine.

I stabbed him in the stomach. His eyes widened.

Will he die if I behead him? I thought at Mel. Obviously, a human would, but he wasn't human.

Maybe not with a normal sword. He can survive the destruction of the physical body he is inhabiting, but your Sith saber of doom is a completely different level of weapon.

I hummed "The Imperial March" as my blade sliced through Gareth's thighs like warm cake, cauterizing the wound before his body hit the ground. I took his arms off too. And to make sure he couldn't magically reassemble himself too quickly, I whacked at the dismembered limbs with the saber until they were nothing but a mess of melted flesh and bone soup.

"Time to move!" I pulled out of my mental spaceship, making sure everyone was awake and standing on their own.

Mel's eyes were wide swirling hurricanes. Her mouth hung open. She shook her head, grabbed Mike, and ran toward the beam.

I pulled a bewildered José by the hand. With Officer Karen, Sister Marie, and Grandpa, we ran to Vincent and the spot where the beam met the bubble wall.

Shadowhulhu roared out of the ground, sending chunks of rock and dust flying everywhere. Lighting sparked at my fingertips, ready to obliterate the tentacled pain in my ass.

"It's just a giant Demon, right?" I asked Mel.

"Close enough," she said.

"I smash. You banish." I sheathed my sword and shot lightning bolts out of my fingertips, lighting the thing up like a thunderstorm. I pulled the monster apart and chucked pieces to Mel who sent them to different parts of the multiverse.

José stared, stunned when the ground quaked. Mel and I each grabbed hold of one of his arms and started running, getting him out of the way just in time for a spike to sprout up where he had been standing.

Thorns flew up everywhere as we tried to run. The group scattered. I screeched when one of the thorns went through my left foot, but the wound closed as soon as the barb was out.

I shut my eyes, feeling the next surge right before it happened and latching onto the energy. The thorns ceased rising as I tangled Gareth up in vines conjured from his own creation.

"Vincent, catch!" I shouted, sending a ball of blue energy at him. His torso and arms solidified. He tore a person-sized hole in the edge of the bubble. I sent everyone through ahead of me, grabbed Vincent, and yanked him through behind me as it snapped shut.

A cockpit formed around us, this one Mel's sleek, slightly retro, but more realistic spaceship. She threw the throttle forward as soon as it was fully formed, and we flew through Between faster than light.

Chapter Twenty-Seven

The most challenging part of being a Demon Hunter was always the day when I had to go back to school, where I was a mediocre student with no friends, after spending the weekend kicking ass with my family

—From the hunting log of Lucy Evanstar, written on June 1st of 2014, confined to the archives after Amelia Evanstar's high school graduation.

The green beam vanished as a horde of Crawlers, Spikes, and Trolls clawed their way over a stone wall that was fashioned out of Between goop.

Mel eased back on the ship's throttle as I harried the Demons with laser fire. I blew up the six that were near the top of the wall, but that also took out a good chunk of the barricade, which only encouraged them to climb more.

"Let me out." I unbuckled my seat belt and ran to the rear of the cockpit.

José blinked. "What are you doing?"

A door appeared in front of me, and I jumped out without answering.

Before my feet hit anything solid, I was shooting lightning bolts at the horde, glad to burn off some of the angry energy swarming under my skin. Blinding bolts forked across dozens of Demons, turning them to snowy dust–even the Trolls.

Mel landed the ship behind me when the last of the Trolls were gone. José clambered out first, hobbled a few feet toward me, and stopped with his eyes wide and his mouth open. Grandpa, Sister Marie, and Officer Karen appeared equally startled, glancing at me as if I were some marvelous, terrifying alien they'd never encountered before now.

Mel let go of the ship, which dissolved to Between goop.

The wall came down next to reveal Aelfric with a broadsword in each hand, standing amid chopped up Demons and their snowy remains.

"That was quick." Aelfric dusted pieces of Demon off his kilt and beard as he surveyed the group.

"Define 'quick.'" I felt like I'd been gone all night.

"An hour." Aelfric sheathed his swords and pulled Sister Marie and Officer Karen into a hug with his bearish arms.

"Have you been fighting that whole time?" I asked.

"No." Light trickled from Aelfric's arms to the women he was hugging.

Anxiety was a cold front plowing through my chest. Panic was an updraft, and thunder rumbled in my chest. I'd gotten everyone home in one piece, but at what cost? Would they ever see me the same again? Did I want them to? I'd never liked how Grandpa, Mel, and José had always thought I needed protecting whether it was from monsters I hadn't known existed or from myself.

Now, I didn't think I could kill myself if I tried.

They'd hardly spoken on the way back.

Mike seemed the most shell-shocked of all them, alternating between muttering equations and theories to silently staring at nothing.

"You ready to go home?" Mel put her arms around him and guided him to the hole. The green light vanished, and Niben appeared in the portal. Mel physically lifted Mike through, and Niben caught him on the other side. Grandpa came next, but he needed no assistance.

The portal was like a television, framing a scene so tender and unexpected that I felt like I was watching a movie, not my own family. Grandpa climbed through on his own, nearly knocking Niben over with a hug and a kiss that made me blush. Aelfric walked Marie and Karen over and hoisted them up through the portal. Marie ran to Niben, who let go of Seamus and kissed Marie. And then Niben kissed Karen.

One day, if Grandpa could stop gawking at me as if I were some ancient deity, we could sit around a campfire how we did when I was a kid, and he could tell me stories about those three women, Aelfric, and all the misadventures he must have had with them when he was young. Preferably the PG-13 versions so things didn't get too awkward.

José hobbled past me toward the portal. His shoulders came within an inch of mine as he passed by me. I wrapped my arms around myself, shivering even though my body felt like it was about to spontaneously combust. My fingers wormed through the tears in my shirtsleeves and dug into the bare skin buzzing on my arms.

He stopped at the edge and turned around. "Erin, are you coming?"

I didn't move. Vincent and I were the only other people left in Between. I knew Vincent wouldn't go through to Grandpa's house even though he was watching like he wished he could but knew didn't belong. Perhaps I didn't belong either.

"I don't need to get past your shields to know what you're thinking," Vincent whispered. "Go see your family."

"What about you?" I asked.

"Sam knows how to find me." He ghosted backward and disappeared into the purplish black.

"Aelfric's holding the door open for you, but he's getting tired." A frown weighed José's face down.

I walked toward him, digging my nails into my arms harder. Jenny was on the other side of that door still pregnant with his kid.

And me? I had bargains to uphold and magic under my skin. I doubted I'd seen the end of Gareth.

José's hand closed around mine, simultaneously comforting and unnerving.

What if I couldn't control my newly acquired power? What if I zapped him to death while we were making out? I shook as I climbed through the portal into the crowded, humid map room. My throat constricted. I was in a sauna surrounded by tears and shock and joy and kissing grandparents.

I couldn't breathe.

"What is she doing here?" José stared at Jenny as she took baby steps toward him with her arms crossed as tight as mine.

"That was how we tracked you." I barely managed to get the words out as my throat began to constrict.

His grip on my hand tightened. "What do you mean?"

"Let go of me," I gasped.

He did. His forehead wrinkled, and his lips pursed together. He backed away from me. "You used my unborn child to track me. Please tell me this didn't hurt it."

José's shoulder's relaxed. "Erin, I'm sorry. I—"

"José, thank God." Jenny threw her arms around José and buried her face in his chest. "Are you okay?"

His arms hung limp at his sides.

She started crying.

He hugged her. Not a soft, awkward pat-on-the-back-hug but a squishing-her-tight-to-his-chest hug.

My throat closed. Tears gushed out of my eyes. In my attempt to bolt, I almost tripped over Mel, who was trying to coax Mike up the stairs.

You laugh in the face of the most terrifying being I've met, but you can't face José and Jenny Dunn hugging. Mel glanced between Mike and me. His tears glistened with the reflection of her light.

Mike needs you more. I climbed the stairs, choking on my snotty tears.

I dashed to the kitchen and tore through the cupboards. There were no Oreos left. No chocolate-chip cookies. No potato chips. There were a handful of cheese curls, which were gone in a second. I grabbed two boxes of graham crackers, a six-pack of Hershey bars, and ran up to my room, slamming the door after me.

I ripped my torn, dirty clothes off, threw the chain mail on the floor, and stood naked, wishing I could rip all my skin off and expand with the raw power buzzing under it. But then what would I be? A ghost? A sentient storm cloud drifting across the sky? Who would stop Mel from burning out? Who would save my family next time the monsters they hunted started hunting them?

I put on a clean pair of underwear but no binder. I couldn't stand something that tight on my skin right now. I pulled on a pair of jeans and kept them on for thirty seconds before I ripped them off. I rummaged through the bag of old Elf clothes and put on a soft, loose red tunic that hung down to my knees without touching my legs. With my glowing skin, flecks of gold swirling through my green eyes, pointy ears, and sparking hair, I resembled some wild creature of myth, not a human.

Footsteps creaked down the hallway. I reached out with my mind. José was halfway to the door. My heart sped up. For four days, all I'd wanted to do was see him, but now I couldn't make eye contact or let him touch me.

I grabbed my car keys and wallet off my dresser, opened the window on the far side of my bedroom, and leaped out even though it was a second-floor window. Mud splattered all over me as I landed crouched in the side yard.

"Erin?" called José.

I ran to my mom's car. If José called me again, it was drowned out by the sound of a whining engine and puny tires squealing up Grandpa's muddy driveway.

*

Pavement scratched my bare feet as I sprinted up the cliff walk. I ran until my legs and lungs ached so bad they almost distracted me from the pressure under my skin.

Furious waves battered the rocky shore, shooting salty spray over cliffs and fence, turning the sidewalk's potholes and crevices into briny puddles. As I jogged on the cliff walk at Fort Williams State Park, mist cooled my exposed skin, tempting me toward the sea.

If it were a calmer night, I might have dived in. If I jumped in with the ocean this churned up, the waves would bash me against the rocks and break me like a fragile shell being crushed by a boot. I wasn't in the mood to die for a second time tonight even if there was a good chance I wouldn't stay dead.

My jog faded to a walk. A tall white cylinder of a lighthouse loomed a few yards ahead of me. The old sections of the keepers' house reminded me of a cat sleeping at the base of an ancient tree. The foghorn was a slow, deep heartbeat.

I collapsed onto a patch of damp grass behind a bench, and I stared up at the sky. The clouds cloaked the stars. Closing my eyes, I was content to simply listen to the rampaging waves and wind, and to just breathe in the salt and let the puddles chill my skin.

The sea sounded as monstrous as I felt.

I should've gone to one of the few sandy beaches where I could've let the chilly waves pound my overheated, overstimulated body without worrying about all my bones getting smashed to smithereens.

"Because riptides and mermaids aren't scary at all."

My eyes opened as I stood. The light behind Aunty Lucy was so bright that she looked like a silhouette. I glowered while my eyes adjusted to Michael the Archangel's searing radiance.

Aunty Lucy wore a tunic similar to mine, only it had a triangle pattern of green leaves. Michael's wrinkled shirt was the same color. His sturdy fingers nervously scratched the sides of his brown cotton pants, which were torn in half-a-dozen places.

Knowing it was Mel's parents didn't inspire me to lower my fists. I would've decked Michael had Aunty Lucy not been between him and me.

"Arch asshat? I've never heard that one before." The Archangel sunk down onto the park bench. His light retreated inside his human guise, revealing his hair sticking up in a dozen directions and circles under his eyes.

I shrugged. "It got Gareth's attention off of Mel."

"We were right outside the bubble," said Aunty Lucy. Her fingers dug into the arms of her wheelchair. "Neither of us would've let that monster kill Mel."

"You said you didn't know where the Bracken Bubble was." I paced circles around him and my aunt.

"When I spoke those words to you, they were true. I had not the slightest idea where in Between the Bracken Bubble was." The Angel ran his hands through his glowing hair, tangling his fingers in his curls exactly like Mel did when she got stressed. "I always know where my daughter is. Had she done what Gareth wanted, had she called me, I would've come."

"Earth would be screwed." Exhaling traces of the anger I held toward him, I stared at his bare feet. "You're not as shitty as I said you were."

"And you aren't the monster you think you are."

I thought he was full of shit.

"I can neither confirm nor deny that statement," said Michael. He stared at me with a smile budding on his lips.

Aunty Lucy burst out into a fit of honking laughter.

How was he confirming he might be lying funny?

"Think more literal," said Aunty Lucy.

I stared, very confused.

Aunty Lucy said, "He was responding to your thoughts, making a crude joke."

I failed to produce a coherent response, unsure whether I was more shocked because in the past three months, Aunty Lucy had never once hinted she could read people's minds or that an Angel had made a poop joke.

Michael winked. "She has no telepathy. I was relaying your thoughts to her."

"If you think Mel is annoying, try spending an afternoon with her father." A content smile made Aunty Lucy look younger. She turned to Michael and whispered, "I've missed you."

He pressed his lips to her temple. "It can't last."

She closed her eyes. "That makes it so much sweeter."

The wind picked up, carrying salt spray across the path to the bench. The waves were chaotic percussions pounding the rocks. Nothing about the moment was silent, but the lack of words made my chest feel like it was getting torn apart by the sea.

"What do I do now? Everyone else is terrified of me."

A mischievous grin spread across Lucy's face. "You call all the pizza shops near Grandpa's and order half-a-dozen large pizzas from each.

"While you sit at the tables, smelling the sauce and cheese, pay for your order, and then drive to the next place, you'll remember that everything on Earth is real, and you're still Erin no matter what magic or energy lurks beneath your skin. And when you get back, you'll need help carrying the pizza in. Humans, especially teenagers, need help, not omnipotent lightning storms.

"You eat and make *Star Wars* jokes, and you tell Mike that the original *Star Trek* was the worst movie ever, and the second worst was *Back to the Future*. Tease Mel about not having wings. Play video games and make sure José wins, but don't tell him you're letting him win. Laugh. Cry. Sleep. Wake up and eat all the bacon."

My stomach growled. "You've done this before."

She winked at me. "Your father and I had our share of adventures when we were young. Some of them made Seamus more afraid of us than for us."

"Thank you," I said, unsure if she could hear me over the growl of my stomach. "You don't happen to have a phone on you, do you?"

"I don't, but José does." Aunty Lucy and Michael vanished in a flash of light that left globs of green dancing in front of my eyes.

*

Running feet scraped pavement and crunched gravel on the path that came up from the gate. I couldn't see shit with all the big spots floating in front of my eyes, so I closed them and focused on listening. Two beating hearts gradually got louder. One veered off to the left. The other, accompanied by the sound of sneakers scratching pavement, kept moving toward me.

"Erin? Hey!" José's footsteps slowed to a shuffle.

"Hey." I blinked a lot, and finally, the big spots faded, revealing José, standing a few feet in front of me with a vice grip on a plate of cookies. The bruise on his jaw was gone, but he still had a nasty welt on his eyebrow.

"You disappeared." He panted from jogging up from the parking lot, but he stood up straight. Mel must have healed some of his injuries before he ran off to find me.

"I thought you'd..." He took a step closer. His lips pressed tight together, and tears wet his eyes. He took a deep breath. "I thought you'd gone off to kill yourself or to fulfill some bargain you made to find me."

His lower lip was swollen and quivering. A threadbare *X-Men* T-shirt clung to his chest and stomach, accentuating his athletic build. My black cargo pants were short on him, not quite covering the top of his sneakers, leaving a sliver of ankle exposed. It was raw and red. At one point, his captors had had a manacle on it.

His heart beat faster. He clutched the cookie plate so tight his finger tore the plastic wrap. "You didn't actually come here to..."

"Kill myself? What makes you think I could if I wanted to?" I put my hands in the tunic pocket.

José inhaled slowly. "Do you want to?"

"No. But I still think you'd be better off if I did."

José's fingers crushed the cookies on the edge of the plate. "Erin, will you just accept that I love you?"

"When will you accept that I am a violent monster?"

"I've always accepted you for what you are." He took a deep breath and forced a smile. "Why do you think I never let you over my house unless I knew Dad was hours away?"

I stared at the strip of raw, purple skin on his ankle. "Because you were afraid he might hurt me?"

José shook his head. "I was afraid you'd murder him."

I sighed. "You don't know how much I thought about that."

"Mel does, and she told me many times. I don't think she would've tried to stop you." José inched toward me until the plate of cookies he was holding was sandwiched between our chests. "If that makes you a monster, then so be it. It doesn't change how I feel about you."

José's breath tickled my lips.

I cupped his chin with my hand. "I love you, but you've always wanted to be normal. You've always wanted out of the supernatural world. You'll never have that with me."

"I don't need normal with you." José's words were sharp knives. He stomped away and sunk down on the bench Michael and Aunty Lucy had vacated not long ago. He stared down at the cookies, taking deliberate breaths. "Erin, do you actually want to be with me?"

"Yes." I sat down on the other side of the cookies. "I love you as much as I can love anyone, but I'm scared."

"Me too." José took the plastic off the cookie plate. "And I'm concerned that you didn't inhale this whole plate before I started talking to you."

"Where did you get these?" I picked up a zombie-shaped gingerbread cookie and bit its head off.

"Sam and I dropped Jenny off at Will's 'apocalypse party' on the way here. I went in long enough to prove I was alive and fill a plate with food." José picked up a chocolate cookie, glared it at, put it back, and crossed his arms.

I finished my cookie. "How is she?"

He cradled his head in his hands. "Coping. On the ride back, when Sam wasn't talking about Vincent, Jenny chattered about the baby. She wanted my opinion on names, and then asked if you had dreamed anything about the baby."

I slipped my fingers between José's. "If we make it, your kid will have your hair and Jenny's eyes."

José's curls tickled my neck as he leaned his head on me. I put the cookies on my lap and scooted closer to him. Tears dripped out of his eyes and tricked down my neck. "Erin, in that vision, were you there?"

I twined my fingers through his hair. "I was. Do you want to see it?"

He tensed and turned his head, so he was gazing at my face. "If you can project a memory into my mind, that means you can hear my thoughts."

"If I dropped my shields while we're touching, then yes, I could potentially hear your thoughts if I made an effort to, which I will never do without your permission. If I attempt to show you the dream, then I might catch a few snippets of your reaction."

"I want to see it but not right now."

"I understand." My eyes stung as I struggled to keep my lower lip from quivering. There could be a million reasons why he didn't want to see it right away, but all I thought of was that he was thinking something he knew would hurt me.

He closed his eyes, moved the cookies, and snuggled closer while we stared out at the dark ocean and the flashes from the lighthouse. It seemed a lifetime ago since José and I had cuddled on this same bench before staging a fight to attract the Incubus we were hunting, the very one Vincent had been trapped inside of.

"Where is Sam?" I took the chocolate cookie José had abandoned.

"Around. She went to find a quiet space to call Vincent." José shivered. "Had I not met him and seen him get us out of the bubble, I wouldn't have believed a word of her story."

"I want to ask Vincent something." I disentangled myself from José and picked up the cookies. "I'm going to drop my shields so I can find them. Don't touch me without shielding if you don't want to risk me knowing what you're thinking."

His Elf stone flared green as he nodded. His eyes widened. "Without my Sight, you appear how you always did, but with it...you used to look like an Elf, but now, your fire and electric Angel light is barely restrained by translucent flesh. You're..."

"Terrifying?"

"I was going to say breathtaking." José pressed his palm to his forehead. "I think you being a telepath will be good for us in the long run because you suck at reading body language and actually listening to words about feelings. Just don't be like Mel with it."

I watched the silvery moonlight break through the clouds. "I will always respect your privacy, but between Mel and me? Even with my shields up, twenty miles away, I can still feel her."

"And without them?" José's scraped hand slid from his forehead to dark curls.

Closing my eyes, I let my mental deflector shields fall away and focused on the piece of annoying brightness I associated with my cousin. "She's tugging-at-her-hair frustrated and anxious because Mike won't speak. He thinks things at her, but everything else in his head is sharp and jumbled images and numbers that she can hardly make sense of."

José's eyes were wide, but the left side of his lip twitched up to a half smile. "What does Mel think of her newfound lack of privacy?"

"I don't think she's had a chance to think about it yet." I wasn't quite ready to think much on its implications either, so I reached out mentally, searching for Vincent's cool hum of energy and walked toward it.

"I have so many questions, I don't know where to start." José followed me up the hill, to a grassy area not far from the lighthouse where I had gotten mobbed by a horde of Demons right before I did my first Tesla-coil impersonation.

I glanced over my shoulder at José. "Then don't start because I'm not ready to answer them."

Sam sat cross-legged on a blanket across from a Vincent-shaped cloud of glimmering dust. I sat next to Sam, so I was facing Vincent. "Who was in control the night we met here?"

Vincent wrapped his snowy arms around himself. "The Incubus. He was much too strong that night. I put forth quite the effort when I realized he was summoning a horde, but I was tied up and gagged in the depths of his dark mind."

I conjured a small sparking orb of blue between my thumbs and zapped him with it. He jumped upright and went rigid, but after half a minute, he'd managed to disperse the energy through himself and appear slightly more solid. "You could warn me next time."

I smiled. "Another zap for another answer?"

"Erin, you don't need to bargain with me for information. We're on the same side now." Vincent settled back down to sitting position across from Sam.

"Humor me."

"Fine. I will answer another question in exchange for another spark of power."

"When did Pedro Estrella cut a deal with your father?"

Vincent closed his eyes. "My sense of time was not perfect while I was confined, but I believe it was a decade and a half at the least."

"Are you telling the truth?" José crouched down a foot away from Vincent.

"I am. Why is this number of so much significance?"

José and I smiled as we made eye contact, simultaneously saying, "Mel."

"Speaking of Mel, I think her parents stole your car," said Sam.

"Her parents? Plural?" Chuckles escaped my lips while I struggled to focus on making a second ball of energy. I tossed it to Vincent.

"Both of them." José lay down and put his head in my lap. "They sped off with some old Green Day song blaring in the background."

Sam grinned. "Whoever said having the voice of an Angel meant someone could sing is full of shit. Mel's father sings worse than a constipated cow."

Laughter shook me like waves would rock a boat if it were out on the raging ocean right now. I might have snorted a couple times. By the time I stopped, my ribs ached, my throat was raw, and a wave of contentment and desire radiated up from José and made my blood buzz faster.

José had dropped his shields.

I was waiting for you to notice.

In my head, the pitch of his voice was softer and a few notes higher than when he spoke out loud. I trailed my fingers across his forehead, tracing the edge of the welt on his eyebrow.

I want to be alone with you, Erin. But here, right now, I feel okay now. If I move, if I think about anything other than my head in your lap and your fingers melting tension out of my head, I might not be.

Then don't think.

The whites of his eyes reflected my skin's volcanic glow. I leaned down and gently pressed my lips to his forehead. I remembered how sometimes Mel shorted out my panic attacks with just a drop of warm, soothing energy. I pulled a thread of my own power, molding it to that soothing temperature and wavelength, and let it slip away from me with the kiss.

He shuddered as tension drained out of his shoulders. His cheeks flushed and his pupils dilated. *You trying to soothe me with Angel fire is* nothing *like when Mel does it.*

José's fingers tickled my neck. They curled around the base of my skull and tugged my head down, toward his parted lips.

Sam cleared her throat. "Um, don't forget you two aren't actually alone because you interrupted *my* moment alone with Vincent."

Mel's laughter chimed in some distant corner of my mind. *Remember this bond of ours works both ways.*

"They'll never truly be alone together." Vincent's eyes solidified as his legs dissolved. "Every time Amelia looks at me, she cringes. She's terrified the Fallen will shatter her like they did me. Tell her as long as she is so tethered to you, she need not worry. You've not scratched the surface of what you're truly capable of."

Did you hear that? I thought at Mel.

It's not as comforting as I wish it were. Do you understand what this means for us?

If I die, you die. And if I never die, we're stuck in each other's heads forever?

Something like that. Mel's presence withdrew from my mind until she was merely a peripheral flash of light on the edge of my awareness.

"I love you, Erin. Whatever you are and whatever you became, remember that." José beamed up at me, oblivious to the conversation Mel and I had just had. He wasn't afraid of what I had and might still become. He was proud. He was safe. I hoped his faith in me wasn't misplaced.

"I love you too," I whispered, truly believing it.

Epilogue

It was a gray, windswept rainy day, but Mom's hair glowed like it was bathed in sunlight. The tips of her ears and sharp points of her jaw, once gray and decaying, were covered with new, pink skin. Mom used to have cataracts as gray as the clouds outside, but they were gone. Her pupils were feline Elven but were surrounded by swirling gold and green irises.

Grandpa and Lucy once assumed that my dad had tried to do something to help my mom not realize what she was because she couldn't process it, but I doubted it was coincidence that it all went away after Nana's curse was broken after she died. In the long run, I thought that would be a good thing, assuming my mom survived the next hour. In the short term, well, if she woke up with her Sight on, she'd think I was a hallucination, not her kid, Erin.

I'd rather have her awake and afraid of me than be comatose forever. I squeezed Mom's hands, kissed her forehead, stood up, and glanced at Mel. "You ready?"

Mel took a deep breath. "As much as I can be."

Brain injuries were the hardest things to heal. Not only did Mel have to be extremely focused and precise, but she also expended twice as much energy. Even with her aura finally back in its hurts-your-eyes-if-you-look-directly-at-it state, something as bad as my mom's brain was an enormous strain—one Mel would've undertaken on her own if she had to.

We joined hands. If everything went as planned, this would take the edge off the energy that was making me want to rip my skin off. I didn't want to think about what would happen if we failed.

Even though there were no sharp objects, this was still brain surgery being performed by someone who hadn't yet started medical school. If Mel put energy in the wrong place, Mom could die, but if we waited, her brain might be impossible to heal. We didn't know for sure if we'd survive that long anyway. We'd delayed the apocalypse, but we hadn't stopped it yet.

We'd weakened Gareth, but hadn't killed or trapped him. My great-grandmother made decisions at the speed of a glacier when it came to fulfilling her end of our bargain. I wanted to find a way to trap him myself without her help. Not only because I was impatient, but also because I didn't trust her.

Mel squeezed my hand. I cleared my mind as best as I could. Her consciousness flowed across synapses and infused my muscles, numbing the pins-and-needle feeling that had been plaguing me all week. I studied her energy as it filled me and mingled with my own, and then I started feeding power to her.

Once we get started, we can't stop until it's done, she thought.

Then hurry up and do this.

Medical jargon, charts, and textbook illustrations filled our heads. There were too many at once for me to understand. I pulled a spark of energy from my core and mixed it with the raw, buzzy energy the dwelt close to the surface and then smoothed it to resemble Mel's power before letting it flow across our bond. Power danced down my arms and split into dozens of tiny light needles before shooting out my fingers and into my mom's brain, a maze of billions of neurons with countless pathways connecting them.

Mel directed the light needles to a part of Mom's brain that was quiet and cold where signals fell into a void between synapses and died, making it hard for other parts of the brain to communicate with one another. Mel revived damaged tissue, and when she ran into pieces that were beyond our ability to save, she woke slumbering cells that had never needed to be used, prodding them until they roused and provided an alternate path for the signals. Light and energy fired faster lasers in an unrealistic space battle.

When Mel's hands pulled away from my mom's head, we separated our energies and consciousnesses as best we could. In spite of using so much energy in the healing, my skin still buzzed how it had five minutes ago.

Mel arched her eyebrows at me. "More like fifty minutes ago."

"Erin?" Mom's voice was raw and raspy, but it was hers; it was the first time she'd spoken in more than two months. It had worked.

"Mom!" Tears rolled down my cheeks. Mom tried to sit up more, but this time, her body wouldn't let her.

She'll need physical therapy to regain her strength.

"Mom. I love you." I flopped forward and wrapped my arms around her and closed my Sight, hoping for a moment where Mom seemed okay.

Her limp arms closed around me and gave a feeble squeeze. "Where—?" Her mouth opened and closed, but she couldn't produce more words.

"You had a head injury. You're in a rehab facility," I said, pulling back enough to see her.

Head injury. It must have damaged my eyes. Lights everywhere. Spots. Erin's hair looks like it is on fire.

Mom nodded. She opened and closed her hands and her mouth and held a shaking, wavering hand to her eyes.

I squeezed her other hand. "You'll get better. I promise."

I hope. How long have I been out?

"Three months. You've been in a coma for three months. Do you remember anything?" I hoped she realized I was responding to her thoughts. Her eyes weren't as damaged as she thought. Her Sight was activated. She'd need to learn things such as telepathy and Angel-Elf-Human-Demon hybrids existed.

"A wall," croaked Mom. *A monster. Your voice over and over again. Trapped. Aware sometimes, nightmares, trapped in a black box.*

"She's talking?" A person in scrubs stood in the middle of the room with a lunch tray. Food still in hand, they turned around. "I'll get the doctor!"

"You're going to be fine," I told Mom, hoping I wasn't lying.

Sometime later, I stepped out into the hall to use the bathroom. On my way back, I saw a light reflecting off the polished tile floor. I stopped and opened my Sight.

With his bound light straining against warm skin, Michael the Archangel leaned against a wall with his arms crossed. His eyes and lips were shut tight before he finally took a deep breath and said, "Chelonia, neither of us is going to war."

Great-Grandmother Chelonia appeared as out of place in the hospital as a tree would if it just pushed roots out of the ground and walked in them wearing a bronze-armored breastplate and a blood-red skirt. Her limbs creaked as she leaned toward Michael.

"Why? Why not defeat the Fallen *and* take the Earth for ourselves?"

My hands curled into fists at my side. My teeth sunk into my lip.

"The Earth belongs to humanity." Michael's words were a low growl pushed through gritted teeth.

Great-Grandmother Chelonia inched closer to him. "Humans are poisoning the Earth. In another century or two, they'll kill each other over resources. Who would stop you from killing half of them to prevent that war?"

Michael rubbed his eyes like a tired human, stretched, and pointed at me.

"Erin."

"Damn right." I crossed my arms so I didn't punch either of them, and stepped the rest of the way into the hall. I turned my glare to my great-grandmother. "If you try to invade Earth, you will regret it."

She smirked. "Perhaps it is time we resume our negations regarding Gareth's fate."

"Soon, but not today." I turned my back on her and stormed toward Mom's room. With me angry but also distracted by my mom waking up, Great-Grandmother Chelonia would get the upper hand too easily.

Today was meant for family, not Faerie politics and violent plotting.

Three doors away from Mom's, I glanced over my shoulder at the ancient Elf. *Three days. Niben's house. Sundown. We'll talk then.*

After putting up my shields fast enough she couldn't respond, I put everything else out of my mind. This was Mom's time, and then I would return home to José' and worry about the world ending another day.

Acknowledgements

Thank you M. A. Hinkle, MJ Beasi, and Abigail de Niverville for your feedback on my drafts and your support throughout the writing process. This draft wouldn't have even made it to my publisher without you.

Thank you to the fantastic people from Reading Excuses for helping with my first chapter and encouraging me to keep writing.

Thank you Ashley, Rae, and the rest of the team at NineStar Press for getting this book out in the world.

About the Author

Sara Codair is an author of short stories and novels, which are packed with action, adventure, magic, and the bizarre. They partially owe their success to their faithful feline writing partner, Goose the Meowditor-In-Chief, who likes to "edit" their work by deleting entire pages. Find Sara online at saracodair.com or @shatteredsmooth.

Facebook: www.facebook.com/Saracodair1

Twitter: @shatteredsmooth

Website: www.saracodair.com

Other NineStar books by this author

Behind the Sun, Above the Moon

Life Minus Me

Power Surge

Half Breeds

Once Upon a Rainbow

Also Available from NineStar Press

Connect with NineStar Press

www.ninestarpress.com

www.facebook.com/ninestarpress

www.facebook.com/groups/NineStarNiche

www.twitter.com/ninestarpress